The Long Way Home

JASINDA WILDER

For Hugh. When Jack and I were just starting out in this business, you were the first author to offer us your friendship, support, and advice. I don't think we would have ever gotten this far without your invaluable and insightful advice, or your warm and genuine friendship. You are, and always will be, one of our favorite humans. Thank you so much for believing in us, for helping us, and for teaching us about the importance of living your dreams. It has been so amazing to watch you live yours. We love you, Huge.

Part 1

1

A handwritten note on Christian St. Pierre's personalized stationery

August 3, 2015

You look at me with blame in your eyes, as if this is somehow my fault; you look at me with disdain, as if I willed all of this to happen; you look at me as if you don't even recognize me anymore, as if all of this has somehow irrevocably altered me on some intrinsic level.

You are not wrong, about any of it.

No, I could not have prevented Henry from dying; obviously I didn't want this—I wouldn't wish it on my worst enemy; of course this hellscape that is our life has changed me—how could it not?

It is not my fault.

Yet still, I accept the blame. I accept the disdain. I accept the distance in your eyes.

I accept it, because I am weak and empty and dead. I am a husk of a man, and it is better to be filled with guilt and self-loathing and sadness than to be so utterly empty and alone as I have been these last weeks.

Ava, my love: you have always been the best part of me, and through you we created Henry, our son, and in him I found completion and strength and purpose. Now that he is gone, I have lost those things, and I have lost you, and thus I have lost myself.

I'm sorry, Ava.

I wish I had the strength to go on, but I don't.

Goodbye.

From Ava St. Pierre's blog:

Confessions of a Working Mommy

August 5, 2015

He's gone. He left. The coward. He just LEFT, vanished, poof…no more Christian.

When I found that handwritten note on his desk, my immediate thought was that he'd committed suicide, but my next thought was to dismiss that notion as utterly preposterous: Christian is nowhere near weak enough (or strong enough, if you look at it perversely) to do something like that. He wouldn't even consider it.

If you've been following my blog for the last nine months, dear reader, you'll know that I've been predicting some kind of third and final blow to my already-fragile psyche. This is that final blow. Neil Gaiman wrote in his amazing novel *Neverwhere* that events are cowards, not occurring singly, but instead running in packs and leaping out all at once; I have found this to be utterly and bitingly true in my own life.

First my blog crashed and I had to have the website totally rebuilt, and then everything with Henry, and now this. My husband, my best friend, my lover, the father of my son…has left me.

I know where he is, of course.

He'll have bought himself a giant ocean-going sailboat, and he'll have boarded it, and sailed away from me, away from Henry's grave, away from our fractured marriage, and away from the chaos of a successful career.

That's the irony in all this: his career is going gangbusters. He's never been in higher demand. Movie studios want rights to his books, his publisher is ordering renewed print runs on at least half of his backlist, fans are clamoring for sequels and prequels and spin-offs…

And he chooses *now* to literally sail away from everything. Of course, he has to be so damned dramatic about it—writing a wrenching goodbye note on his custom stationery, using his Mont Blanc fountain pen.

What am I supposed to do?

Please, guys, sound off in the comments if you have any suggestions; at this point I'll consider just about anything. Do I go after him? Let him go? Send him a sternly worded email? Oh yes, he'll have his email connected; that man can't live without internet any more than I can, and you all know how I feel about my interwebz—call me nasty names, take my house, take my car but, dear god, at least leave me my social media; it's all I have left, now.

So.

Do I forget him and move on?

Mourn him, and the loss of our son—alone?

Become a crazy cat lady?

Get heavy into drugs? I could be a druggie. I could totally rock the heroin diet and lose those last twenty pounds I've been wrestling with since giving birth to Henry. I could rock the heroin-chic look, the old ratty clothes, the too-big canvas jacket, maybe even a pair of fingerless gloves...wait, I think that's hobo-chic, which is a different aesthetic entirely. I don't know, though. I've tried drugs before and they just make me twitchy and paranoid. That one time I smoked pot back in college, I ended up sitting on the roof of my sorority house eating Cool Ranch Doritos and waiting for the mothership to come take me. Of course, I later found out that the pot had been laced with something else which contributed to the bad trip, but that was enough for me—I've known ever since that I'm just not cut out to be a stoner, tweaker, or any other type of drug addict.

I'm content to be addicted to Twitter, Snapchat, Instagram, and a good dry cabernet. And 70% dark chocolate. And Darcy, my labradoodle puppy, my best buddy. And Bennet, my calico kitten, my *other* best buddy. Those are my addictions, and I'm sticking to them.

But will they be enough to get me through this chapter of my life?

We shall see, dear reader. We shall see.

PS: People have been asking about a Kickstarter page, and I honestly considered it. But I don't really need money, so in lieu of monetary donations please send contributions in the form of dry red wine to my P.O box, the address of which can be found under the "Contact me" tab. Yes, I'm dead serious. Dry red wine, the drier the better, and it doesn't have to be expensive, but no two-buck Chuck, if you please.

3

From Christian's computer journal

January 10, 2015

Henry is sick, and they don't know what's wrong with him. It started as a low-grade fever that wouldn't go away, and then he became colicky, crying literally all the time, nearly every moment of every day, barely even sleeping. Which means I'm not sleeping, and Ava's not sleeping. Ava is out of her mind with panic. Something's wrong with him, she claims. Something serious. She *knows* there is, she says, she just doesn't know what. We've taken him to the doctor; we've taken him to *several* doctors. He's been X-rayed, MRI'd, CAT scanned, poked, prodded...they just can't figure it out.

Even when Henry finally manages to fall asleep, I can't find rest. My eyes close, my body demands rest, but my mind will not quiet. The only way I can slow or quiet myself enough to sleep is through medication, which leaves me groggy and unable to wake up, or self-medication by way of excessive amounts of scotch. I don't care for either option, and Ava says I'm a different man when I've been drinking.

But without those options, I don't sleep.

It's four in the morning right now, and I tossed and turned from the moment I laid down at eleven until finally giving up and opening my laptop to this journal a few minutes ago.

I have the baby monitor beside me, and I can hear Henry fussing. Tossing, turning, mewling, as if he, too, cannot rest.

I'm not a praying man, but I've found myself begging any deity that might exist to give me Henry's illness, to take it from him and give it to me. He's an innocent little boy, not even a year old. He doesn't deserve this—no one deserves this, but a baby?

I think about that, and I get angry, and I'm reminded why I've never been a praying man.

Bad things happen to good people, and good things happen to bad people. There is no justice.

I know this is ridiculous and selfish and petty and horrible, which is why the only place I'll ever voice this complaint is here, in this digital journal, but...

Ava and I haven't had sex in months. Since before Henry was born. I know, I know—she gave birth, she needed to heal. No problem. But then once she got the okay from Dr. Gupta, she didn't feel ready. She still had the baby weight, she said, and she felt like she looked like roast beef down there—her words, not mine—and didn't want me anywhere near it. And then Henry started crying all the time, and that's taken all of our time and energy, and now she's too panicked and exhausted and stressed to even think about intimacy.

And I know I shouldn't be thinking about that, but I can't help it. I *need* that intimacy with her. Yes, I also need the physical release and relief, but it's more than that. It's the connection. The closeness we find, especially in the afterglow.

God, I feel like such an asshole, but the need for her is yet another stone on the pile weighing me down. And I dare not say anything to her. Dare not make a move. It would hurt too much to be rejected yet again, and would only upset her more than she already is. I know she doesn't mean it as a rejection of *me*, per se, but that's still how it feels.

Now more than ever we need each other, yet…I feel us drifting further and further apart.

4

January 20, 2015

Let's talk about sex.

Ha, now you've got that song stuck in your head.

But for real, I've got some dirty thoughts I need to muse on, and you naughty vixens out there seem to enjoy getting glimpses into the inner workings of my fucked-up mind, for some reason, and so you're going to be my sounding board.

Henry was born seven months ago.

The last time I had marital intercourse with my husband was exactly twenty-four days before that;

I know the exact date only because I blogged about it (which you can find <u>here</u>). So, it has been eight months since I last had sex.

Eight months without any nookie whatsoever.

Ya'll.

That's not okay.

NOT OKAY.

Mama needs her nookie, all right?

I mean, yeah, the first three months or so are understandable: I had just pushed a human being out of my vagina, and Henry was *not* a small baby, at nine pounds six ounces. So yeah, six to nine weeks of recovery for poor Ava St. Pierre's hoo-ha is to be expected.

And then…and *then*…?

Nobody tells you about the hemorrhoids, nor what I've been calling the Arby's poon—which is when your lady bits rather closely resemble a sandwich from the aforementioned purveyor of meat-like-substance imitation sandwiches. Yeah, I'd like to have learned about *that* shit in the My Baby and Me class. Screw Lamaze, let's talk about roast beef pussy. Yeah, sure, of course Chris told me I looked totally normal and was more beautiful than ever; he *had* to say that because he knew I'd kill him—

The other thing nobody talks about is that your hormones don't go back to normal right away either. I mean, yeah, you hear all about how you'll be hormonal during pregnancy, and you'll have weird cravings and alternate between loving your hubby more than ever and wanting to strangle him with his shoelaces—which you couldn't reach because hello, you're pregnant. Do you ever hear about still feeling like an unhinged lunatic months after the baby is born? NOOOOOO. I didn't, at least. Yeah, they talk about postpartum depression, but what about postpartum homicidal rage because you're not getting laid? What about feeling stabby because your baby is three months old and you haven't had wine or coffee in almost a fucking year, and now they're telling you that you *STILL* can't have it because you're breastfeeding?

Switching Henry to formula so I can have wine and coffee would make me a horrible mother, wouldn't it? Yes, I know I can have beer while I'm breastfeeding because of something to do with lactation or something, but honestly, *beer*? Probz not, folks.

But I digress.

Sex.

Which I'm not having.

Why?

Because I'm still twenty pounds away from my post-baby goal weight, and it seems like a goal I'll never reach because Henry is colicky and difficult and I think he's sick but they can't find anything wrong with him. But I'm his mama, dammit, and I *know* he's sick. I've been around colicky babies before. My sister's son, my nephew Alex, now *he* was a super colicky baby. He was just cranky all the time, and hated life and hated being put down and hated being hungry and hated being wet and REALLY hated being poopy, and guess what he was all the time? Hungry, wet, and poopy. That was colic. He grew out of it, turned into the sweetest, cutest, happiest little walking, talking kid you could ask for.

This, with Henry? It's not colic.

There's something wrong, and nobody knows what.

So that's not helping the get-Ava-laid program.

Also not helping is the fact that Christian is under deadline and took two months off from writing to help me with Henry and take care of me. God bless the man, he did so much in those two months, and I don't know how any woman has ever survived those months without my Chris, because he made me breakfast in bed, brought me endless mugs of herbal tea, brought me snacks, held Henry so I could sleep, changed diapers, went to Walgreens whenever I ran out of Tuck's pads AND brought back chocolate. He had pizza and the Thai place on speed dial, and could get in and out with our order in less than ten minutes, so I wouldn't be alone with Henry for too long while I was still so sore I could barely walk.

Yeah, they also don't tell you about that. Giving birth hurts—that's not news; what's news is that it continues to hurt for weeks and weeks afterward.

So yeah, Christian was an actual angel from heaven,

and now he's got sixty thousand words due in six weeks and did I mention that Henry cries ALL...THE...TIME? Poor man isn't sleeping, and he's still trying to be there for my every want and need, and he's got insane stress from the due date.

The only thing he can't do for me is make me capable of sex.

See, that's the issue. I WANT sex. I NEED sex.

My man and I have wicked powerful chemistry, okay? I've blogged about this before (here and here). Chris and I? We're, like, world champions at sex.

But...my body is all like *NO, AVA, NO SEX FOR YOU* and my mind is like **FUCK YOU, BODY, GET WITH THE PROGRAM! RIDE THAT DICK!** And my heart is like *I just want intimacy. I want him to whisper sweet nothings and tell me how beautiful I am and kiss me and make me feel desired and needed.*

And I'm freaking out about Henry. Freaking out seriously hardcore, and that's just shut down my mojo completely.

Even worse is, I know Chris is feeling it too. He needs it as much as I do, if not more so simply because he's a dude and dudes require crazy amounts of sex to function. My point is, he needs me. He needs *us.*

And I can't give it to him.

I wonder if he ever reads my blog?

If you're reading this, Christian, then please know it's not you. I love you more than ever and want you more than ever, but I just...*can't*. And I feel horrible about it, and I'm sorry.

Who am I kidding? Christian's never read my blog, and never will. Not because he doesn't care—he does, and he supports me, so don't get the wrong idea, here.

I don't know, though. Don't let my pithy blog style fool you, dear readers: I'm a damned mess right now.

5

From Christian's journal

February 14, 2015

Valentine's Day.

Fitting that this would happen today, on Ava's and my least favorite holiday of all time.

Henry has officially been admitted to the pediatric oncology ward. It's 2:30am, and I haven't slept in forty-eight hours, haven't eaten in sixty. Ava is curled up on the chair/bed thing beside Henry's hospital crib, her hand over his, a troubled expression marring her features even asleep.

God, I love her.

I just took a candid snapshot of her with my phone,

and I'm staring at it, memorizing her features. It's not like I don't have a trillion photos of her, and it's not like I couldn't sketch her from memory, if I could draw for crap, that is. But for some reason, this feels different.

She's medium height, five-six in her bare feet, which are size six and adorably tiny. She has black hair cut in a smart chin-length bob, and stunning, vivid blue eyes. She's svelte, delicate. She has a perfect body, in my opinion. Hour glass figure, a hip-to-waist-to-bust ratio most other women would kill for. The few extra pounds she's kept on after having Henry actually adds some softness and curve to her body, if you were to ask me, but she doesn't want to hear that. She has a prominent Jewish nose, which she hates and which I love, a feature courtesy of her Orthodox paternal grandparents. Her fierce azure eyes are compliments of a dominant gene on her mother's side, or so she says. She has a penchant for cursing which I find at once funny and amusing and erotic. The way she says "fuck" when she's pissed off is so completely different from the way she says it when she's turned on and encouraging me in bed. She's wildly intelligent, insightful, a talented wordsmith…and she's cuttingly funny. As in, her tongue is by far her greatest weapon, followed closely by her pen—metaphorical and literal.

I'm ruminating on Ava because it's easier than thinking about Henry.

They're talking about a brain tumor. Scans show a

mass in the very center of his brain, diffused in such a way as to have made it hard to detect and impossible to operate on.

Radiation and chemotherapy will extend his life by a matter of months, if that, and those months will be fraught with horror and agony and sickness.

Ava refuses to accept what the doctors are saying. Insists there has to be another way. A cure. An experimental treatment. *Something*.

They insist there isn't.

Prepare for the worst, they have told us.

Worse than what we've already gone through?

Their suggestion: medicate him out of the pain, and allow the cancer to run its course.

Dope him up and let him die, they mean.

But Ava...god, Ava. My sweet, fierce Ava. She's crumbling. Trying to stay strong. Trying to keep her chin up. Trying to be cheerful for Henry. But then he falls asleep again, and the false cheer falls away, replaced by a vacant, haunted stare.

And I can think of no words to soothe her.

Because I'm crumbling just the same. Except I cannot summon false cheer. To keep the sobs at bay is all I can manage, and that requires a total shutdown of my emotive capacity. I am a blank wall, a breathing, moving statue of stone. It's not fair to Ava, who needs me to be strong, but I have no strength.

Ava knew there was something wrong with Henry

all along, so this isn't as much of a shock to her.

To me, it is an earthquake of a magnitude no Richter scale can measure.

I have to put some kind of food inside me. I have to sleep.

But how can I think of such mundanity as food and sleep when my son is dying?

6

From Ava's blog:
Confessions of Working Mommy

March 17, 2015

I haven't blogged in weeks, and for that, dear readers, I apologize. I probably won't be on again for some time to come, and I'm only putting this up because I feel I owe my dedicated readers a bit of an explanation.

Henry has a brain tumor.

Inoperable.

Incurable.

Fatal.

We are near the end, now. Another week or two, at most, they're telling us.

So…yeah.

I've already decided that I won't be changing the name of my blog; he'll be gone, but I'll still be a mommy. Just…a mommy without a child.

I don't have anything else, right now. I won't be replying to comments or emails any time soon, but I'll say thank you in advance now for your prayers, thoughts, well-wishes, and eventual sympathies. Thank you.

When I am capable of writing again, when I'm capable of my trademark humor and sarcasm, I'll return to blogging. Maybe.

But for now,

For now…

I don't know.

I guess for now I have to figure out how to survive my son's death.

Blunt, but that's what it is. I'm not one to shy away from the truth, and by now y'all know I'm also not shy about putting the truth up on my blog, whether everyone is comfortable with it or likes it or not.

This is bullshit, and I would like to take this opportunity to extend a pair of raised middle fingers to God, Mother Nature, the universe, whoever and/or whatever is in charge of this kind of thing.

FUCK YOU for taking my child.

Because in the process, you're taking Chris, and myself, and everything I am and everything I have away from me. And it's not fair.

So fuck you for that.

Okay, the rant is over. Again, I'll be radio silent for the foreseeable future, and I can't guarantee you I'll ever be as funny as I used to be.

April 5, 2015

Christian scoops up a handful of rich brown soil, steps to the edge of the grave, and lets the dirt trickle over the edge of his palm. The soil makes an echoing, thudding sound on the small casket of polished mahogany.

Ava stands a few feet behind him, a wad of Kleenex clutched in one fist, which is trembling and pressed against her lips. Tears trickle down her cheeks. Ava's older sister Delta and her son Alex stand with Ava's parents, nearby. Christian's mother, his only living family, stands close to Ava's family. A few friends and some of Ava's extended family are also in attendance. The minister has said his words, and waits nearby, looking appropriately somber, his hands folded over his well-worn leather Bible.

Christian glances back at Ava, stretches out his hand for her. She refuses with a soft shake of her head.

"Come on, Ava. One last goodbye."

"I can't." Her voice is a whisper, lost in a hot Florida breeze. "I can't. I already said goodbye to him. I can't do it again."

Ava turns and walks away, the thin black spikes of her heels sinking into the thick green turf. Her back is straight, and a pair of oversized black Brighton sunglasses cover her face, hiding her tears. Except those that drip from her chin, that is. She reaches their car, a glossy white Range Rover, climbs into the passenger seat, and waits with the door open to allow the heat built up inside the vehicle to vent out.

Christian spends another moment at the grave, staring down at the tiny wooden box. "Goodbye, Henry. I love you." His voice breaks on the final whispered word, and then he strides slowly across the grass, his once-broad shoulders now thin and stooped, as if he is bent to breaking under some invisible, enormous weight.

Ava watches him. He's as handsome as ever, only… now he's thin and haggard. Once, he was powerfully built and bursting with vitality, radiating charisma and charm, his chiseled features exuding life and joy and vibrant intelligence. His hair is greasy, unwashed, and shows strands of gray, where before there were only glossy, wavy, sandy-brown locks usually left artfully messy. His eyes, though. Those show his sorrow the most clearly.

Blue-gray, the color of polished steel, or the sea in the distance on a cloudy day. They once shone brightly, warmly, they once welcomed you to approach him and invited you to sit down and talk to him, and for Ava, they once begged her to kiss him, to interrupt his writing, to come up with something quippy and sarcastic just to see those eyes of his blaze with humor. Now, they're dead and flat. More steel than sea. Sorrowful rather than sanguine. Hard, rather than inviting. Sunken, dark circles, bags. Lines, deeply carved around them and between them. Anger lines and sorrow lines, rather than laugh lines.

Ava is as much changed as Christian, and she knows it.

Her heart is cracking, shattering, but for the first time in her life she can find no way of expressing any of it. She has no words. She was voted "most talkative" in high school, but now…what is there to say?

Christian climbs into the Rover, starts it with a push of the button. They pull away, and leave the cemetery. The radio is off. Her hands are folded on her lap, fingers twisting and tangling and tightening and releasing compulsively. Christian drives with his right hand at twelve o'clock on the steering wheel, the fingers of his left hand propped at his temple, pressing hard.

It's a thirty-minute drive from the cemetery to their condo on the beach north of Ft. Lauderdale; those thirty minutes pass in complete silence.

And when they arrive home, Ava trudges listlessly to their bedroom, leaving one of her shoes in the den and the other in the hallway, discarding her purse at the foot of the bed. She climbs into bed, on the right side, under the covers, fully clothed, staring at a small framed photo on her bedside table.

In that photograph, Henry is in cradled in her arms, a bright, happy, innocent grin on his little face, lighting up his eyes, which are so much like his father's. In that photograph, Ava is just as happy, the smile on her face so wide and so bright she is utterly transformed. She doesn't recognize herself, in that photograph. It doesn't match the woman she sees in the mirror.

Once through the door, Christian does three things in a specific order, with practiced familiarity: first, he sets his keys on the center of the island, along with his phone and wallet; second, he flips open a cabinet over the refrigerator and grabs a bottle of Johnny Walker Black Label; third, he goes into his office, closes the door, and sits behind the desk with his scotch. He takes a long pull directly from the bottle, and stares at a photograph on the left side of the desk: it is a selfie, snapped early one morning on his phone. Ava is asleep on her side, Henry cradled carefully in her arms, nuzzled to her bare breast, his chubby little fingers curled against her pale skin. They both share the same peaceful half-smile, mother and child. The selfie features half of Christian's face, the right side of the photograph slicing directly down the center of his face, and his smile is one of pride and happiness and joy at the sight of his sleepy little family.

His laptop, a thin silver MacBook Air, remains closed in the middle of his desk. On the top of it, just below the Apple logo, is a yellow Post-it Note, in his handwriting: *last 20k words due 4/7.*

The date is April 5, 2015, and he has never missed a deadline, not once in his life, academically or professionally.

Even if he opened his laptop, he knew there would be no words waiting to flow through his fingertips.

When his father died, Christian wrote. He channeled the rage and confusion and relief into a marathon eighteen-hour writing session, in which he produced twenty thousand words of the most poetic and powerful prose of his entire life.

When his beloved dog died, he wrote.

When he and Ava broke up their senior year of college, he wrote.

And he wrote even more when they got back together, and only stopped to spend forty-eight hours making up with her. He'd then made omelets and toast and had gone back to writing.

This time?

There was nothing.

Silence.

And that, in some ways, was the most terrifying thing of all.

For a writer, that mental silence which signifies a damming up of the creative flow is death by torture—excruciating, slow, and terrifying.

Christian takes another slug of the Johnny Walker, a long glugging drag on the bottle, and then slams it down with a growling hiss as the whisky burns down his throat.

He coughs, and then twists the cap back on.

A sudden, fierce need seizes him, and he gives it rein. He stands up suddenly, leaving the chair spinning as he moves around the desk, out of the office, and up the stairs. He pauses in the doorway of their room, staring at the slight bump under the duvet that is Ava. She must know he's there, but gives no indication. The blanket doesn't rise or fall visibly, and fear blasts through him, spurring him to lurch over to her side of the bed and crouch beside it, peering at her—she's alive, she hasn't suddenly and inexplicably died. She's just…there. Barely. Her eyes are open, staring at the photograph. Tears trickle now and then down her cheek, into her eye, onto the pillow. She doesn't wipe them away, doesn't sniffle.

Christian stands up. Rips off his tie. Tosses the suit coat aside. Kicks his shoes away. Sheds his dress shirt and the undershirt with its faint sweat stains at the underarms. Steps out of his trousers and underwear. Slides into the bed behind Ava. He clings to her, pressing himself up against her.

She doesn't move.

"Ava." His voice is a murmur, a low, rough, ragged

plea. "Look at me."

She doesn't respond. If he hadn't seen her blink a tear away, if he couldn't feel the warmth of her skin and the subtle expansion of her torso as he clings to her, he would think her dead.

"Ava. *Please.* Talk to me." His palm clutches at her belly, his nose buries between her shoulder blades. He heaves a shuddering breath. "Please."

Silence.

Christian remains behind her, clinging to her. Breathing her scent. Begging her—silently now—to respond, to turn to him, literally and metaphorically—for comfort.

But there is only silence.

From Christian's journal

May 3, 2015

Ava is completely unresponsive. She leaves the bed to use the bathroom and drink a glass of water now and then, but that's it. I've brought her meals three times a day for over a month, and she hasn't touched any of them. She is wasting away before my eyes. I can do nothing. I tried to physically sit her up and somewhat force her to eat, and she flat out punched me. She didn't say a word, didn't curse or scream, just struck me across the face, and then when I released her out of sheer shock, she resumed her place in the bed, curled up on her left side facing the photograph of her and Henry.

I've spoken to our family physician, Dr. Lucas, and he says a healthy adult—even one still with a "normal" body mass index like Ava—can go months without food without significant or lasting damage. As long as she's drinking water regularly, she won't die of starvation any time soon.

So medically, nutritionally, there's nothing to worry about. She'll lose some weight, but that's about it.

Mentally, emotionally? Dr. Lucas said everyone deals with grief in their own way, and this is hers. I should be there, I should remind her that I love her, continue to offer her food, continue my attempts to reach her.

And so I do.

I bring her sandwiches and soup and salads, and I set them on a tray on the bed behind her, and I sit near her and beg with her to eat. To respond to me. To speak, at least. She hasn't spoken a word in weeks, and I beg her to speak to me three times every single day.

I'm beginning to feel desperate. Undone. I too am grieving. I want to climb in bed behind her and stay there with her and just not ever wake up.

My body won't let me. I feel a physical desperation to move. A panic if I remain still for too long. And I cannot sleep, because worry for Ava consumes me, overwhelming all thoughts and needs.

I watch her breathe, just to know that she's still alive. I still fear that one day I'll bring her a meal and she'll be staring into space as she always is, but she won't be breathing, her skin will be cold, her limbs stiff, and her lips blue.

Panic is a tangible thing. It's in my heart, crawls on my skin like lice, scurries through the dark corners of my mind like roaches fleeing a beam of light. It causes my legs to writhe out of my control, sends my feet to carry me away at the oddest hours of the night.

I find myself walking my neighborhood alone at 3am, naked but for a pair of gym shorts, barefoot, shivering, struggling for breath even though I'm barely walking.

I'm drinking too much. It's barely noon as I write this, and I'm fighting the urge to grab the bottle of whisky. I'm losing the fight, too. I'm afraid I will succumb, and become the worst kind of Hemingway—all the booze, none of the prodigious talent.

What do I do? How am I to cope? How am I to grieve? My wife is...gone, for all intents and purposes. All but dead. I cannot reach her. And I am...crumbling. I don't know a better word for this.

How long can I go on like this? I'm trying to be strong. I'm trying to be what she needs.

I'm trying.

I fear I'm going to fail, and soon.

From Christian's journal

June 10, 2015

Two months have passed, and Ava has finally begun something like normal life once more. She took a shower. She ate a very small meal—a few pieces of sliced deli turkey, a few slices of Havarti cheese, some jalapeño-stuffed olives, and a mug of black tea.

She was always a svelte woman, but now she is... worrisomely thin. Her ribs show, as do the bones in her wrists and forearms. Her cheeks are sunken. But she is upright, moving, and eating.

She still won't speak, however.

I sat at the kitchen table with her and watched her

eat, tried to engage her in conversation, but she completely ignored me.

I haven't written a word in months. I fear I might never again.

I went into our bedroom to strip the bed so I could wash the bed sheets, and when I came back, Ava was gone. She'd taken her Mercedes and left.

I know where she went: to Henry's grave. So I set the sheets to washing and went after her. I found her lying on the thick green grass over his grave.

God, that was difficult, seeing that headstone:

Henry Christopher Michael St. Pierre
Beloved son, gone too soon.
June 24, 2014—April 3, 2015

I sat beside her, traced the letters of his name on the marble. Touched, tentatively, Ava's shoulder.

She jerked away. "Don't touch me."

"Ava, please, we need to—"

"Go away."

"I'm hurting, too, you know."

"Then go have another drink."

"That's not fair," I told her. "He was my son. I loved him, and I lost him, too. You're not going through this alone."

"Yes, I am." Her fingers dug into the grass, clawing as if to dig through the earth to cradle his tiny form beneath the soil.

"Well, you don't have to. I love you. I need you, Ava. Let's try to get through this together."

She shook her head, but said nothing.

I stayed with her as she lay on the grave, hour by hour. The sun began to set, and I grasped her hand. "Ava, let's go home. Please."

She shook her head again. "You go. I'm staying here."

So I sat with her hours more. The air grew cool, and she began to shiver beside me. I went to my Rover and retrieved the blanket I keep in the trunk, settled it around her shoulders. For the first time in the months since Henry passed away, her eyes met mine. Briefly, a fleeting touch of her eyes on mine; in her vivid blue gaze I saw a woman I did not know. Gone was the vibrancy, the life, the fierceness, the humor, the sweetness and compassion and the touch of arrogance, gone was the giver of zero fucks—her words, not mine—and gone was the woman who once convinced me to walk out of our philosophy class together so we could—as she put it—fuck like teenagers. Which was exactly what we had done. We had excused ourselves to go to the bathroom, her first and then me, and we fucked like crazy in the handicapped stall. Then we got into my restored and beloved 1988 Ford Bronco and drove to the beach where we fucked in the surf.

I would put it more eloquently, more poetically, but in truth, that afternoon, it was exactly that: raw, rough, and dirty fucking. There was no sweetness to it, no soft sighs in the candlelit darkness, no hands clasped and trembling as we found union in each other's arms. We discovered all those things together, certainly, and many many more times over the years. But that afternoon…I don't know. There was something in the air, I suppose. A fierce and wild drive to devour each other.

This evening, at 8:38pm, I looked into Ava's eyes and did not see that woman.

(When I looked away, because I could take no more of her gaze, my gaze fell to my iWatch, and the digital readout told me the precise time when I knew my wife was gone.)

In her eyes, I saw only a vacant and haunted being, a withered and bitter emptiness. A woman I did not know. She was cold. So, so cold. I would say there was "distance" in her gaze, but that would not be a strong enough word; "distance" is the space between New York and Los Angeles. When we broke up our senior year, it was because she was afraid of falling in love with me as deeply as she felt herself doing, and panicked—a tale as old as time. She shut me out, and eventually walked away. But a month later, she knocked on my door and asked if we could talk. That day, in my apartment in Miami, there was distance in her eyes. She couldn't stay away, but she was still afraid. It took months more for that ice to thaw, for the distance to close. That day, I saw distance—as if I was standing in Miami and she was physically present there with me, but emotionally, she may as well have been in Seattle.

When I met Ava's gaze this evening, we were both sitting in a cemetery in Ft. Lauderdale, but emotionally and mentally Ava may as well have been sitting on Pluto, spinning in the farthest reaches of our solar system. That is not mere distance—that is something so much more that I do not know a word in any language to encompass it.

I got into my car and I drove home. I took the bottle of Johnny Walker and went out onto the beach and I buried my toes in the cool sand, and I drank myself into a stupor.

I am writing this at 4:24am, because I woke up on the beach, freezing. I vomited into the sand, and then went inside. Ava was asleep, and remained so as I took a shower and changed into sweatpants and my University of Miami hoodie. Instead of joining her in our bed—what had once been our bed, at least—I slept on the couch in my office. Or...tried to sleep. The couch is comfortable enough, which I know from experience, as I've slept there a few times after particularly nasty arguments. I couldn't sleep. Not anymore.

I'm writing this journal, because it's all I know how to do.

Perhaps if I can write here, I can manage to write fiction.

Perhaps not. I don't know.

The only thing I do know for sure is that it feels as if I have died and am now trapped in purgatory.

How do I escape? Because escape I must, or…

Or what? I don't know.

A common enough phrase to hear: I'm going crazy; I'm going to lose my mind.

But what does that look like when it really happens? What will I do when I can take no more?

From Ava's blog
Confessions of a Working Mommy

July 3, 2015

Three months.

It has been three months since…

God, it's impossible for me to even write the words. Let me get some wine and I'll try again, a bit less sober. Hold on.

Okay, let's try this again, now that I'm lubricated with some cab sav.

It has been three months since Henry died.

FUCK.

He passed away on April 3, 2015. We buried him

on April 5.

I didn't eat for the first two months; I think I've said a total of a hundred words maximum in these past ninety days. I mean that very literally. I didn't speak, didn't eat, barely got out of bed. I drank water and I had diarrhea, and I cried.

Friends stopped by, and I ignored them. My sister called me a thousand times, and I ignored her calls. Her voicemails are still on my phone, not listened to. My voicemail icon has a little red 28 next to it, which is the number of voicemails Delta has left me. My text message icon? 128 unread messages. My parents called too, but I've never been very close to them, and I have nothing to say to them, and there's nothing they could say which I'd want to hear.

The good news: I'm under my pre-pregnancy weight by 18 pounds.

I was 135 before pregnancy, 156 after, and I'm now 117. Which, I suppose is worth mentioning, puts me officially underweight for my height.

Yay!

That's all I've got for good news, dear readers.

Waking up is hard. Putting on clothes is hard. Breathing is hard. Making myself eat food is hard. Not drinking myself into a catatonic stupor every day— which is Christian's current coping methodology— is really really really *really* motherfucking hard.

In fact, it's so hard I'm failing completely. See, I too

am prone to long bouts of intensive alcohol consumption. The truly sad part is we're not even coping via alcoholism together. He drinks in his office or on the beach out back, and I drink in our room or in the den in front of the TV.

Judge me all you want, readers, IDGAF. For the uninitiated, that stands for "I don't give a fuck", FYI.

And FWIW, Christian has tried his damnedest to connect with me, but I just can't seem to function or understand him or feel any emotions other than rage and grief and depression and guilt and listless apathy. I guess I only say that so you guys don't feel the need to crucify him in the comments or anything. He's trying, and I see that. I just…don't know how to care.

Also, is needing to drink myself blind an emotion?

I'm sorry to be such a downer, peeps, but it's all I've got right now.

How did you cope with a debilitating loss? Sound off in the comments.

For now, I'm going to finish this bottle, and probably drink another bottle or three before passing out in a pool of my own vomit.

JKLOL, I don't puke when I'm drunk. No need to worry about me, Christian won't let me die like that.

Probably.

I'm out of fun acronyms, so I'm ending this blog post with a rare request:

If you pray, pray for me; if you believe in the power

of positive thinking, then think good thoughts for me;
if you're an activist who believes in taking action to
solve problems, then send me more wine and possibly
Xanax.

11

July 25, 2015

Ava is passed out on the couch, *Judge Judy* muted on the TV. Two empty wine bottles sit side by side on the coffee table, silent witnesses to her wine-soaked sorrow. She has spent much of the past month like that, drinking, watching TV, and picking at the occasional meal.

Christian has not been idle. He sold his Range Rover for close to market value, cashed out all their investments, sold the condo in LA, sold the apartment complex in Miami and all the other properties he owned. When his books started selling and the cash started rolling in, he decided to invest in real estate rather than letting it sit idle, or trying to monkey with the stock market. Ava knew about it, but had always been content to let him do what he wanted as long as they could afford the payment on her SL550 and splurge on the occasional purse. He'd invested wisely, it had turned out: he'd netted himself a net profit on the sales of all the properties to the tune of well north of twenty million.

He paid off the Ft. Lauderdale condo he and Ava currently lived in, paid off Ava's car, purchased a life insurance plan for himself, and set up an auto-payment plan for the utilities and Ava's car insurance. He split the remaining income streams—percentages from the film deal, which included merchandise royalties and gross sales percentages—between their joint account and his new personal one. The real estate money was his, so he kept the remainder after setting Ava up for financial solvency in his impending absence. Their personal account had contained a nest egg of savings, which he left alone; after setting things up he had enough cash in various offshore accounts plus royalty payments that he could function in luxury for a long time.

Then, he bought the boat. He'd come across the listing quite by accident—as an idle pursuit, he'd searched sailboats for sale online, and had come across a gem: a brand new, ocean-going catamaran for sale, with a ridiculous list of amenities and custom features, operable by a single experienced occupant.

Christian was nothing if not an experienced sailor: he'd left home at sixteen, hitchhiking and walking from rural Illinois all the way down to Miami, where he'd found work at a mechanic's garage, which specialized in boat motors. Christian knew motors better than he knew anything, since his father had taught him everything there was to know about fixing an engine…along with how to take a beating. He'd shown aptitude and willingness to work, and had ended up finding a berth aboard a sailing yacht a couple years later, doing engine maintenance and learning to sail. He'd circumnavigated the globe aboard that yacht, and eventually became an expert sailor. When he was nineteen, he'd accepted a position as first mate aboard an antique schooner, and sailed from the Caribbean around Tierra Del Fuego and up the Pacific to Los Angeles, and then to the Far East sailing West. By that time he was twenty-two and didn't even have a high school diploma. The owner and captain of the schooner, a reclusive millionaire, had offered to pay for Christian's education, and so Christian found himself in Miami, finishing his GED and enrolling at the University of Miami.

He'd worked aboard a fishing charter while studying, and had planned to save enough for his own boat. But then he'd met Ava. One day, six months after they began dating, he'd written her a romantic little short story, just for fun, on a whim. Not a big deal, and he hadn't even considered it very good. It had just been meant to make her swoon a little, laugh a little, and get him laid. Well, it had done all three with admirable success, and had also sparked an interest. So he wrote another short story, and another. And another. And then, a few months later, he realized he had nearly fifty short stories, and collated them into a single volume. On a whim, he'd sent it out with a query letter to a few dozen agents—and to his immense shock, he'd been accepted by one, an exclusive and premier agent who had immediately sold his short story collection with a caveat that Christian follow up with a full-length novel within a year.

He'd taken an idea he'd had for a short story, expanded it, and had a full-length novel within six months. It had sold as well. Not for a lot, but enough to prompt him to write another novel. Which had also sold, and through luck, timing, clever marketing, and aggressive touring, had ended up earning out in a year. By this time, Christian was twenty-six and in his senior year of college.

Then, toward the end of his senior year, his father had died. This sent Christian into a tailspin, but not out of grief; rather, out of a bizarre sense of relief, which had birthed a large dollop of guilt, which had in turn incited confusion and self-loathing, and like any writer or other artist, he'd turned to his craft for solace.

He'd produced a full novel within three weeks, and his agent had sold it in another week, for a huge advance, and that novel had gone on to go through several print runs, earned out swiftly, and garnered him praise and adulation...and a Hollywood film deal.

It had all been very surreal, and there the breakup with Ava in there, which had also prompted a magnificent piece of angst and heartache driven prosodic brilliance, which had only cemented his status as a hot new star, one whose every work turned to gold.

He'd gone after success like a man possessed, churning out sequels and standalone novels with crazy speed, and they'd all done remarkably well, two more novels getting optioned over the next four years—of the four books he'd had optioned, two had been made into films, the first and second books in a planned trilogy, and it was the third and final book in that trilogy for which his editor was now clamoring so desperately. Producers were already sniffing for the manuscript, hoping to capitalize on the heat of Christian's momentum.

Six years after that first novel, Christian has eight titles to his name, six of which were bestsellers. Two movies, both of which had done hundreds of millions at the box office, meaning massive payouts for him, since his film agent had been a wickedly savvy negotiator.

Six years. Eight books. Two movies. Millions of dollars.

And one dead child.

One ruined life.

One ruined marriage—well, one might argue two ruined marriages, since it's Ava's marriage as well as Christian's, and they seem to be approaching it differently, at the moment. Namely: Ava is drinking and avoiding and curling further and further into herself, and Christian is about to leave her.

He buys the sailboat, rechristening it *The Hemingway*. He's not exactly sure why he chose that name, only that it seems apropos.

His life has come to an abrupt halt, and it's now crashing into a million pieces around him. He can't write, can't sleep, can't do anything. His wife is lost to him, utterly. She won't speak to him, won't look at him, won't even respond to the slightest stimuli. She drinks, and she stares listlessly at the TV.

He checks her blog regularly. She's posted once since Henry passed, and that short post, all five hundred words of it, ravaged his heart and soul. He doesn't know how to fix her.

He can't fix himself. He's not cried for his son. He can't. He hasn't slept more than three hours in a row in nearly a hundred days. He has no appetite.

Worst of all, the very sight of Ava makes his heart bleed, makes him shake uncontrollably. He isn't sure if it's hatred or love or a confused mixture of the two, but her presence makes him physically ill. Not out of disgust, but…well, he's not sure. He can't pinpoint it or describe it or make sense of it, all he knows is that she won't even *look* at him. The few times she has, her gaze has been that vacant, icy stare she'd given him at the cemetery.

She goes there, every day.

He doesn't. He can't. His feet won't carry him there.

Sometimes, he can't breathe. His heart palpitates wildly. His hands tremble. He feels as if he might vomit, but doesn't.

Everything hurts.

Henry's nursery is exactly the way it was when they left to take him to the hospital. Nothing has been touched. The door remains closed. Once, while Ava was passed out, he tried to go in, intending to clean it out, but he couldn't. One look at the rocket ships on the walls and the stuffed lamb and the spare binkies and the open container of dried-out baby wipes, and Christian had fled, closing the door behind him. He'd finished an entire bottle of whisky, and woke up alone on the beach once more, still drunk at 2 a.m.

Everything hurts.

The only thing Christian knows, now, is that he has to leave. He can't stay anymore. He just can't. He's dying. Suffocating.

The guilt over leaving Ava will eat him alive, he knows this already. But if he stays...

Well, that's just not an option.

He's taken possession of *The Hemingway*, stocked it, moved the majority of his clothing and personal effects over to it; he's gone over every inch of the boat a million times from bow to stern, double checked all the arrangements to make sure Ava will be provided for into perpetuity, for as long as the royalties keep coming in. There's nothing else left to do.

He tries to wake up her. Shakes her shoulder.

"Ava."

"Mmmnnnngg."

"Ava, wake up."

"Nnng. Lemme 'lone."

"Ava, please. Wake up for one second."

She squints one blue eye at him. "What, Chris?"

He hesitates. Hoping she'll give him a reason to stay. "I love you, Ava."

She stares at him for a long moment, as if uncomprehending, and then she closes her eye and rolls away from him.

"Ava?"

"Don't." Her voice is muzzy, slurred. Sleepy.

More than likely she won't remember this when she wakes up.

"I love you, Ava. Never forget that."

"Mmmm."

A sob tries to jag through him, and he clamps down on it, so it only emerges as a soft, whining exhalation. Had she heard it, she would have said it sounded like a hurt puppy.

There's one last arrangement to make: Ava hates being alone, but more than people, the company she craves more than anything is a pet, but there simply hasn't been time in the past few years for pets, and Christian never wanted one; it was a constant sore point between them, and a source of conflict.

So, he finds a labradoodle breeder nearby, Ava's favorite breed. He buys a puppy, brings it home.

Ava is awake, drinking wine and watching *Mad Men* reruns. "Who's this?" she asks.

"I've been calling him Darcy."

"After Pride and Prejudice." Ava slides off the couch, moving sloppily to sit on the floor, scooping the puppy into her arms.

He'd known exactly what Ava would name a puppy, if she were to get one.

The next day, he's out running when he sees a little girl sitting at a table on the apron of her driveway, with a large transparent storage crate in front of her, filled with calico kittens; there's a handwritten sign—*free to a loveing home only take one if you will really really love it.*

Christian takes one, brings it home, snuggling it against his chest as he jogs back to the condo. Once again, Ava is awake when he returns, a little after three in the afternoon, although she is visibly intoxicated already.

"This is Bennet," he says, settling the warm little bundle of fur in her hands.

Ava stares at him, but says nothing.

Yet, she cuddles the kitten to her chest, nuzzling her nose into its fur. A tear slides down her cheek into the kitten's fur, and yet Ava still only stares at Christian.

Darcy sniffs the kitten, and Ava scoops the puppy onto her lap, letting the two animals meet. It's a heart-rending scene, and Christian finds himself unable to breathe. Eventually, he turns away, returning to his office. It is empty, since he's already transferred most of his books and his laptop to the boat. There's nothing in the office, in fact, except the desk, chair, and a half-empty bottle of scotch.

Which he finishes, slowly, sitting at the desk, fighting the urge to smash the bottle against the wall.

He pens a note for Ava, using his personalized stationery and Mont Blanc fountain pen—once prized possessions which he now finds…gauche and pretentious.

August 3, 2015

Ava wakes up on the couch. It is dark outside, but there is a hint of gray on the horizon, prophesying the coming dawn. She is still drunk. Her head throbs, and her stomach is roiling, and her hands tremble. Darcy, the little labradoodle puppy, is asleep at her feet, curled into a comma, his nose tucked under his tail; Bennet, the kitten, is draped along the back of the couch, wide awake, staring and blinking and watching Ava as she rouses herself to a sitting position.

The cable box shows the time in bright orange numerals: 5:08 a.m.

Something is amiss.

Her gut clenches, and it has nothing to do with

the alcohol curdling in her system. Any home is quiet and still in the predawn hours, but there is a new texture to this silence, a foreboding, an echoing sense of... otherness.

Ava shuffles from the living room into the kitchen, peering sleepily around. Then to the hallway and the bathroom. She hesitates outside Christian's office, but lacks the courage to open that door just yet. Their bedroom is empty, the bed made, fresh sheets turned down, pillows plumped; Christian learned how to professionally make and turn down a bed while working on that rich guy's yacht, and has always been a bit anal retentive about it. She checks the master bathroom—something is missing. But what? It takes her bleary, wine-fogged mind a moment or two to figure it out.

His razor is gone. His shaving cream is gone. His deodorant and hair paste and cologne and toothbrush are gone. She checks the cabinet, and any item he used frequently is gone along with his stuff from under the sink.

She pads into the walk-in closet: his clothes are gone, the hangers empty and neatly arranged against one side of the closet, the shelves empty. His dresser drawers are empty. His watch collection is gone, and even the ceramic dish he'd made in fifth grade in which he keeps spare change is gone. All of his effects and belongings are gone.

Finally, she can avoid his office no longer. She stands outside the door for a long, tense moment. Her hand trembles on the knob. And then, abruptly, she twists the knob and shoves the door open, and it shudders and slams against the wall and drifts back toward her, catching to a stop against her bare toe. Empty shelves, clean desk—he was a messy writer, with pages of handwritten notes scattered everywhere, reminders on Post-its, bills half out of envelopes. His laptop is gone. The drawers are empty.

She doesn't see the note at first. On a desperate hope, she half-jogs out the back door and out onto the beach. She scrunches through the sand to the place where he'd always sit and drink, as of late, a few feet up from the surf, close enough that water would lap at his feet but not get him wet.

Nothing but sand.

Back inside, to his office, and this time she sits in his chair. And that's when she sees the note:

You look at me with blame in your eyes, as if this is somehow my fault; you look at me with disdain, as if I willed all of this to happen; you look at me as if you don't even recognize me anymore, as if all of this has somehow irrevocably altered me on some intrinsic level.

You are not wrong, about any of it.

No, I could not have prevented Henry from dying; obviously I didn't want this—I wouldn't wish it on my worst enemy; of course this hellscape that is our life has changed me—how could it not?

It is not my fault.

Yet still, I accept the blame. I accept the disdain. I accept the distance in your eyes.

I accept it, because I am weak and empty and dead. I am a husk of a man, and it is better to be filled with guilt and self-loathing and sadness than to be so utterly empty and alone as I have been these last weeks.

Ava, my love: you have always been the best part of me, and through you we created Henry, our son, and in him I found completion and strength and purpose. Now that he is gone, I have lost those things, and I have lost you, and thus I have lost myself.

I'm sorry, Ava.

I wish I had the strength to go on, but I don't.

Goodbye.

"Christian?" Her voice is tremulous.

Rushing, now, she rechecks everything, as if his belongings might suddenly reappear. As if *he* might suddenly appear.

Darcy is worried, following Ava around, sniffing her heels and nudging her calves with a wet, cool nose, whimpering. Ava stoops, picks up Darcy and cradles him to her chest. He licks her chin, and then her cheeks, and that's when she realizes she's crying.

She collapses onto the couch, clinging to Darcy, her shoulders shaking.

"He's gone, Darcy."

ErrrrrRUFF?

"What do I do now?"

Darcy's head tilts to one side, and he whines in his throat.

For the first time since Henry's death, Ava cries audibly, loud sobs wracking her thin frame.

13

A handwritten letter from Christian to Ava

postmarked August 9, 2015

Ava,

I realize now that I owe you more of an explanation than my short and rather melodramatic note provided.

As I'm sure you have probably surmised, I bought a sailboat and have embarked on a solo journey around the world. I am not planning to circumnavigate. At least, not yet. At first I am simply going to wander wherever the winds take me, to reacquaint myself with life at sea. It has been a few years since I last sailed, but I am finding the skills return swiftly.

I have named my vessel The Hemingway.

I could not continue as things were, Ava. I just couldn't. You were all but catatonic for two months. You refused to eat, to speak to me, to even look at me. In the wake of losing our son, your withdrawal from life cut me deeply. I needed you, Ava. I tried with all that I was to be there, to remind you of my love, to support you as best I could, to be what you needed. But I too was grieving. I am still grieving—I wasn't able to indulge in true grief because my worry for you eclipsed even that.

I am angry with you, Ava. So very angry. You lost Henry the same as I did, but you claimed all the grief for yourself, leaving none for me.

And then, when you finally emerged from your catatonic state, you sank into heavy drinking. And still you wouldn't speak to me, wouldn't look at me, wouldn't interact with me. I know your pain, Ava, for it is mine as well. But you added to my loss by removing yourself from me.

And I'm afraid that was a loss too great to bear.

I feel as if I have died, these last months. I am dead. My body lives, but my mind and my heart have perished, and rather than being numb—which would be bliss, I think—I am feeling the pain of an excruciating death.

Enough of my self-indulgent, solipsistic rambling.

I have arranged things for you so that all you will need to do to take care of yourself is buy food and put gas in your car. The utilities are all on auto-pay, deducting from an account created for that purpose, which will always contain the requisite funds—you are an account holder, so should you wish to alter this arrangement, simply visit our bank. The condo and *your car are both paid for in full. Car and health insurance are both part of the aforementioned auto-pay system. You will have plenty of money in our joint account, and you have your own personal account to draw from as well, so you are, in every way, financially solvent. Meaning, you are taken care of. I hope you did not think I would leave without seeing to your needs, first.*

I love you, Ava.

That has not changed. That will not change.

I know you must have questions for me. I don't have many answers for you, however.

I do not know how long I will be gone. I do not know when or if I will come back. I do not know where I am going or where I will be. I do not know if I will ever be okay, if I will ever recover from this. From losing Henry and then losing you.

In truth, I think I lost you before Henry ever died; his passing was merely the final nail in the coffin, so to speak—and I apologize for the macabre metaphor. I began losing you when you couldn't bring yourself to seek intimacy with me after his birth, and I lost a little more of you when he was ill and the doctors couldn't identify the problem, and I lost a little more of you yet when he was admitted to the hospital for the final time, and I lost the rest of you when he died.

I hate myself for being so weak as to leave you like this, but I could see no other course of action. I was dying. I couldn't take it anymore. I just HAD to leave. I'm sorry.

To send me letters via post, i.e. "snail mail":

Christian St. Pierre % Jonny Núñez

P.O Box 136

9846 Estate Thomas, Charlotte Amalie, St Thomas 00802, USVI

I cannot guarantee how often I will receive post, however. As impersonal as it may be, if you wish to contact me directly, email is the best bet—you know how I am.

I wish I knew what the future holds, Ava. The only thing I know is that I love you. I will always love you, no matter what. I hope you find a place of healing, a place of peace. However you get there, whatever that looks like.

Email me.

14

Email from Ava to Christian

3:23 a.m., August 11, 2015

Chris,

I'm just going to sort of unload on you. No rereading, no editing, no filtering. I'm just going to type until I feel like I've said everything I want to say.

FUCK YOU.

You left me, you piece of shit.

I needed you. I STILL need you. I was trying, god-dammit. There's no guidebook for how to cope with this kind of thing, Christian. I get that you were in pain too, but couldn't you have just hung on a little longer? You say you love me, but then you vanish in the middle of the night like this was a one-night stand or something? Like I'm some barfly you hooked up with and now you're just done, buh-bye, gone. Seriously? No warning, nothing.

I'm starting to think I don't know you as well as I thought I did. The Christian I thought I knew, the Christian I thought I'd fallen in love with and married would never have just fucking left me like this. I had to get stitches once, do you remember? I'd cut my finger dicing onions, and I needed stitches. You drove me to the ER, and you sat with me, distracting me, teasing me, and then you insisted on going with me to get the stitches, and you refused to let me out of your sight, even though it was, like, eight or nine stitches and totally routine, but you wouldn't let me out of your sight. You've always protected me. Taken care of me. Even now, even in this, you're taking care of me.

Thanks for making the arrangements. That was pretty thoughtful of you. Demonstrates how far ahead you planned this abandonment. Two thumbs up, fucker.

Darcy is amazing. He's so smart! Sitting on command, even rolling over, and he's already potty trained. Bennet is an asshole, but then all cats are assholes, which is why I love them so much.

Honestly, I'm not sure why you brought me a kitty AND a puppy, but I'm not complaining.

Wait. I think I'm understanding this a little: you brought me them so I wouldn't be alone after you left, didn't you? You know how I am about being alone, I guess. So...again, thanks. It's sweet, in a backhanded sort of way. Like, you knowingly abandon me in the time of my greatest need, but you have the foresight and thoughtfulness to make sure I'm financially set...AND you get me a puppy and a kitten to keep me company, *AND* you give them the perfect names. That's so messed up I can't really prise apart the conflicting emotions. Is it *prise* apart, or *pry* apart?

I hate you.

But I also love you.

If I saw you right now, I'd probably punch you straight in your perfect Roman nose and then kiss your stupid perfect lips. And then ugly cry, snot and all. And then rip your clothes off and ride you like a stallion. Or maybe all of those at once. Kiss you, punch you, and fuck you, all while ugly crying.

I can't believe Henry is gone. Sometimes, when I've gotten really really drunk, I'll wake up in the middle of the night thinking I hear him crying. It's an audible thing, like, I seriously *hear* him crying, and I get up and go to his room, but the second I put my hand on the knob, I remember that he's dead.

It fucks with my head super hard, TBH. It's like... phantom pains, I think. You know what I'm talking about? When an amputee feels pain in the limb or extremity, even though it's not there anymore.

I think I'm so used to writing in the 500-word

blog-post format that I'm almost incapable of anything else. Because…i'm out of words. I'm just…lost. Lost without henry, and lost without you.

I'm lost.

I know I deserve this, but it still hurts, Christian.

I want to beg you to come back, but I won't. I can't. If you're capable of leaving me, then it's best you stay gone.

I'm not sure how to sign this email off.

Love?
Yours truly?
Best?

Wait, I've got it.

I love you, and fuck you,

Ava

15

Email from Christian to Ava

12:33 p.m., August 13, 2015

Ava,

I apologize for the delay in my response, I was making the crossing from Jamaica to the Yucatan. I spent some time in Kingston, and now I'm in Tulum, which is a tiny little town south of Cancún. There's not much to it, but it's less crowded than Cancún. The accommodations are much less…well, everything, but since I'm on the boat, it's a non-issue.

I appreciate the bluntness. Never filter yourself. Your honesty, even your sometimes crude unfiltered transparency is something I've always loved about you. I always know exactly where I stand with you.

Yes, I left you. I wish I could make excuses or give a better reason, but I can't. I accept your hate, because I deserve it. I abandoned you, as you said, in your time of greatest need. But it was also my time of greatest need, and I was utterly alone. I remained with you, giving you everything I had for three months, and I got absolutely nothing in return except a couple blank stares, and that was literally it. Not a word, not a glance, not a touch. How was I supposed to cope? What was I supposed to do? Sit around waiting forever? Bring you food you never ate, 3x a day every day until you died of starvation? And then when you did finally start functioning like a human being again, you drank yourself stupid every day. I know, I know, I did too. I'm not passing judgment at all, I promise. But you did it alone, you didn't talk to me, didn't acknowledge that I even existed. And when you did, it was with a stare that made me feel like a bug.

It was torture.

I struggled to stay sane, literally every moment of every day for three months, and I just couldn't do it anymore. It was utter hell. Because I was grieving, only I couldn't give in to the grief, because you needed me. But...you didn't, really, did you? You pushed me away. Shut me out utterly and completely. Why should I have stayed? For what?

Maybe I'm not the man either of us thought I was. I

know I don't feel like it. I feel...I don't know, it's hard to put it all into words.

If you want the raw, unvarnished truth, Ava, I cry myself to sleep some nights. I lay out on the trampoline between the hulls of my catamaran and I stare up at the stars and I miss you—as you were, once—and I miss Henry, and I miss us—as we were, once. I miss our life. I miss feeling whole. I miss feeling loved. I miss feeling like part of an *us*. I miss all of that, alone out here on the vast ocean, and I cry, as I have never cried in my life.

And another truth, since we're disclosing them: if you are capable of shutting me out as you have, then you are not the woman I thought I knew, the woman I fell in love with.

We've both been altered by this, Ava. I accept the blame that is due to me. But it's not all mine.

You don't deserve this; *I* don't deserve this; *we* don't deserve this, as a couple. But yet it's what has been placed upon us, and I think we've made a hell of a mess of it.

It seems we're doomed to unburden ourselves of our darkest thoughts and feelings 500 words at a time, since I'm nearly done with this missive as well.

All that's left to say is that I'm sorry, once again.

That I love you, once again.

But love isn't always enough, is it?

Where do we go from here? I don't know.

Also, for what it's worth, I didn't hide anything I was doing. You just missed it. You shut me out so thoroughly you didn't notice me carrying loads of clothing and books out of the condo right in front of you. You didn't hear me making phone calls from my office to set up the arrangements. You didn't see any of it, because you blocked me out. I did it all in plain view, during the day. And I said goodbye to you, but you were too drunk to know what was happening. It was ten o'clock in the morning when I woke you to say good-bye. I told you I loved you. I begged you to wake up. If you had spoken to me, acknowledged me, given me the slightest reason, I would have stayed.

I would take a hundred punches and all the ugly crying you needed to do, if I could have one more kiss from you, or a single loving, affectionate touch. Do you know the last time you touched me? The last time you kissed me?

I dream of that. Of us…of you, Ava. I dream of the way you used to touch me, the feel of your hand on my skin. You were always so eager, so passionate, so fiery and fierce. Needy, hungry for me. The first time we progressed past kissing—do you remember, Ava? Your dorm room. We skipped class together. You skipped a lit class I think it was, American literature from Hawthorne to the modern era, possibly? I skipped an ethics class, the first time I'd ever skipped a class in my entire life. It was noon, broad daylight. We'd met for coffee before class and decided to go back to your dorm room instead of class. My heart was palpitating wildly as we entered your room. I wanted you so badly. You locked the door so your roommate couldn't surprise us, and then you kissed me. I pushed you up against the door, and I buried my fingers in your hair—it was long, then, past your shoulders, and you had a purple streak in it. You dug your fingers into my shirt, and I thought you were going to claw into my skin and leave marks. You tore my shirt off as we kissed, threw it across the room, and it landed in the sink. And then you tore open my jeans and shoved them down, and I was so painfully hard I could barely stand. You saw how hard I was the moment my zipper was down. Your eyes went wide and you literally licked your lips in anticipation.

I couldn't breathe, and my hands were shaking, and my knees were knocking—not because I was nervous, since it was neither our first times by a long shot, but because I needed and wanted you so damned badly. I wanted you naked, but you were a woman possessed. I tried to take your shirt off, but you just laughed and went after my underwear. I was still wearing those horrible Joe Boxers, remember? They were terribly uncomfortable, but it was what everyone was wearing, and I've always craved approval. You yanked them down so my erection sprung free.

You giggled.

At first, I was embarrassed, because I thought you were laughing at how small I was, but then I saw the look on your face. The awe, the lust, the raw hunger.

I've never forgotten that look. You looked at my cock like it was the Holy Grail, Ava. And when you touched me? Jesus. I could have died and gone to heaven, in that moment. There are no words for the bliss I knew in that moment, at the touch of your hand. The way your delicate, pale fingers wrapped around me, stroked me. God, I'm getting hard as I write this, remembering. That touch, Ava. I remember it, vividly. I think of it, often. I dream of it. I wake up throbbing, aching, leaking, and I think of the way you touched me, that day. I warned you that I wouldn't last long, and I didn't. I told you again and again that if you kept touching me that I was going to come. I tried my damnedest to hold out. You stopped touching me long enough to let me get rid of your shirt, jeans, and bra, and that was my undoing. You, naked but for a pair of skimpy red panties?

It was my undoing. You touched me again, and I told you I was about to come, and you said you didn't care. Do you remember, Ava? Do you remember the way you stroked me, slowly, deliberately, staring into my eyes, ignoring my warnings? Do you remember what happened, then? At the last possible moment, in the very instant of my orgasm beginning, you sank to your knees in front of me and you swallowed my seed, and I had never come so hard in all my life as I did then, watching you on your knees, naked, breasts swaying, fierce blue eyes wide and startled and lascivious and mischievous. I wasn't expecting that, and you knew it.

It's why you did it, I've always thought. You wanted to shock me, and you succeeded.

And then, when I was weak-kneed and gasping, you led me to your bed, and you lay down and wiggled out of your panties, and you fingered yourself while I watched. But you weren't content with that, and neither was I. You crooked a finger at me, and I crawled above you, and you shoved my head down between your sweet, pale, luscious thighs, and I devoured your essence like a dying man's last meal. You came with a deafening scream.

I continued to devour you until you came again, and by that time I was hard for you once more.

We made love. I made you scream twice more, and someone in the room next to yours applauded, and we laughed together, and then I finally came again, buried deep inside you. Your legs curled around my waist, and you bit my earlobe as I poured into you. It wasn't until after that I thought to ask if you were on the pill, and thank god you were, because I'd been so helplessly eager to feel you that we'd forgotten a condom.

Do you remember, Ava?

I relieve myself of the ache, reliving this memory.

I guess I had a bit more to say after all, didn't I?

Don't sign off at all, Ava. Think of this as an ongoing conversation, like we used to have. Perhaps we can get to know each other—and ourselves—as we are, now, in this strange, painful new world of ours.

As an aside, I will not use the phrase "I love you" again, until—unless?—I am able to say it to your face. It feels too disingenuous, at this point.

Xoxo,

C.

16

Email from Ava to Christian

8:23 p.m., August 15, 2015

I really hate you, Chris. For real.

I absolutely *hate* you for making me relive that afternoon.

Do I *remember*? How could I forget? It was the single most erotic experience of my life. I'd expected you to be well-endowed, having obviously noticed the size of your hands, which are large enough to engulf mine almost completely. But I was in no way prepared for the reality. I was stunned stupid, TBH. I hadn't intended to suck you off, actually; that was a shock for both of us. Once I got my hands around your big beautiful cock, I couldn't stop. It was like…I don't even know. Magical? Addicting? I wanted to have sex with you, that's what I wanted. I wanted to come. I wanted you to touch me too. But then I touched your cock and I couldn't stop. It was just so soft and warm and hard and big and you were groaning, making these rumbly bear-like sounds and your eyes wouldn't stay open, and you just watched me touch you like it was the most amazing thing you'd ever felt, but all I was doing was touching you with my hand.

When I went to my knees, that was a spur of the moment thing, totally unplanned, because I realized at that last second that you were about to come, and I wanted to make you feel even better than I already had. When you came in my mouth, I nearly orgasmed myself. It was so fucking sexy, your groans, the way your hips flexed, the way you felt in my mouth, the way you looked at me.

God, I'm horny now. Which is why I hate you for bringing it up in the first place. Because I'm horny and I'm alone, and you know how much I hate masturbating. I hate you for being able to turn me on even now, from Mexico, via email. I hate you for not being here to touch me. I hate you for knowing exactly how to turn me on, how to make me forget how much I hate you—at least long enough to daydream about you, and touch myself while thinking about you.

Darcy must think I'm crazy. He's sitting at the end of the couch watching me. I'm sitting here on the other end, my laptop on my legs, and I've got my fingers between my thighs. I'm stopping every few seconds to type a little, to tease myself, to draw this out, and then I put my hand back down there. I think about you. I think about all the times I would lay on our bed, checking emails and FB notifications from my phone while you showered, and I'd always stop and watch you as you got out and dried off. I'd watch the way your thick hard muscles shifted under your skin as you wiped yourself dry with the towel, and I'd watch you ruffle your blondish-brown hair and you'd scrub your junk a little, and I'd bite my lip when you did that, because I've always been so insanely attracted to you, always, always, always. The attraction never let up. I never took that for granted, or got used to how hot you are.

And sometimes, you'd catch my eye, see me looking, see the expression on my face, and you'd prowl from the bathroom to our bed, and you'd climb up and crawl over me, and you'd tug the sheet and blanket down. You'd be hard by then, because you know I always sleep naked. The moment you looked at me, from the bathroom, it was over. I was going to have you. It was always inevitable, from that first look.

The moment I met you, on the quad at Miami, I saw you tossing a Frisbee to some bro, your hair was all messy and perfect, and you had these amazing laugh lines and you were so tan and weathered, not like some douchey country club bro, but the tan and weathered lines of a man who has spent countless hours and days squinting into the sun, being blasted by the wind, and weathering rainstorms and who knows what else. That moment, that very instant I saw you, I wanted you. If you had walked over to me then and asked me to blow you, I would have. No questions asked. I would have fucked you, right then. That's how bad I wanted you, instantly. And then you really did come over and say hi. You said your name was Christian, and did I want to go out with you. So hot, so confident. Rugged. You were wearing khaki cut-off shorts and a tank top, barefoot, no shoes anywhere to be seen. It was instant lust.

That has not abated a single iota since that day on the quad at Miami. Not a bit. Not during pregnancy or after, not during Henry's illness and death, and not after.

I just…I've lost myself.

I was trapped, Christian; I *am* trapped, still.

And I have a question:

What happened to you? When did you become so pretentious and artsy-fartsy? Since when do you prance around the subject, use flowery language and use words like "missive" and "panties" and "seed"?

What happened to you? You used to be this man who was so different from anyone I'd ever met. You were practical, down to earth, a man who appreciated simplicity, a man who was present in the moment and enjoyed every second of life for what it was. You used to be a man who didn't really give much of a shit about possessions.

You were this guy who'd seen the world. You'd been to all these exotic places...Tortuga, Madagascar, Jakarta, Cape Town, Johannesburg, Tierra del Fuego, Rio de Janeiro. You talked about those places with authority because you'd been there. You would describe such amazing sights. Like when the pod of whales porpoised next to your boat for an hour. Or when the volcano erupted not half a mile away. You were truly worldly, in the realest sense of the word. Yet you were also educated. There was a hint of a Midwestern accent. You drove a Bronco you'd restored yourself. And by restored, I mean you rebuilt the engine and left the rest alone, so it was a squeaky, rusty, cracked-pleather, smelled like cigarettes, old ass piece of shit...which could haul some serious ass.

You would talk about Arthur Miller and Hemingway and Homer and Archimedes just as easily as you would chill on the beach drinking Natty Ice by the case. You rarely wore shoes. You would show up to class barefoot, and the professors would have to remind you to put on a shirt at least half the time. You would discuss Heisenberg with physics majors and some obscure biology principle with the biology students, and you would have long winding passionate discussions of Degas and Dali and Van Gogh and Pollack with the art majors, and you would gleefully geek out over Herbert and Clarke and Asimov and Heinlein. And then you'd go play Frisbee with the jocks and drink a shitload of beer with the frat boys and sorority bitches, and you never thought any of it was at all strange. You fit in everywhere, and you were effortlessly cool.

And us?

We would go out for coffee and end up at a bar six hours later, and we never ran out of things to talk about. We've never lacked for conversation, though, have we? Even up until recently, we could talk for hours.

Do you remember the conversations we'd have while I was pregnant? We'd go to our favorite little Italian place, and salads and pasta would turn into three desserts and you'd drink cup after cup after cup of coffee, and we would just talk and talk and talk for hours. What did we talk about? I can't even recall the conversations, the subjects we discussed. Everything, right? Sex, politics, movies, books. You'd tell me about your books and I'd tell you about the stupid comment threads on my blog and Facebook group. You'd bitch about how slow the editing process is. It wasn't *a* conversation, like one and then another, day after day. It was one conversation, interrupted.

And now?

You write melodramatic faux-suicide goodbye notes on personalized stationery with a $500 fountain pen. You drive a Range Rover and wear $600 sunglasses and $2000 watches and iron your Armani shirts to go grocery shopping for designer kale at Whole Foods. You've lost that adorable hint of an Illinois accent and you haven't touched a Frisbee in years, or had a rambling conversation with a stranger about some obscure particulate of history or science or art.

You write in purple prose and speak in arch, pat phrases like a modern-day aristocrat.

We stopped talking, at some point.

I bet you felt proud of your dirty little email, and using words like cock or panties.

Never say "panties." Never write "panties." It's a nasty, ugly, horrible word. Just as an FYI.

I bet you couldn't write a dirty email without making it all flowery and eloquent. You'd try to make it a Pulitzer Prize winning piece of *ART*.

You used to write for the love of words, for the love of telling a story.

Who are you, now, Christian?

I want the old you back.

Also, xoxo? Really?

No. Just…no. You don't get to xoxo me, not when you left me to go gallivanting about the Caribbean.

A.

17

Email from Christian to Ava

6:04 a.m., August 20, 2015

I got lost in success. That's what happened to me. I was that man in college because that's all I knew. Then success started happening to me, and I could suddenly afford things I'd never had before. Nice things. Cool things. And I just got lost in it all.

I was on the beach in Cancún a couple days ago. I anchored out a ways and took the dinghy to shore. And you know what I did? I played Frisbee with some douchey college bros on vacation before classes start. And then I sat in the sand with an older couple and talked about the Golden Age of Jazz and our mutual love for the poetry of e.e. cummings.

I'm finding that man again, Ava. I miss him too. I realized recently how pretentious and obnoxiously materialistic I'd become, and I took all my fancy, expensive clothing and I packed it into a suitcase, and I brought it to the university at St. Thomas and I gave it to the first young man who looked like he was of a similar build as me. He was baffled, at first, and then he set the suitcase on the ground, opened it, and saw what it was and tried to give it back. I just told him to keep it and have a nice day. He was wearing torn up sneakers and ripped, stained jeans. I even put in my favorite dress shoes.

I still have the stationery and pen, though. They're useful items, and I will use them again, if only to doodle or write grocery lists, and they'll be a reminder of who I don't want to be ever again.

I haven't had a drink since leaving Ft. Lauderdale. I wasn't an alcoholic, in that I intentionally chose to drown myself in booze. But then, they say denial is the first sign of addiction. Either way, I've quit drinking, for now.

I told my editor I was going on indefinite leave. The reason this reply is so long delayed is that I put in at Belize City and spent four days in the cabin of my boat, finishing the book. I finished it, and I sent it to Lucy, and I told her I would be unavailable for follow up revisions or rewrites. They could have it as is, or they could have their advance back—I didn't really care which. I've lost the touch, I think, lost the drive to write. I have no stories. Maybe I will again, someday, but right now…it's still hard to wake up, most days.

I'm surrounded by beauty, but sometimes all I see is gray. I'm on the trampoline, watching the sunrise, and thinking about all the times we used to lay on the beach all night long, and wake up to watch the sunrise together, the air cold, our bodies warm under the blanket.

Our vacation to Iceland, you remember that? We lived somewhere it was sunny and hot all the time, so we wanted a vacation to somewhere different, a different climate. So we went to Iceland. It was so fucking cold, but we loved it. We dressed in thick wool sweaters and wool hats and fur-lined boots…and the locals were looking at us like we were crazy, because it was spring, and getting nice and warm for them. To us, though, it was frigid. Our room in the B-&-B? You remember how damn cold it was all the time? God, that was amazing. We stayed naked and piled on the blankets and huddled in that little bed in that little room, keeping each other warm, watching Netflix and drinking wine all night long.

I want that back.

Huddling together, keeping each warm through the long dark nights.

God, I miss you.

C.

Email from Christian to Ava

11:48 a.m.

I'm en route down to Rio now and I found myself thinking about you, as I so frequently do. Thinking about your last email some more. The beginning of it, most of all.

That first day we met, I'd had my eye on you for a few days, actually. I first saw you three days earlier, on the beach with a few other girls. You were wearing a blue bikini, sunbathing. I was surfing by myself. That bikini, or more accurately, your body in that bikini, god, it was like I'd been struck by lightning. I saw you as I carried my board down to the water. You were just laying there, big sunglasses on your face, arms at your sides, and your body was…god, so perfect. Your breasts were just the right size, big and juicy enough to sway to either side and almost spill out of the top, and your waist was trim and your abs taut, and your hips were a perfect bell curve. Your bikini bottom could barely stretch around your hips, and the tiny triangle of indigo fabric was being devoured by your pussy. Yes, I stopped, and I stared. I stared helplessly, probably creepily. I could see the outlines of your nether lips—you're probably cringing as you read that phrase—and my mouth watered. I had to go run into the water then, or risk embarrassing myself at the beach with a monster hard-on in my swim trunks.

I tried to forget you, tried to get you out of my mind, but I couldn't. I surfed, and you slept and sunned on the beach, and when I finally came in from surfing, you were gone. I was forlorn. I'd been sure it was going to be love. But alas, you'd left. Imagine my pleased shock, then, when I saw you crossing the quad at my university. I was sure all over again, then, that it would be love. You were just as gorgeous as I'd remembered, even wearing more clothing. And god, I wanted you. I walked over to say hi and ask you out, and inside my head, I was thinking about how badly I wanted to get you naked and do all kinds of dirty things to you. If I'd known how bad you wanted me too, I very well might have asked you to get on your knees and suck me off right there and then. I thought about that, actually. We went out later that day, and it was a totally average first date. Wonderful, and amazing, and fun, and I fell for you even more, and we went our separate ways afterward without even a kiss.

But I went back to my room and I imagined you in that blue bikini, and then I imagined myself tugging the string of the halter top and watching it fall to the floor of my room, and your luscious tits fell out and I pictured myself sucking on your nipples. In my imagination, I should point out, your nipples were nowhere near as plump and your areolae nowhere near as dark as they are in reality, and that was a pleasant surprise indeed. I jerked off twice thinking about you, after our first date.

I jerked off thinking about you every single day, and

sometimes more than once in a day.

And then, after six dates, you finally let me kiss you on the beach. On the seventh date, we waited until we got back to your room, and you locked the door and my heart went crazy, beating in my chest so hard I thought I was having a heart attack. And then you kissed me with such aggression that I was shocked by it, by the fervor and suddenness of it. Within seconds of that kiss, you had my shirt off, and you wouldn't let me at your clothes, wouldn't let me undress you. You were too eager, too voracious. And then…oh god, and then you shoved off my shorts and yanked down those stupid boxers, and you took hold of me, and I almost came right then. For real, I nearly did.

I'm hard as a rock, right now, thinking about this.

Jesus, what a mess. I'm thinking about you naked, touching me, and I'm remembering how your hand feels, and your body. I'm remembering the way your breasts taste and the sound of your moans as I make you come. I'm remembering all this, and I'm jerking off. Typing one-handed, one-finger hunt-and-peck style, imagining you. Us. The away things were.

And I've made a horrible mess all over myself.

God, Ava. How did we get to this place?

C.

18

Email from Ava to Christian

August 21, 2015

I don't know if I can do this, if I can survive the sex-ting-emails, whatever you want to call them. I fucking miss you, and I'm so angry at you, and I can't sleep at night and I can't stop drinking and I fucking hate you as much as I fucking love you.

How did we get here?

I don't know. I wish I knew. I have no answers.

If you were here, I'm not sure what I would do. Beat you senseless, or fuck you stupid, or both.

I'm just…

SO ANGRY.

Not just at you, though. At life. At God, or Fate, or Destiny, or who the fuck ever or what the fuck ever is in charge in this life, if anyone, if anything. I'm just angry and I don't know how to cope. I miss you, and I don't want to. I understand why you left, and I don't want to understand. I want to wallow in my rage, but I get it.

I still wake up in the middle of the night, sometimes, and reach for you. Or listen for Henry. But then I remember that I'm utterly and completely alone.

Except for Darcy, of course, who now sleeps where you used to.

Everything is a mess.

Do you remember that time we both had too much to drink, and I couldn't come because the alcohol had desensitized me, but you were hard and horny, so I told you I'd suck you off? I sucked you off like a damn champ that night, for real. It must have been a good ten minutes I spent going down on you, and then, on the spur of the moment, instead of swallowing, I took your load on my face and tits. You were so shocked, and you didn't know whether to be turned on or disgusted, which was exactly how I felt. Equal parts of both, is what it was. God, what a mess.

I would do that again, right now. Take your cum all over my face. All over my tits. I would…god, Christian, I would do absolutely anything for another taste of you, for one moment with you.

But then all the other stuff comes back, and I feel

this irrational hatred of you. I know it's not your fault. It's not, and I know that. I'm just as much to blame, and it's also just one of those things that no one is at fault for, a horrible horrible awful tragedy no one could have prevented. But I still hate you for it, and I don't know why, and I don't know how to fix it.

I'm not blogging. I can't. My readers expect humor, and I have none. None at all.

I think I'm going to need some time to figure things out, Christian. The tug of war between needing you, wanting you, loving you, and hating you, loathing you, reviling you…is just too strong and too painful. I need to figure it out. I need to decide what to do, how to get clean, how to live again, how to stop drinking, how to stop missing you. I want to beg you to come back, but I'm terrified of what I'd do if you did.

Nothing is okay, and I don't know what to do, and emailing you, hearing your voice even through email is too painful, too difficult.

I'm not going to email you again. I don't know for how long. I don't know if I'll ever get past all this.

I'm not saying goodbye, I'm just…I'm done for now. I don't know what else to say. What else to do.

P.S.: that vacation to Iceland remains one of my top ten favorite memories of my entire life. Top five, and number two or three in that top five. Our wedding day is my number one favorite memory. We did it so cheap, a little arbor on the beach wreathed in white lace and white roses, you barefoot in your tux and me barefoot in that incredible Vera Wang I bought off the rack. I walked down the aisle to you to Edwin McCain's "I'll Be" which was so great and ridiculous and just perfect. My parents were there, your mom, Delta, Lucy your agent, and that's it. It was perfect. So romantic.

What's number two? I'd really have to say the Iceland trip. We ate fish every meal, and I think I still have an entire storage crate full of wool sweaters. The locals thought we were so crazy for being so cold all the time, but sixty degrees is cold to us, whereas sixty to them is downright frickin' balmy. I mean, I remember everything from that trip. Hiking for days, riding a motorcycle together around the coast, all the way around the whole island. Deep-sea fishing with Captain Didrik, but his name was actually spelled with that rune-letter-thing that looks like a "d" with a cross at the top of the upper part. Going out drinking, getting lost, and trying to find a cab to take us back to our B-and-B, but we couldn't remember the name of it. Out of all that, though, yes, I remember the nights best. I was on my period for half the trip so we couldn't have sex, but we had such an incredible, memorable time doing what we did, drinking and watching movies in that fucking frigid little room all night every night. It was amazing.

Number three is having Henry. Giving birth, I mean, they say you forget the pain, but I haven't. It was so, so, so worth it to me, the moment I held that warm squalling, mewling, nuzzling little bundle of warmth in my arms. Fuck, now I'm crying because I miss him so damn bad. His little hands, his little feet. The way his chin would tremble when he cried, and his little fists would shake with outrage because he'd shit his pants for the twentieth time in 24 hours. I miss all of it.

For real. I'm done with these emails. I need time. I have all those fucking memories running through my head and I need you and I miss you and I love you, and then I remember that you FUCKING LEFT, and I'm just filled with rage all over again and I don't know what to do. I don't know what to do, Chris.

So, until I figure that out…I just can't do this anymore. I don't know. I don't know anything. Don't email back. Just…give me time and space. Please.

A.

Part 2

19

Puerto la Cruz, Venezuela

September 1, 2015

A hundred yards from the dock, I haul at the line hand over hand until the sheet is furled, and then belay the line around the cleat. I pull up to the mooring the rest of the way using the motor, and Jonny is there on the dock to tie me off.

He's my best friend, Jonny Núñez. The first friend I made on my first voyage out. He was the experienced, worldly, hard-as-nails, tough-talking first mate and I was the new kid from rural Illinois who didn't know a clew from a cleat from a coxswain. I knew engines, but I knew nothing about sailing, and I suppose my eagerness to learn endeared me to Jonny, who'd learned sailing and deep-sea fishing from birth. He likes to joke that he was born with a bowline in one hand and a fishing line in the other, and that he hasn't let go of them since. He could captain his own boat, but says he doesn't want the responsibility, which I think is true enough. He signs on for a voyage or two or three with a captain, and then ends up staying wherever he feels like staying for as long as he feels like it. He might be in Jakarta for a few months, and then sail for a few months, and then end up in Grenada for a spell, and so on around the world. We exchanged emails on and off over the years when I was in school and then landlocked in Ft. Lauderdale with Ava; he kept me apprised of his voyages and described the people he met, and I in turn would tell him of the joys of pedestrian, home-bound, landlubber life. I don't think I was fooling him any more than I was fooling myself.

Every single day that I was at university and then living in Ft. Lauderdale, I missed the sea. I loved Ava, obviously, but the sea was always calling me.

She'd hate that turn of phrase, though. Melodramatic, she would call it. But then, she doesn't know the ocean the way I do, hasn't lived upon the sea. She doesn't know the caprice of the sea. That's a common phrase in literature, to the point of ubiquity, if you study literature as we both did. But, like all clichés, it is deeply rooted in truth. The sea is a fickle beast, a harsh mistress—all that bullshit. It's all true, though. Live on the sea, and you'll find out.

These are things I've spent the last few weeks thinking about. Even more so since Ava quit corresponding with me.

I miss her emails, dammit; I miss *her*, dammit. But like she wrote, I'm also pissed off at her. So, so, so angry. At her, at life, at God, at everything.

It was torture, living so close to the ocean but never being able to venture out; Ava hates sailing. I took her once, during college. I rented a Sunfish and took her out, staying within sight of shore the whole time. She was a native Floridian who had somehow never gone sailing, which just seemed weird to me, and I thought I'd rectify it. She hated every second of it. She couldn't remember to stay out of the way of the boom when we tacked, couldn't remember which line to pull or when, even when I told her. It was just a mess. We spent an hour sailing, and then I finally relented and took her back to shore. We saw a movie and ate dinner and never discussed sailing again. She doesn't mind boats, likes the water, loves swimming, enjoys fishing once in a while… but hates sailing.

Which is the one thing I love more than anything else. Except for Ava, I'd usually say.

But lately? I'm not so sure.

Which makes me a horrible person, I think. It may be just the events of the past few months, the renewed joy I feel at simply being out to sea again, after years stuck on land. I'm a nomad by nature, I think. I'm not made to stay in one spot, and I'm certainly not made to live on land. My heart and my soul come to life at sea.

Ava doesn't understand that.

She calls it melodramatic horseshit, and tells me to go surf, like that'll get it out of my system. Which is rank nonsense.

Surfing is to sailing as reading is to writing: surfing is a watersport, something you do on the ocean, and so is sailing, but they are not even remotely equal; reading uses words, and so does writing, but they are not the same, they are not equal; I cannot expunge my need to be on the sea by surfing.

"You gonna sit there stewing all day or are you gonna get out of the damn boat and say hello?" Jonny says, snapping me out of my train of thought.

I shake my head to clear it, and grin at him. "Yeah, yeah, I'm coming. Hold your horses, old man."

He's not old: at forty-two, he's only ten years older than me, but I like to tease him about it, and he in turn acts like I'm still the teenager he first met way back when.

I step onto the dock and clasp forearms with Jonny, and then embrace him. "Been a while, *amigo*." I don't really speak Spanish, and I only call him *amigo* to annoy him.

"Too long, my friend, way too long." He wraps an arm around my shoulders and guides me toward downtown Puerto la Cruz, Venezuela. "I wish I could say it was good to see you. It is, but I wish it was under different circumstances."

I shrug. "It is what it is."

Jonny rears away and stares at me. "That don't sound like you."

I pull away. "Maybe I've changed."

Jonny doesn't follow me. "You're livin', you're changin'. That's just how things are. But what you been through? You don't just shrug it off and say it is what it is. That's stupid, and I ain't stupid, Chris. Now for real this time. What gives?"

I slow my steps, and Jonny catches up. I walk beside him in silence a while, and he lets the silence stand. He nudges me around a corner and across a street, and then into a dingy dive bar, where he orders us drinks in Spanish. We sit at a table outside under an awning, and we sip local *cerveza*, and I finally find words.

"Sorry, Jonny. You deserve better from me than that answer. It's just hard for me to talk about."

Jonny is sitting close to me, close enough that my American sense of personal space leaves me feeling uncomfortable, but it's just how Jonny is, and it's comforting in an odd way, being uncomfortably close to him, like old times.

He shrugs, and then pats my forearm. "You been through a lot. You're allowed to feel what you feel, right? But you gotta talk it out. I know you, man, and know you wanna bury it and pretend it ain't there. Can't do that, Christian. Won't work. Not somethin' like this."

I sigh and nod. "I know."

Jonny stares at me, expectant. "So? Talk."

I shake my head. "Not yet, okay? Give me time."

"Why? So you can bury it deeper?" He takes a long drink, eying me sidelong. "You been out there on that sexy new boat of yours alone for what, over a month? Stewing, thinking, brooding. You've had time. Now you gotta open up."

I glance at him, taking stock of my friend: he looks much the same as he always has, except there are new streaks of silver creeping in at the temples, encroaching on his jet-black hair, which is, as always, a little too long and combed straight back. His features are weathered and craggy, his eyes set in a permanent squint. The lines in his face are etched more deeply than the last time I saw him, and he has a new scar on his jawline, slicing through the permanent ten-day scruff. But despite all this, the guy is seriously handsome—even as a straight guy, I can admit that much about him. That, along with the fact that he tends to be a man of few words, makes the ladies go crazy for him; the whole tall-dark-and-handsome, strong-and-silent type and all that, I suppose. Jonny fits all that and then some.

"What do you want me to say?"

"What happened? Why are you way down here, alone?" He picks at the label of his bottle. "I thought you and your old lady were tight, thought you two had that real-deal kinda love goin' on. Now suddenly you're on a fancy new boat by yourself. So...what happened?"

"A lot happened. I thought we had that too, but...I guess I was wrong. I don't know." I try to put things into words, but it's too big, it's too much. "Jesus, man, where do I even start? So much happened. Like, between Ava and I, and then Henry, and..." I shake my head, trailing off. "It's too much, Jonny."

"Start small. You and Ava."

I laugh. "That's starting small?"

He raises his eyebrows at me. "You'd rather talk about your boy, then?"

"Fuck no."

"Right, so start small. You and Ava." He lifts a hand, and then points at our nearly empty bottles, and a server nods, brings us fresh ones.

"I guess I feel like things just...changed. Snuck up on us, sort of. She got pregnant, and I was happy, you know? I mean, I really was. I loved her, and I felt like we were ready. We were in a good spot financially, we both worked from home, and it just seemed like the best next step for us. We weren't trying, but we also weren't trying *not* to. The pregnancy itself was...I mean, it was a pregnancy. You know how that it is."

Jonny laughs and shakes his head. "No, I don't, man. Had a few girls try to tie me down, but it don't stick. Don't know what a pregnancy is like."

"It's when your wife turns into an alien creature. She eats weird shit, eats all the time, pees all the time, and goes through more mood changes than you can possibly believe. There's puking in the morning, and there's when she suddenly wants to drink Squirt all the damn time when she never liked it before, and hates salmon, which used to be her favorite thing. She alternates between hating you for knocking her up and putting her in this position, and loving you more than ever for creating a life inside her. Then she starts to get big and her back hurts and her feet hurt, but the baby kicks and it starts to really feel real when you can feel that little foot pressing against the inside of her belly." I sink into remembering. "She could barely walk by the end. He was such a big baby, and he kicked her all the time. Right in the spleen, she said. *Bam, bam, bam, bam*—like he had some kind of vendetta against her poor spleen. And she peed literally every twenty minutes, and seriously ate her weight in cucumbers, rice cakes, and Laughing Cow cheese wedges."

Jonny stares at me. "Sounds awful. Why would anyone go through that on purpose?"

I laugh. "Because when it's time, you go through this weird space of like two or three days where there is no time, there's only the hospital and the contraction monitor and the heart monitor and all that, and she's in labor and you eat hospital food and drink shitty coffee, and don't really sleep."

"Still not seeing why you'd go through that on purpose."

"Because you watch a human being come out of her, Jonny. For nine months it was just your wife's belly getting bigger, and ultrasound pictures, and the occasional weird flutter against your hand when you touch her belly. But then…a *person*, someone who didn't exist before, a person you and your wife created together…comes out of her. It's incredible. We were two, and then three." I push back against the darkness I feel encroaching on me. "Makes it all worth it."

Jonny laughs again. "Maybe for you. You didn't have the person come out of you."

I nod, and shrug, and laugh. "That's true. But even Ava said it was all worth it, the second she saw him."

Jonny's gaze is sharp. "So, how'd that lead you here?"

"I don't know. We became parents. Our lives suddenly revolved around this tiny helpless little person. We ate, slept, breathed, and existed for him. He was literally everything. All the time."

"Yeah, man, you're not making a great case for parenthood, here."

I groan, and slug back some beer. "That's not what I'm trying to explain. If that was what I was trying to do, I'd be telling you about what it's like to hold that helpless little bundle on your chest and feel him breathing, feel his little hand clutching your finger, and knowing you'd do literally anything for him." I have to pound back more beer, because the darkness is too strong, now.

Jonny doesn't miss it. "You don't gotta filter yourself around me, Chris. You know that."

"I'd have done anything." I blink hard. "But there wasn't anything."

"That's rough."

"You have no idea." I finish the second beer, and wave off a third before the desire to drown myself in liquor takes over. "We were two, and then we were three…and then suddenly we were two. And now I'm just one."

"Not anymore."

I clap him on the shoulder. "I know, Jonny. And that means more than you can know."

"Ain't the same, though, I'm guessing."

I shake my head. "No. Not at all." I fight the urge to run, or drink, or start a fight—anything to lessen the pressure inside my skull. "Being a parent to a newborn takes everything you have, both of you. You don't have time for yourself, or each other. That was part of it. Parents go through that all the time, and they find ways to reconnect. And in some ways, the utter focus on that child brings you closer, because you're united in that common cause. But for Ava and I, we didn't get the break once he got old enough to sleep through the night and didn't need to eat every two hours. He started getting sick. Just crying all the time. He wasn't hungry, didn't need a diaper, was too young to be teething, didn't have gas, he was just…he just cried all the damn time. We never got a chance to just…find each other, and ourselves, in that new space of being parents. It was all about Henry, all the time. That was a wedge, I think. Plus, even if he did quiet down for a while, Ava felt like shit. About herself, I mean. Physically, mentally, emotionally, she was just… wrecked. Didn't feel like she was beautiful anymore, like how could I want her. I did want her, but she couldn't feel it, and even after she got the all-clear, she just couldn't… she didn't want that."

"What do you mean, the all-clear?" Jonny asks.

"After giving birth, a woman typically needs about six weeks to heal before having sex."

Jonny stares. "Six weeks? *Jesus Cristo*. How did you live through that, man?"

I laugh. "There wasn't time to even think about it, at first. Too tired, too delirious from not sleeping." I fidget, restless and uncomfortable. "You think six weeks is bad, though? I'm not sure I want to admit how long it's been, in that case."

Jonny glances into the mouth of his bottle, as if assessing it. "Then I think maybe we need something a little stronger."

I shake my head. "Not sure that's a good idea, bud."

He frowns at me. "Why not? We used to get shitty together all the time. You become an alkie when I wasn't lookin'?"

I tip my head side to side. "Yes and no."

Jonny's snort is derisive. "Alcoholism don't work like

that, man. Either you are, or you ain't."

"Yeah, no shit, Jonny. My old man was a boozer, remember?"

"Right, so why you talkin' about yes and no like it's a guessing game, then?"

"I guess I'm scared of becoming my dad. When Henry…um—after all that…" I twist the bottle in place, staring at the grain of the wood table under my hands, seagulls cawing overhead. "I started drinking all the time. Like, all day. Morning, noon, and night. A bottle of whisky a day sort of thing, if not more."

"But you quit."

I nod, lift the bottle. "Yeah, this is the first drink I've had in weeks."

"Your old man, his drinking—was it because of a tragedy, or was it just because?"

I shrug. "He was a miserable bastard. Hated life. I don't know. If it started because of something specific, I never knew what it was. My mom took care of him, cleaned up after him, stayed loyal to him no matter how much he knocked her or me around. Which I've never understood, honestly. Point is, if he had some reason for being such a miserable, drunken, abusive bastard, I couldn't tell you what it was."

"But point is, he just never bothered to quit," Jonny responds. "You did. I ain't encouraging you to be a drunk, Chris, but I like to think I know you pretty damn well and, sure, maybe you could put away the booze with the best of us, but you also knew when to call it quits. You drank to unwind, and when it was time to work, you were sober and you worked. You went through something most people can't even imagine, *amigo*, and that shit leaves deep hurt. And you know, sometimes I think the only way we can get through the worst of the pain is to numb ourselves to it until we can figure that shit out." Jonny slid his half-finished second beer away. "You tell me you ain't drinking no more, then I'll quit drinking too while we sail together. But I don't think that's what it was for you. Just my input, man."

I shake my head at him. "You're crazy. But you're a good friend, Jonny. Don't know what I'd do without you."

"How about this." Jonny takes his beer back, lifts a hand for a server, and requests something in Spanish— hard liquor, most likely; after a few minutes, the server returns with four shot glasses full of tequila. "If you look like you're startin' to have a problem, I'll kick your ass. And unless that's what it takes, you're gonna drink some tequila with an old friend, and then we're gonna prep that fancy-ass boat of yours and we're gonna sail to motherfuckin' Africa together. You and me and the Atlantic, bro."

I take a shot glass, lift it, and clink it against Jonny's. We toss it back, lift the second shot, clink, and slam the glasses onto the table. "It's been fourteen months," I say, and then chase the tequila with a swallow of beer. "No, wait…fifteen. Almost sixteen."

"Since what?" Jonny says. And then his face twists into a horrified expression. "Since you had sex? Fuck no. No. That ain't possible. No way."

"Way." I shrug a shoulder. "Since just before Henry was born. After he was born and she got the all-clear, she just couldn't—or wouldn't, I'm not sure. Like I told you, she didn't feel sexy, didn't feel beautiful. Which, I mean, I get it, as much as a guy can. She had a baby. She put on some weight and…other stuff. Then he got sick, and I was under deadline to finish a book, and then he got diagnosed with cancer and that was the last thing on either of our minds, and then he…he died, and we were both just…fucked-up, as you hopefully cannot even begin to imagine. And then suddenly I'm out here on the boat realizing I haven't had sex in almost two years."

Jonny seems at a loss for words. *"Jesus Cristo, amigo.* Sixteen months celibate? What are you gonna do?"

I shrug. "Hell if I know. Ava and I—things are a mess. It's not like I can just pop back up to Ft. Lauderdale and be like hey babe, let's bang." I finish the beer, a little too fast. "I don't even know if I'll ever see her again. It's a mess, Jonny."

"How were things when you left?"

I snort. "She spent the better part of two months essentially catatonic. In bed, not eating, just sleeping and crying. Unresponsive to me completely. And then when she came out of that, she pretended I didn't exist. She drank wine and watched TV all day. And then she started visiting his...the cemetery. Didn't talk to me. She's spoken...maybe a hundred words to me since Henry was first admitted to the hospital."

Jonny eyes me. "And so you left?"

"I wasn't sleeping, wasn't writing, couldn't eat, couldn't function. I couldn't grieve because Ava was...I was so worried about her. I brought her food, tried to talk to her, to comfort her, to distract her, and all she would do was snap at me. She actually hit me once. I was going crazy."

"And so you...*left?*" His voice sounds...skeptical. Judgmental even.

"You don't understand."

"I'm trying to."

I stand up. "I don't need this. I didn't want to talk about this."

Jonny stays where he is. "Siddown, Christian." His voice is hard, sharp; I clench my fists, release them, but resume my seat. When he speaks again, he unloads with both barrels. "I'm just tryin' to understand things, is all. Sounds to me like you left your wife when she needed you most. And that just ain't the Christian I know."

I wince, and hiss. "It was fucking *hell*, Jonny. I was totally alone. My son had just died. My wife was starving herself in front of me. I was trying to keep it together, trying to be strong. But I just couldn't. I *couldn't*. I was going crazy. I hated myself, hated the drunken bastard

I was becoming. Waking up on the beach, drunk, puking into the sand, and then going back inside to drink more, just so I could forget how bad it hurt for another few minutes? Watching my wife lay in bed for days on end, only getting up to use the bathroom and drink some water. Watching her waste away, watching her cry. She looked at me like—like she *hated* me. It wasn't my fault, but she hated me for it. I couldn't cry. I couldn't...I couldn't *breathe*." I meet his eyes. "So yeah, I left. Yeah, she probably still needed me. Maybe if I'd been stronger, I'd still be there, and we'd still be together."

"Chris—"

"Maybe if I'd gotten him to the right doctor sooner, they'd have caught the tumor when it was still operable, and he'd still be alive. Maybe we should have had him go through the treatment. I mean, they said it would only extend his life by a few months at best, and those months would be worse than torture. But maybe it would have— maybe there would have been a miracle. He might be alive, still. Maybe...Maybe there was something I should have done or said that would have helped Ava cope." I stare at him, and he's the first to look away, now. "I've gone over all this a million times. It's all I think about. What if, what if, what if—maybe, maybe, maybe."

"Chris, listen—"

"No, *you* listen." I lean forward and stare him down once more. "I was going *insane*. I mean that very literally. If I didn't leave, I would have..." I force the words out, an admission I haven't even really made to myself, much less anyone else. "I was starting to think about suicide. How being dead would be better than what I was feeling. Alcohol wasn't numbing me enough. I couldn't do a goddamn thing to fix *anything*. I couldn't fucking sleep, I would be awake for days at a time, until I started to hallucinate. And I started to think, like, *anything* is better than this. Anything is better than watching my wife just…sink into this—this shell, this morass of despair that I wasn't capable of pulling her out of. What the fuck was I supposed to do? She would have found me swinging from the ceiling fan if I hadn't left, Jonny. And not even she knows that."

Jonny leans back, flags down the server, mutters something, and waits. Within a minute or two, the server returns with a dusty old bottle of tequila and two rock glasses. He pours us each a generous measure. Returns my gaze steadily. "Since you were eighteen I know you, Christian. I taught you to sail, I taught you how to charm the ladies like a Latino. I taught you to fish, taught you to drink, and I taught you to tell shit like it is." He slides me one of the glasses, raises his. "So here's what it is. You need to dig deep and figure yourself out. You love that lady like I think you do, you owe it to yourself and to her to get past whatever this is that's got you running. And until you do, brother, I'll be running with you."

I'll drink to that.

EPISTLE #1

8 sep 2015

Ava,

I have no intention of sending this to you. It is more of a diary or journal than anything else, but addressing it to you makes it easier to be honest, since I am, as you may no doubt be aware, rather facile at lying to myself, whereas I could never lie to you. Thus, I am beginning an epistolary journey, in which I attempt to discover myself. Revive myself. Syntactical cardiopulmonary resuscitation. Prosodic self-diagnosis and -medication.

I've journaled most of my life, and I brought those

notebooks with me, and read the backlog of journals on this computer's hard drive. I recently read through them all, and I don't really like what I have read, for the most part. I tell only one side of things. I indulge in what you, my love, call my purple prose. I am guilty of that, I admit; and further, I don't think that will change. I enjoy far too much the flavor of words, the delicate tang of syntax and the musky earthen aroma of grammar and the heady floral bouquet of prose. I love to swirl my words like a sommelier with a well-aged wine, recently uncorked, sniffing for the nose and sipping for the notes. I am not eloquent in my speech; I am still far too much the Midwestern farm boy for that.

No matter how far I sail, I cannot escape that part of me. If I close my eyes, I can walk the acres, freshly furrowed, the dirt sun-dried and fragrant and skritching underfoot, rows and rows and rows of evenly spaced lines spanning in every direction as far as I can see. The sun will be hot on my neck and if I kneel, in my mind's eye, I can scoop a handful of that rich brown dirt and run it between my fingers and I can smell it, recall the grit of it on my palms. The bellow of Dad's voice from the pole barn, where I will lay under the tractor which Grandpa drove and great-Grandpa drove, which Dad expects me to fix, because it's a family tradition to plow the garden behind the house with that tractor, rather than the enormous new one they'll still be paying off fifty years after I'm dead.

See? Self-indulgence.

The man in those journals, the boy, the young man, the adult—I don't like him. I don't remember being him.

I recall our most recent emails, Ava. A few quick digital correspondences, and then silence from you. It hurts. I deserve it, but it hurts. I love you. God, I love you. I sit at this very laptop and I open a new email message and I address it to you, and I get nowhere. I don't know what to say. I want you back. I want *us* back. But I don't know how to get that. If I saw you, right now, I wouldn't know what to say. I would stare at you. I would steal glimpses down your shirt, and if you turned around, I'd stare at your ass. If you walked away from me, I'd enjoy the view, the swinging sway of your hips and the gentle bounce of your ass. If you bent over, I'd enjoy the glimpse of your luscious mounds. I include that phrase for you, because you would hate it. Oh, you would hate it so much.

"I do NOT have 'luscious mounds', Chris," you would insist, and you would use air quotes with your fingers, and a sharp irritated snap in your voice.

You've never been able to stand falsity, pretensions of grandeur. You're proud of me, as a writer, I know. But I think, secretly, you hate my writing style, especially what it has evolved into over the years. When I first started writing, it was for fun, as a challenge, as an expression. A way to create art, when I have always been more technical, mechanical, and social. I can fix an engine, I can sail a boat, I can plow a field, start a fire, kill, skin, and cook my own food whether fish, fowl, or mammal. I can discuss—as you pointed out in one of your emails discussing the man I used to be—any number of subjects with facility and enjoyment; I am enormously well-read, after all—stuck in Festering Shithole, Illinois, there was little to do but read, and then after I left, books became my steadfast companion during my travels. But while I have always been able to appreciate and love and discuss art, until I discovered writing, I couldn't produce any of my own. So now that I know I can paint with words, yes, I am going to indulge in it. Thick, great, iridescent and textural glops of words smeared across the page in fat eager brushstrokes.

God, Ava. I need you. This is a specific need, however. Yes, I miss your intelligence and wit and vulgarity and blunt-as-a-hammer honesty and your easy way with words, spoken and written; and yes, I miss our relationship, as it was before Henry.

I hate myself for that phrase—as it was before Henry. But it's true, and it cuts me to the quick to admit that. Cuts as deeply and sharply as a nanoblade.

Henry changed us. Me, you, and us. He was our ending, Ava. God, what a vile thing to say. But it's true, isn't it? That doesn't negate the bone-deep, soul-shearing love I have—had? Have? I don't know, dammit—for him. But he changed you. He changed your body, and he changed your psyche, and he changed your focus. I don't mean that selfishly, my darling. Truly, I don't. I loved your body as it was post-birth, even in the months when you were complaining about not being able to get rid of the "extra baby weight". I loved that version of you. Softer, lusher. More curve to your hips and thighs. From the point of view of the man who looked at you and desired you day in and day out, naked in the shower and in three-day-old yoga pants alike, you were so lovely, so sexy. Motherhood suited you. If only you could have enjoyed motherhood. I can't even allow myself to imagine our life together had he not been ill. The few times he was happy and content, as a baby should be, it was heaven. But those moments were so few and far between, love. Overshadowed by pain and horror. Tears, and frustration, and desperation, and Pain. God, the pain.

I digress.

I need you, Ava.

I am desperate. For *you*. For touch. For a kiss. For the scrape of your hand down my stomach. For the slide of your lips across my hipbone. The sweep of your thigh against mine in the dulcet, drowning darkness. For the warm huff of your breath on my skin and the wet suck of your mouth around me and the building pressure of need reaching release. Ava, I need the sweet cream of your cunt—and oh yes, love, you'd hate that phrasing as well; you'd shudder and curse me if you were to read it.

I am mad with need.

Wild with it.

I cannot have you. I have lost you, as I have lost myself.

And so I go in search. Of myself, and thus the man who might return to you, and take you in his arms, and love you from the plunging red of sunset to the birthing gold of dawn. I yearn for that reunion. But I am not that man.

I am no man.

I am…Un. As in Undone. Unmade. Unrestored. Unremarkable. An Unmitigated disaster…that one was a stretch, I admit.

Un.

Nix.

A no-man. A being writhing in the vast empty spaces of the world, a wicked and twisted creature scrabble-clawing through the endless dark of despair, faceless. No, not faceless—possessed of eyes with which to see the ruin of self. Mouth stitched closed, sewn shut with thick black poisonous thread. To scream is to groan, to speak is to moan, to weep is to hiss, and all these sounds are eldritch and ravaged, scuttling up from beneath the mossy lichyard stones.

Ava, I need you.

But I do not deserve you. I still dream of darkness, still desire sometimes to drown myself in the bottom of a bottle. Sometimes, as *The Hemingway* sculls across the waves, I stare down into the wine-dark sea and I think of the peaceful oblivion I might find there, floating down

down to the blackest crushing depths, the silence I might finally possess if I threw myself overboard. Silence, I say, because my mind is a place of cacophony, a lampshade full of banging and burning moths, each fluttering desperate winging thing a doubt, a sorrow, a desperation, a need, a curse, an angry tirade, a vitriolic diatribe against the flimsy vagaries of this venomous thing called life. I cannot silence them, Ava.

You have your own moths.

And, in the long sleepless nights beneath a countless million stars, those moths become dragons, long massive draconian fire-breathing demons, unkillable and monstrous.

I loathe each of the thousands of miles between us, but I cannot wish them away, for I hope at the end of my journey I shall find you. Or rather, find myself, and thus…you. Myself, and thus us.

I am taking the long way home, Ava.

21

Off the coast of South America

October 23, 2015

Jonny and I decide to wait until late November to make the crossing from the Caribbean to Africa. It's a challenging trip, with difficult winds and crosscurrents, and that's under the best of conditions. Until then, we opt to, as Jonny puts in, "bum around a bit." I think he's angling to take on another crew member or two, because a west to east trip with only two people, even on a catamaran designed for minimal crew, is tricky as hell, and would be made safer by additional hands.

Fine by me, just don't expect me to be best friends with any of them.

We left Venezuela and followed the coast, for the most part. We put in at Trinidad and Tobago for a while, and then took another short jaunt up to Grenada, where we stayed for a few days, drinking rum like it was about to be discontinued. Just like the old days, which was exactly what I needed. We'd hit bar after bar, making friends and telling outrageous stories. We left Grenada, and Jonny convinced me—which didn't take much work on his part—to hit up Barbados. So then we ended up staying in Bridgetown for most of a week.

Which is where we met Martinique. A French expat, an experienced sailor, and the only woman I've ever met who could go shot for shot with Jonny. Shit, not just the only woman, but the only *person* aside from myself. Going shot for shot with Jonny Núñez is a competition I only attempted once and vowed never to repeat. Martinique, though? She did it three nights in a row, at three different bars, and it was Jonny who put the kibosh on a fourth.

It is four in the morning, we've been drinking since nine the previous evening, and we are currently on *The Hemingway*, in the saloon, playing a drinking card game that doesn't really make sense for three people.

Martinique is shuffling the deck. "I have a question," she says, bridging the cards and then rifling them into a stack to shuffle them again.

"I'm sure one of us has an answer," I say. "Maybe not the right one, but *an* answer, at least."

"Where are you going after you leave Bridgetown?" She eyes me, cutting the deck with one hand and pouring shots for each of us with the other.

She's in her early thirties, maybe late twenties—it's hard to be sure. She has the air of a woman who has seen much of this world and a lot of life in a short span—worldly-wise, knowing brown eyes, long blonde hair she keeps in a loose braid. A killer body, a yoga body, a swimmer's body, strong, athletic, toned, but curvy enough that I find it hard to not stare at her. Over the last three days, she's worn what seemed to be a kind of uniform for her: short khaki shorts that barely covered her ass, a tank top or V-neck T-shirt, and Teva sandals and a pair of mirrored sunglasses on top of her head, the arms shoved into her hair.

Jonny shoots me a glance, telling me silently it's mine to answer.

I waffle on how to answer. We've spent a lot of time over the past few days trading stories of our various voyages, and it's clear Martinique knows her way around a boat and the open sea. She would be a valuable asset on the transatlantic voyage, both as an extra pair of hands and as someone new to break the monotony. She's funny, sharp, and has no problem keeping up with Jonny's acerbic and sarcastic sense of humor, or my often-stony silences. Plus, she's beautiful.

But on the negative side, she's beautiful. She's a distraction. A potential problem. The last thing I need in my life is a funny and beautiful woman.

I know, intellectually, that I should tell her we aren't looking for any additional crew. I know it. I don't need the distraction, the temptation.

But I'm sick of being haunted by the specter of what used to be. I need something new in my life, and this is a new chapter, right? It doesn't have to be a thing. She's just someone to make the transatlantic trip more pleasant.

"South," I answer, eventually. "Georgetown or Paramaribo, most likely."

She deals, and nods, then fixes me with another look. "And then? Long term, I mean."

"Africa."

She nods again, and each of us examines our cards. "I am trying to make my way back to Europe. I 'ave been gone for quite a few years, and I think it is now time to go back to Marseilles. See my family. See my father, before he is gone."

I nod, and glance at Jonny. He shrugs a shoulder, his expression closed. I know he approves of her for the voyage, or we wouldn't have spent the last three days drinking with her, but it is my decision, in the end.

I fidget with my cards and sigh, knowing I'm probably making a mistake. "The crossing, then. I don't know my plans beyond that."

She smiles at me, warm and bright and sharp. "The crossing. Wonderful. Thank you, Christian."

I keep my smile in return small and somewhat cold.

"Looking forward to the journey, Martinique. We'll have a lot of fun, I think."

Her gaze glitters, and her grin is enigmatic. "Oh, I'm sure we will." She plays the first card, takes a drink, and winks at me. "Call me Marta."

Later, after she's left for her hostel, Jonny pokes his head into my quarters; I'm lying in my bed, letting the room spin, and wondering exactly what I've gotten myself into by agreeing to have Marta make the crossing with us.

"You are sure about this, Chris?" Jonny asks.

"About what?"

He snorts at me. "Don't play stupid. Marta— you sure it's a good idea bringing her?"

"Why wouldn't it be?"

Jonny expels a breath. "Because she's a nice-lookin' lady and you're two years into a dry spell. And you're not in a good place in your head or heart. And because I saw the way she was lookin' at you."

"She wasn't looking at me any kind of way."

He blows a raspberry. "Yeah, okay, bro. Whatever you say."

"Fine, I'll bite. How was she looking at me?"

"Like she wanted to eat you for dinner."

"She's just along for the transatlantic."

"So you say now."

"So I say now, and so I'll say all the way across. Not looking for that, Jonny."

"Good. Because that would be a complication you don't need."

"No shit."

He hesitates. "Look, Chris. I'm your friend. Maybe even a mentor in some ways. I've got your back. I'll check your shit when your shit needs checkin', okay? But I ain't your papa. I'll tell you how I see it, but I ain't gonna police your ass, okay? You make that mistake, it's on you. This is me warnin' you—that girl has her eye on you. Don't go there, *me etiéndes, amigo mio?*"

I throw a pillow in the direction of his voice. "Yes, yes, yes. I got it. Fuck off so I can sleep."

150 miles east of Rio de Janeiro

November 18, 2015

We'd made good time from Barbados to Rio, which was our last stop on this side of the world. Marta had proven herself to be every bit as valuable as I'd predicted, and the three of us had meshed well together, falling into an easy sync as a crew. Jonny and I had discussed the possibility of a fourth person, but I'd squashed that idea after some thought. For me, it was hard enough having one new person aboard, and the thought of two new people made me queasy. I liked Marta, but I kept my distance, as much as one could on a relatively small boat such as this.

I'd overestimated myself, I was realizing. Jonny is a known commodity, to me. An old friend, someone with whom I have a history. Someone who knows me, knows what I am going though.

Marta? She knows nothing. I've resolved to keep it that way. She doesn't make it easy, though. She's a natural conversationalist, and it used to be my nature to let the talk flow freely, let the conversation go wherever it ended up. And for the most part, it was fine; we would talk about music and art and the exotic locales we've been to and favorite drinks and favorite cuisine, and eventually she would find something to do somewhere else. And then I would breathe a sigh of relief, because I'd weathered another moment alone with her; each time it was just Marta and me, I would feel as if I was being tempted, and then I would tell myself how stupid that was, how greatly I was overestimating my own attractiveness. I wasn't attracted to her or her to me. I may not currently *be* with Ava physically at the moment, and we may be experiencing a deep and agonizing separation, but I was still committed to her. Marta was just a passenger and deckhand on my boat for a few weeks. No reason for any weirdness.

But sometimes…she would get curious. About me. And that's what I struggled with. I didn't *want* to talk about any of that, with anyone. I wanted to pretend it hadn't happened. I wanted to keep pretending this life on the sea was all there was, all there ever had been. But then Marta would ask a probing question.

Like now. She sits opposite me. I'm behind the wheel, feet kicked up, an e-reader in hand. The sails are trimmed and bellied out taut in a favorable wind carrying us eastward toward Africa. The sky is blue and clear, the waves rolling past and around and beneath us, the sun is high, just past the midpoint. And Marta is on the couch a few feet away, eying me over the top of a magazine, which looks like a French version of *People*. She's got her mirrored wraparound sunglasses on, making her expression unreadable. She's in her customary too-short shorts and a tank top. Jonny is forward, earbuds in, sunning himself.

"So, Christian. May I ask, why are you making this voyage?" She asks it casually, seemingly as passing conversation. But yet I feel her attentiveness as a second skin upon my flesh, wrapping around the moment.

"I've only been to Cape Town twice and Jo-burg once. I've always wanted to go again." I shrug. "Now's as good a time as any." Truthful statements, all, and vague enough.

She flips a page of her magazine. "I meant..." She waves at the sea around in an expansive, all-encompassing gesture, "in a more...philosophical or personal sense. More deeply. The voyage as a whole. Not merely this leg of it, only. Why are you sailing? You and your friend, the very funny Jonny."

"I can't speak for Jonny, necessarily, but I've known him long enough to know the sea and sailing and fishing are all he's ever known. He's sailing because it's what he knows."

"And you?"

I shrug, trying for nonchalant. "I...needed a change. A big one. I sailed with Jonny awhile back, and when I decided to do this, I knew I needed him along for the ride."

"You are trying for a circumnavigation?"

I shrug again. "Eh. Not in the particular sense of the word, no. I hope to get all the way around eventually, yes, but...I'm in no rush to get anywhere in particular. Last time I was out, we sailed west to east, from the Caribbean down around Tierra del Fuego and then up to Indonesia by way of Hawaii. This time, I want to see things going in the opposite direction."

She flips another page, the sound of the paper snapping seeming irritated; I may be attributing too much meaning to the turn of a page, however. "So you're sailing just to sail?"

"More or less." I don't give her time for another question. "Why are you out here?"

"I left home very young. I read too many stories of young boys who went out to seek their fortunes on the sea and I thought, I could do that. I was a naive little girl. I did not realize how different our world is now than when those stories were written. I lied about my age and convinced a fishing boat to take me on as kitchen help. In time, they let me work on deck with the men. That was almost twenty years ago, and I have spent the years in between on fishing boats, on the antique tall ships, on anti-whaling expeditions, scientific research vessels scouring the Antarctic. Any ship I could find berth on, anywhere it was going. I have accumulated very little money, but a great many stories and a lot of wonderful friendships. A greater fortune than a bank vault full of Euros, I think." She gives a very Gallic lift of a shoulder. "Now I go home, finally. For how long, I do not know. Until Papa is dead, perhaps."

"Is he sick?"

"Not in any particular sense. He is just very old and has lived a very hard life. I was an accident, you see. My next oldest sibling is fourteen years my elder, and my parents began having children late. So even though I am only thirty, my father is eighty years old. I was…an after-thought." She twirled the end of her braid between her fingers. "When he is gone, I think I will set out again, and this time, I will not return to Marseilles. It is not really my home. The sea, she is my home."

I nod. "I think I understand."

Marta gestured at the waves again. "The sea, is she your only home, too?"

I debate my answer for a little longer than I probably should. "For now, *The Hemingway* is home."

"Why that name? I have wondered."

"I enjoy writing. Ernest Hemingway is one of my favorite writers, and a wonderfully complex figure. A man of great courage, great talent, and many faults. A true man of the world." I can't help but let my mouth run away from me. "He was an alcoholic, and he committed suicide. But his life and his writings left behind an indelible mark on the world. I think I named her *The Hemingway* so that I would be reminded of...well, many things. The beauty in the written word, the importance of truly living in each moment and of having courage, and that alcohol alone will not exorcise one's demons, or eradicate one's ghosts. In committing suicide, Hemingway stole from the world a great many more works of fiction, and that, to me, is a great tragedy. Same with any suicide. It is theft, to steal one's self from the world in that way."

I can feel the speculation in her gaze, even though Marta's eyes are hidden behind her sunglasses. "You have thought much on this."

I let too much slip, I realize. "Not much to do *but* think, sometimes."

"Suicide is not something one thinks upon for no reason," Marta says.

I feel the wind shifting. "Prepare to come about," I say, by way of evasion.

I don't miss the smirk on Marta's lips as she sets her magazine aside, and I'm careful to keep my eyes on the sheet flapping loosely for a moment as we come about for a new tack, and then on the waves, on the wheel, on anything but her as she moves about the boat, tightening and tying off lines with efficient grace. Once our new tack is established and the sail is taut, I busy myself with my e-reader, doing my best to look absorbed as Marta resumes her seat and her magazine page-flipping.

Minutes pass in silence, and then Marta's ability to remain quiet slips. "My sister killed herself. When I was eleven. So many people acted shocked, but I was not. Marie, she was a very upset person…disturbed, you would say, I think. Much in her own mind, sad, or angry, and always alone. Why, I do not know. She was twenty-five when I was eleven, and I suppose there may have been things she experienced which I have no idea about. I was so young, after all. I just remember seeing her walking along the docks near our flat, and thinking that she was just so sad, so sad, always so sad. And then one day Papa was at work and I came home from school, and I found Marie. In the bath, her eyes open wide, but seeing nothing. The water was red, and there was a razor blade on the floor. I didn't understand at first. Or, perhaps I didn't want to. I left the flat, and went to find Papa. He worked on the docks, loading and unloading ships. I found him, and I told him, and he only nodded. Kept me with him, and called the authorities. That was it. When we returned home some hours later, she was gone. Someone had cleaned the bathtub, erased all of the evidence."

"I'm sorry you went through that." I can't figure this girl out, why she would tell me that.

"No sadness is so great that to die is the only escape." She sets her magazine down on her thighs and I can feel her stare hard and sharp on me once more. "This world, it is so wide, so vast, so complex and filled with so much beauty. To die before it is your time, you miss all the beauty. All the wonder. The happiness that is out there if you only have enough courage to go find it."

"And sometimes, the world is so full of ugliness and pain that beauty has no meaning. Sadness, tragedy, it can consume you. Blind you. It obscures everything, Marta. Drags you down like an undertow." I stare out, watch waves crest white to starboard. "Yes, the world is full of beauty, sometimes. Yes, there is happiness, if you look for it. But sometimes…just waking up is a struggle. Being alive, facing the world, facing life, facing yourself, it's too much. Too hard. Sometimes, it's impossible to see past things to the beauty and happiness there is out there. How are you supposed to find something if you don't know what it looks like, what it feels like?"

Marta is silent, then. "You have known such pain?"

"Yes."

"You do not wish to speak of it." She states this flatly, but her head is tilted to one side, inquisitive, and she toys with her braid as if nervous.

"Not really, no."

She doesn't push any further, thankfully.

I pretend to read, and so does she, but I don't think either of us is seeing the words.

The silence is broken by Jonny's voice. "Look port side!"

Marta and I both move to the port railing. At first I don't see anything but the rippling blue-green of the Atlantic. And then a curve of something mammoth slices the surface of the sea, a dark shadow breaching up from the depths. Another. And another. And then a whale's tail spears out of the water and slaps down, sending a white gout of water pluming into the sky.

Marta and Jonny have already reefed the sheet, and we coast to a rolling stop in the middle of the pod. I count at least a dozen, probably more, as it is hard to keep track as they surface and dive again, a few tail sailing—leaving its tail above the surface to catch the wind, its body under the water.

Marta has vanished below deck, and returns with an armload of wetsuits. "Have you ever swum with them before?" she asks, handing me my suit.

I shake my head as I begin donning the rubber suit. "Seen them, sailed with them, but never swam with them."

She gestures at the pod, individuals breaching and tail slapping, tail sailing, sliding past just beneath our boat, huge eyes visible for a moment. "They are curious creatures. To be this close to so many is a rare treat."

Within a few minutes I'm suited up, my tank on and mouthpiece in, tumbling backward into the water, and my worldview shifts.

Beneath the surface is a wonderland of life, titans of the sea twisting and squealing, tails drifting lazily, fins flicking. I kick away from the boat, and within a few strokes of my fins I'm parallel with a gargantuan creature. It is breathtaking and terrifying all at once, my stomach dropping away and my heart slamming in my chest. It sees me. It rolls onto one side and tilts away, bringing an eye to bear on me, watching me. I cannot breathe. The surface, the boat, Ava, all of it fades. It's just me and this whale, a wild, gentle, curious beast fifty feet long and something like fifty or sixty tons. It drifts, and I kick my feet, extending my hand carefully; the whale watches, and drifts. Its fin lifts, floats toward me. Breathless, I touch the fin with a fingertip only, at first. And then run my palm along the rubbery surface. Its eye follows me as I inch closer, brush a hand along her side.

I cast a glance around me, and realize I am surrounded. A mother and her calf sidle closer, curious. The calf remains tucked near its mother's fin, against her side. The whale closest to me gives a gentle flick of its tail and drifts away with slow easy grace, breaching the surface. I follow her up and watch as she spouts, her blowhole whuffling and sputtering and then inhaling a whistling lungful of air before sinking back down. The mother and her calf are a few feet closer, drifting cautiously toward me; I tread water to stay in place as they approach, my fins flicking now and again to keep me from sinking downward. Mother and calf, a wonder of new life. They're less than twenty feet away now, and I have to remind myself to keep drawing oxygen off my tank, keep breathing. The calf wiggles its fins, and then flicks its tail, leaving its mother's side finally; the mother watches, alert as her baby approaches me, circling around to keep an eye fixed on me. I see intelligence in that calf, the curiosity, the wonder. This creature has a personality, a soul. It is a life. Not just another creature in the sea, but an individual being moving through life, thinking thoughts I cannot fathom, but thoughts nonetheless.

After a few circles around me, I hear the mother make a sound, a low rolling, rumbling murmur shuddering through the water, and the calf darts back, ducking underneath mama's fin once more. Mama angles away, and the calf follows, and then pauses, as if glancing back at me one last time.

It makes me think of a human mother and her child I saw once. My first trip to Africa, we put in at Bata, a port town in Equatorial Guinea. We only spent half a day there, but I remember prowling around a market, wide-eyed, still green, just a kid who'd never been east of Illinois. A woman was at a fruit stall, bartering for mangos and coconuts. Her child, a tiny, frail-looking little girl with wide eyes and a hundred thin braids in her hair, crouched clutching her mother's colorful skirt.

The girl watched me, curious, as I paused at a fish seller's stall a few feet away. I bought a fish, took the paper-wrapped package, and then turned to the little girl, squatting, smiling. The girl tugged on her mother's skirt, and the two exchanged words, and then the little girl had skittered cautiously closer to me, stopping just outside of arm's reach. I extended the package to her, and the girl took it, eyeing me warily. I only smiled, and waved at her. She inched closer, clutching the fish to her chest with one hand, and ran her finger along my forearm, marveling at the white skin. Touched my hair, and then hers. And then she waved at me and scrambled back to her mother, hiding behind that bright yellow and red and black skirt again, and the mother took her fruit and moved away, her free arm herding the daughter along with her.

And, like the whale calf just now, the little girl had paused, stopping to look back at me, a moment of awareness between us, eye contact between two souls. The mother paused, meeting my gaze steadily, and then she called for her daughter. I obviously had not known the language, but the context had been clear—*come, child; let's go.* Gentle, loving tones. Mother and child had gone their way, and I'd gone mine. A momentary interlude, a brief interaction, remarkable in the moment and easily forgotten amid a million such moments over the years, but remembered now for the similarity.

A whale and her calf; a mother and her

child—moments of beauty. An interaction that touches the soul, reminding me that I am not alone in the world. If that mother was to lose her calf to some tragedy, she would grieve. Prowl the waters, clicking and mourning and howling her grief, and perhaps other mothers would drift beside her for a while, comforting her.

I return to the boat, and Jonny and Marta take their turns in the water, and eventually the pod breaches, blows, sucks in great drafts of air, and then dives down and we lose sight of them.

We resume our eastward tack, and I sit behind the wheel with my wetsuit around my waist, remembering the whale mother and her curious calf.

My thoughts are myriad, and tangled.

EPISTLE #2

19 nov 2015

Ava,

I swam with a pod of southern right whales yesterday. A mother and her calf. The calf came right up to me and swam around me, and I felt the soul of the animal. It was a beautiful moment, my own curiosity mirrored by that of the baby whale.

   I am adrift. I am a whale scudding alone through the deeps, surfacing for breath now and again, far from anyone, far from land, from my own kind or any other. Who is there to know my thoughts? Who is there to hear my sighs in the night?

No one.

I wonder, in the sleepless hours of starlit predawn, what you are doing. What you are thinking, what you are feeling? Do you miss me? Do you long for me?

Do you still mourn?

Do you still cry yourself to sleep?

Do you touch yourself and wish it was my touch? I cannot indulge in even that. Even self-pleasure falls flat without you, Ava.

I am not alone on the boat any longer. It is a confusing thing, to have others present, but to still feel so utterly alone. I cannot speak of you, cannot even think of Henry—to write that name, to type those five letters... it is raw agony. Impossible to speak of it, even to Jonny, who knows everything. Or nearly everything.

He does not know that I dream of you. That when I do manage sleep, I wake having dreamed of you. Just this past night—it is five in the morning as I write this, and I am awake for the day, sitting on the trampoline with my laptop, watching the sky lighten—I dreamed of you. Do you want to know?

It was a bizarre, erotic dream.

It began with an all-pervading sense of blue—*blueness*. Soft, delicate, warm azure. The color of ocean water lapping in an inlet somewhere on the coast of Bermuda, Hog Bay, perhaps. That was all there was, for an eternity or a moment, that lazy lapis lazuli. It surrounded me, enveloped me, breathed in me and through me and was me. I was the blue, and the blue was me.

Then I floated. Like lying on my back in a pool, eyes closed, sun bright and warm on my eyelids, water lapping at my cheeks and lower lip, just breathing and floating. I sank into that blue, into the peaceful swirl of a gentle current.

Then, slowly, the floating drifting blue…shifted. It was a subtle transition, a gradual becoming. Motion, before random and idle, now breathing with purpose. The blue, before like water, now swallowed me. Slid along my flesh with purpose. Alive. Not a fearful or frightening or alien life, though; this was familiar, and lovely, and comforting. All I knew was that the touch of the blue was like curling up in my own bed after a month of hotel sheets. And this too was lovely and comforting; yet there was a new element, a new feeling, now. Softness and the slide against my skin was less the slick wet splash of water and more the deliberate tracery of palm on thigh, cheek on chest, breast on mouth, tongue on hip, breath on core.

This too pulsed with the soul-calm of home.

An eternity passed as I drowned in that touching kissing licking embracing breathing blue. I gave myself over to it, let it consume me. I became one with it.

Eternity after eternity, and still I convulsed and writhed and sighed in that roiling flesh-slick blue of touch.

Never end
Never end
Never end

Those two words were my only thought, my only awareness. I was home, and I wished never to leave. I needed it.

And then all morphed again, another slow imperceptible shift.

The blueness became a gaze. Awareness. Intelligence. Sentience.

Blue desire.

A vibrant blue, vulpine and ravenous.

And so, so familiar. Home. All that is me, all that is known, all that is comfort and solace.

The sense of touch became more. More everything—more real, firmer, needier, hungrier. Aching. Clawing.

All within that blue, such a sweetly familiar shade, a flavor of blue I knew with my mind and my heart and my soul and my body and into my pores and down through my cells. I *knew* that blue.

It touched. Demanded. Possessed. Became.

Again, I gave myself over to it. Abandoned myself to being possessed. The touch expanded, and I expanded with it. The touch slid along my neck, tracing the tendons. Carved a furrow down the center of my chest, like a teasing fingertip scraping from breastbone to navel.

Another long slow touch, this one beginning at my toes and brushing up my calves, to my thighs, to my belly. Palms on flesh. Need. Ache. And that blue, blue gaze. It was a gaze, now, and I knew the eyes. Such vivid, vibrant, ensorcelling azure. Tracing my body with hungry needy fever, fervor, furor. A tempest of touch, a tangling, sighing dream-silk of whispers winnowing awareness from sleep.

The touch became...aggressive.

My balls ached, throbbed. I felt my manhood engorge. Felt it stiff and hard as nails and dripping with need. The blue, it saw my need. Felt my desire. Tasted my desperation.

I looked into that blue, into those eyes, and assented to anything, everything. Begged for touch. For the bliss of release. Pleaded for more.

And so the blue caressed me, intimately. A sweet slow affectionate brush of hands over my cock. Gentle and unhurried.

I breathed a whimper of pleasure, and the blue breathed back, lips whispering against mine, words I couldn't make out, whispers like a breeze in the treetops, licking against my cheekbones, ruffling my hair.

And I recognized as well the texture of that whisper. It was as blue and familiar as the eyes that gazed at me, into me.

For time without end I lay in that drowning blue, basking in the touch, the breath, the presence. Letting the blue caress me, unhurriedly squeezing and sliding and stroking until I was unable to breathe properly, unable to be still, until I could only writhe and beg for the dulcet beautiful torture to end, to let me find release.

Whispers met my plea.

Words, this time.

Give it to me,

I heard.

Never end,

I heard.

Opposite, but complimentary. The blue and I both wished for this to never end, but we both knew it must, and so we both wished for the ending to be...a song so glorious even the most distant stars would hear and feel jealousy.

And so it was. The build-up was slow and my arousal was painful. The touch and the blue gaze grew hungrier and needier and I could not resist the need to release any longer. I became aware of the touch as a real physical thing, a hand wrapped around me and sliding slowly and grinding at my base and twisting around the top and sliding and caressing unceasingly until the moment of release was upon me, undeniable, heat and pressure boiling through me fiercely enough to melt me from the inside out, and I stared into those blue eyes and whispered back—

To you.

As I came, it was you touching me, Ava.

Only at the end as I exploded with a wrenching groan did I know you as the owner of those blue eyes and the perfect touch. But it was always you. Always the shade of your eyes, the texture of your voice, the sweetness of your touch. You, Ava.

You.

When I awoke, my come was a sticky hot pool on my stomach.

If you had been there…oh, love. You would have gloried in the mess. Teased me, tasted it, perhaps. Cleaned me with a loving touch.

I woke, messy, and you weren't there.

It had all been a dream.

But I choose to believe it was you, still, somehow.

Perhaps our dreams are tangled.

I wonder if you dreamed of me, that night. Was I there, in your mind, in your sleep? Touching you? Licking your core, tasting your essence, gathering the sweet slick dew from deep within you on my fingers and licking it away like the nectar from a flower, like honey dripping from a golden comb? Pleasuring you as slowly as you did me? Teasing you to the edge and denying you the release—just as you love so much in reality.

Pluck that dream from my mind, Ava. Take it, make it real. I push it out into the æther, waft it toward you with all the impetus I can impart it. Take it, drown in it. Drown in my touch. Relish my whisper as you sleep. Glide languorously in my presence, imagined though it may be, and drown in my touch, in the sweep of my tongue against your seam, swirling against the hard bud of your clit, my fingers squelching inside you, finding that secret place that drives you to helpless screams and writhing whimpers.

God, I could come again thinking of it. Writing this, I am aroused.

I torture myself with this, Ava.

Pray, love. Pray that I am strong enough. That I can withstand what I fear comes my way.

23

Jamestown, St. Helena,
Ascension and Tristan de Cunha

December 24, 2015

We're moored at Jamestown Bay, sitting in the saloon just past dawn, sipping coffee, and pretending it's not the holidays. We spent Thanksgiving riding out a nasty storm, and only celebrated it with an exhausted meal after some twenty hours on deck. Now, it's Christmas Eve, and none of the three of us seem inclined to bring up that fact.

Jonny has no family that I know of, his parents both having passed years back, and if he has siblings he's never mentioned them. Cousins, maybe, but a lifetime at sea means he probably won't be calling them up to wish them a merry Christmas. Martinique sent out a postcard with a care package of expensive coffee grown and roasted here on this remote island, and some other odds and ends, but that was it.

I'm debating what to do.

Part of me demands I call Ava, just for Christmas, and part of me says I should keep my distance.

I'm waffling.

The morning passes in a somewhat awkward silence, all of us absorbed in our own thoughts. Jonny is uncharacteristically taciturn, spending his time alternating between carving a block of wood into a small sparrow, and staring out over the vista of the city spread out before us; Jamestown is built in a crevice between mountains, extending in a long, narrow strip up and away from the water's edge.

Marta, well…she's an enigma, as ever. She has a seemingly inexhaustible supply of magazines, and flipping through the pages seems to be her favorite pastime, although I've never been sure if she actually reads anything. I think she just uses it as an excuse to…I don't know. Watch me? Watch whoever is around? Something to do with her hands and part of her mind while ruminating on whatever it is that goes on in her head, possibly.

That's what she's doing now, and I feel her gaze as always. She watches me frequently, though not obviously.

I just...*feel* her gaze. I can't ever parse her thoughts, her intentions, but I just feel her watching me.

Eventually, she rises from her customary place in the corner of the couch in the saloon, and heads down below deck; I hear a door close.

Jonny eyes me. "Call her, *amigo*."

I flinch at his words. "What?"

He laughs. "You might as well have your thoughts written on your face, bro. I can read you like a book. You're thinking about calling Ava. Thinking maybe you shouldn't, maybe you should."

"Jesus, Jonny. Are you telepathic?"

He nods. "Yeah, 'course I am. Didn't you know that already? Come on, now." He grins, waves me off. "Nah, you're just obvious, and you forget how well I know you."

"And you think I should call her?"

He holds up the partial carving, a head, beak, eyes, and part of a breast of a sparrow, examines it. "Yeah, you need to call her. Wish her a merry Christmas. Tell her you're alive."

I blow out a breath. "If this goes bad, I'm blaming you."

He just chuckles. "Fine by me."

I dig out the sat phone and the calling card from the drawer beside the wheel. Enter all the requisite numbers and then replace the card in the drawer and take the phone forward to sit in the sun. It rings half a dozen times, crackling and spitting static.

And then the ringing stops, replaced by a brief silence. "Hello? Christian?" Ava's voice, soft, quiet, sleepy—6 a.m. here, which means it's…shit, it's two in the morning in Florida.

"Hi. Sorry to wake you. Forgot about the time difference."

"Mmm. 'S fine. Where are you?"

"Jamestown, St. Helena."

"And that's where? South Pacific?"

"Wrong ocean, babe. South Atlantic. Off the coast of Africa, about twelve hundred miles west of the border between Namibia and Angola."

"I see."

God, the silence between us is awkward and thick and tense and painful. "I just…I wanted to call you and wish you a merry Christmas."

"Oh. Ah, thanks. And merry Christmas to you." More silence, and then her voice again. "So…what are you doing for the holiday?"

"We're just going to spend today in port and then we'll probably head out tomorrow and spend the actual day itself making for the continent."

"We?" Her voice isn't suspicious, exactly, more just… curious. Which almost hurts more.

"Oh, um, Jonny. I know I've mentioned him before."

"Yeah, you sailed with him for quite a while." She lets out a breath. "Just you and Jonny then?"

I hesitate. "Um, no actually. We brought an extra hand on board for the crossing back in Barbados."

"What's his name?"

I hate how this will feel, how it will sound, even though there's no reason for it to. "Um, her name is Martinique. Marta."

A long, long silence. "Oh. I see. A woman."

"Just for the crossing. It's good to have at least three people for a major crossing."

"Young and beautiful, probably?"

I can't deny the truth of that, but I don't have to acknowledge it either. "Ava, she's a deckhand. An experienced sailor to help make the crossing, nothing more."

"Right."

"Ava."

"What?" She sounds defensive, and then sighs again and starts over, resigned, now. "I've got no reason to be this way. We're not together anymore, I guess, huh? You can have anyone aboard your boat you want. You don't owe me any explanations."

"That's not what I meant, Ava. We may not...physically be in the same space right now, and things may be a bit...unsure, I suppose you could say, but...we're not— *not* together. Not like you meant."

"Then what are we?"

I groan. "I don't know. I don't fucking know. I'm trying to figure that out. Us. Me. You. Everything." I rub my face with my free hand. "Jesus, this is exactly what I didn't want. I just wanted to wish you a merry Christmas and—and hear your voice. I miss you."

"We're not there, Chris. You can't say you miss me. You left, remember?"

"Goddammit." Against all my best efforts, my heart squeezes and my throat clogs with heat and my eyes burn. "Fine. Whatever, then. I'll call you—I don't know. After I round the cape, maybe. I plan to stop in Port Elizabeth for a while before continuing east."

"Chris, I'm sorry. I'm just…angry. Hurt. Confused. Things are really hard for me right now, and I don't know how to feel about anything."

"You think I do?"

"Well, you brought a woman on board your boat. It's just you and Jonny and this Marta person. And I notice you didn't deny her being young and beautiful. And what, French, too? Out there having the time of your life. Sailing the world, like you've always wanted to. I remember the way you used to sit out on the beach staring at the sea. I could feel you…*wishing*. Longing. Like…like those old Irish tales about selkies. Like I'd captured you and stolen your sealskin to keep you prisoner away from the sea."

"Felt like it, sometimes. The way I loved you, still love you—it was freedom and liberation and beauty and comfort and everything perfect in the world…but then if I thought about the sea, it…it did sometimes feel like a cage. Although your description of the selkie legends is more apt."

"You're where you belong. Just…without me."

"How do we reconcile, this, Ava?"

"Fuck if I know, Chris. Maybe there is no reconciliation. No healing. No new chapter in the story of us. Maybe Henry dying was life writing 'the end' on our story."

"I don't believe that," I say, spitting the words, vehement. "And I sure as hell hope you don't."

"I don't know what to fucking believe, okay? I don't know what I feel. Everything all at once, most of the time and it's too much, and hearing your voice just makes it worse."

"Ouch."

"Sorry, but it's true."

"I know what you mean, though. This isn't us, this kind of conversation."

"It is now, it seems." She lets out a breath, long and slow and shaky. "One question."

"Okay."

"Have you fucked her?"

"No, Ava. I told you, it's nothing like that."

"Would you tell me if you had? Or if you do?"

"Would you?" I shoot back.

"Unless you asked specifically, probably not."

"Well I'm asking specifically," I say. "I didn't think that's what this is, the kind of separation where we see other people. That's not what I want. It wasn't when I left and it's not now."

A brief, sparking pause. "What if it's what I want?"

"Is it?"

"I don't know. I've thought about it."

"In general, or someone specific?"

She huffs a weird, harsh laugh. "How about I answer that if you answer me this: your *deckhand*, Martinique the sexy French girl. Have you thought about her sexually? Are you tempted?"

"She's attractive, yes, but have I thought about her sexually? No. I keep my distance. We don't really talk all that much. Am I tempted? It's hard being away from you, feeling this separation, this sense of…us being broken, and I'm lonely. So…yes, in a way, but not the kind of temptation I'd ever do anything about." I turn it back to her. "Your turn."

"The sense of separation and us being broken and being lonely, that's exactly where I'm at. It's hard, and I hate it. But it feels like…like our lives have changed. Gone separate ways. You're out there, now. You have your boat and the sea, and you know how I feel about sailing. I just…I don't see us being together after this."

"That's not the answer to the question."

"There's no one specific. I still barely leave the house. I still drink too much. But I'm seeing a therapist, now. It's helping, and making me start to think about the future."

"That's improvement. Seeing a therapist, I mean.

And thinking about the future. Just not…" I trail off, unsure how to finish.

"Just do me a favor, Chris, please?"

I clear my throat, because it's still clogged with that odd, hard heat. "Um, yeah. What's that?"

"Never lie to me. Don't keep anything from me. If it goes that way for you, tell me."

"You have to promise the same thing." I clear my throat again. "But that's not what I'm—it's not—can we agree that we're not there, not yet?"

"I don't know, Chris. I just don't know." She inhales, holds it, and lets it out shakily. "But we'll be honest with each other, at the very least. I will, and you will."

"I promise."

"I promise too."

Silence.

"This sucks," I say.

"It does. It sucks really hard." When she speaks again, her voice is tiny, achingly thin. "Why'd you have to go, Christian?"

"I was dying inside." I realize this is one of those truths I'd just promised to give her. "I was considering suicide. Not considering, really, that's not exactly true. More…thinking about it as a what-if."

"Jesus, Chris. You're just now telling me this?"

"Well, before, you weren't exactly in a place where I could tell you anything. You weren't even looking at me, for fuck's sake."

"About that, Chris, I—"

"That's a different conversation, Ava. I don't want to talk about that right now. Not after everything else we've already talked about. This was supposed to be me just wishing you a merry Christmas."

Another tension-engorged silence.

"Okay, well…merry Christmas, happy New Year, and all that," Ava finally says.

"You too." I have to pause again, gather the courage to ask the next question. "Should I call you again, sometime?"

"Sure. Just…maybe not on Valentine's Day, huh?"

"Yeah, maybe not Valentine's Day."

She laughs, a quiet sound, bitter but amused. "How about we make a pact that we'll both get colossally wasted on V-day, in effigy, as it were."

"I can agree to that," I say, my own voice laced with amusement.

We used to get hammered on Valentine's Day. She hated the whole idea of that day, and refused to acknowledge it as a holiday, refused to let me get her flowers, chocolates, presents, or anything, or even take her on a date. Instead, we'd order in and drink a few bottles of expensive wine together, and intentionally not have sex until after midnight when it was no longer Valentine's Day. It had been our thing.

"Okay, well it's two in the morning and I'm tired, and now I'm emotionally wrung out on top of that, so

I'm going to let you go." She sighs yet again. "Goodbye, Christian."

"Talk to you again soon, Ava."

There's no click as she hangs up, just a different kind of silence. One possessed of a kind of finality.

Merry fucking Christmas.

The Selkie and the Sea

A short story by

Christian St. Pierre

Brighid considered herself a widow. There was no news for certain, but then, there probably never would be. That was just the way of things. Her husband Calum had taken a berth aboard a whaler two years ago, and hadn't returned. Nor had he sent any letters—which wasn't all that surprising given that Calum could barely write his own name—but on the voyages before this one he'd at least sent money, and sometimes a note in the hand of someone to whom he'd dictated his thoughts.

Perhaps even a parcel containing a bolt of calico or lace as a token of his regards.

Two years, now, and not a word. Ships came and went month by month, some with news from other men in the village: Michael O'Halloran had taken ill with malaria, and was stranded in Barbados until he'd healed; Sean Murtagh had lost his leg and was bound for home on a company ship; Tommy Dooley had been lost at sea and was thought dead. No news of Calum, however.

So Brighid carried on as best she could, alone. Herded the sheep and goats from pasture to pasture, fed the chickens and collected and sold the eggs at market, sheared wool at the appropriate season, milked the goats and made cheese, mended fences.

And watched the sea.

She had a ritual, performed daily. Once the day's work was done, she would follow the narrow path from the field behind her little home and over the dunes and through the tall dune grass waving in the ever-blowing wind and down to the sea. She would kick off her shoes when the trail ended at the sand, and she'd pause there, digging her bare toes into the cool sand, wiggle her heels, fill her lungs, and let her hair down. The wind would play with her hair, blowing the long red locks this way and that, draping a strand across her eye. The wind would play with her skirt, too, flirty and presumptuous, tugging at it, pressing the linen against her thighs. It would pry at the edges of her sweater and mould the sweat-damp cotton against the mounds of her breasts. Then Brighid would gather the hem of her skirt up to her knees and knot it there to leave her legs bare; there was no one to see, after all, since Calum had built their home miles from the village, right up against the sea on the west, in a green sward boxed in by hills to the east and south, accessible only by a narrow, rocky path to the north. It was a place of solitude and solace, their little farm. Far from any prying eyes. And so Brighid would tie her skirt up indecently high, because only the gulls were there to see the white flash of her thighs and calves.

She would traipse down to the water's edge, and let it tickle her toes. Her eyes would scan the horizon, east to west, watching for sails, praying that the next she saw would have word of Calum, but knowing in her breast that no ship would come, not with word of Calum. But still she spent her evenings at the sea's edge, hoping. Letting the sea foam drag at her ankles, biting achingly cold on her bones. If she went too deep, calf-deep, as she sometimes did, on warm days, her ankle would throb, a reminder of the time she broke it as a girl, chasing a sheep away from a cliff's edge.

She liked the ache, secretly. The cold was bracing. Sometimes, in the depths of her heart, she wished she had the courage to strip all of her clothes off and delve beneath the waves and let that delicious icy ache spread through her whole body. She never did, though. She'd gone thigh-deep, once. She'd had to hike her skirts up to her waist, and had stopped when the water began to lap and lick in an indecently intimate way. She'd splashed ashore trembling, and had made her cook fire in the hearth that evening especially hot.

Day after day, Brighid went down to the sea, waded in the cold brine, and watched the horizon.

And then, one evening, after a day of particularly brutal rain, Brighid as usual followed her path down to the sea, kicked off her shoes, and waded ankle-deep in the icy water. She followed the shoreline a ways, kicking at the waves, her hair let down to flutter behind her like a copper banner. The wind was sharp and strong, pressing her clothes hard against her body, tossing her hair this way and that, more aggressive than flirtatious. And the sea was full of ire, still, sending an occasional wave crashing against the shore in a spray of cold white foam to surge calf-deep. So Brighid tied her skirt up around her thighs to keep the hem dry, and followed the shoreline. She whispered a prayer to Brendan moccu Altae, saint of the seas and mariners, more as an idle pastime and a vaguely remembered habit than real faith in the saint to bring her husband back.

Hear my prayer, Saint Brendan, she prayed. *Assuage my loneliness. Return him to me. Show mercy to me.*

The whispered words upon her lips, she felt the wind scraping in from the sea, harsh and cold, sending shivers down her spine, and the sea roared and crashed, and waves licked at her calves like a cold tongue. She

continued along the shore, mindless of distance, heed-
less of time.

Her eyes cast down, following only the restless advance and retreat of the surf, she was thus startled when
she heard a footstep in the wet sand. She looked up just
in time to see the nude form of a man, turning from
her and leaping into the sea, a bounding splashing step,
a second, a third, knees driving high, taut dark buttocks
driving him powerfully into the surf, and then he dove,
a graceful shallow plunge headfirst into the waves. Her
vision of him was brief, but his form was immediately
imprinted upon her mind. He was tall, taller than Calum
even, who stood head and shoulders taller than most
men in the village. His back had been muscled and firm,
his shoulders broad and his waist narrow, with the powerful legs and buttocks of an athlete or warrior. His hair
had been long, unkempt, wild, wet and dark black and
pasted to his spine and shoulder blades.

Brighid stared after him, waiting for him to surface,
to rise up and gasp and splutter at the cold, to poke his
head up over the waves and glance back at her. For long,
long minutes Brighid stood and stared, with the cold
brine pooling around her ankles with the inrush of the
evening tide. Longer than anyone could hold a single
breath. Had he drowned? Brighid moved deeper into the
water, sucking in a deep breath at the icy ache at her
knees.

And then, far, far in the distance, she saw a shape

breasting the water, leaving a V-shaped wake in the white-capped waves; a head, perhaps, ducking and rising back above the surface. Too far to tell for sure, but it could have been him. Or perhaps it was just a seal, startled away by his presence—they liked this stretch of beach, Brighid knew, because it was remote and rocky and contained tide pools where fish became trapped, and fishermen rarely ventured here, preferring other easier places to ply their trade. It suited Brighid, and it suited the seals as well, and she often saw them sunning their bellies in the distance, and as she approached they would bark and splash into the waves and surface only when they'd put a healthy distance behind them.

A seal, or a man? From this distance, there was no way to know.

Brighid was cold, now. The wind still blew damp with the day's rain, and the surf was rough and angry, dampening her skirts even bound up as they were, and now her legs ached with the dull insistent throb of the sea's icy teeth. She trudged through the encroaching tide into the damp hard-packed dark brown sand and then up to the dry tan sand, where her feet sank in and were engulfed by the relatively warm grit. She looked back, but the sea was empty again, except for the omnipresent gulls, hawing and wheeling, skreeing and floating head-on in the wind, riding the currents and crying their discordant discourse.

She went home and stirred the fire into blazing heat

to warm the ache from her bones, and ate the last of the mutton stew; she'd have to make more for dinner the next few days, which meant slaughtering another sheep, a chore she loathed. Her mind wandered, that night, as she drifted off to sleep.

Calum was floating beside her. She was lost in the waves, drowning. She could feel her hair billowing in the sea currents, but she could breathe and he couldn't. He was sinking out of reach, and she was weeping, soundless under the surface of the waves. Above, a storm raged; she saw the lightning flash, saw the vengeful churn of the sea. Calum reached for her, his fine blond hair a yellow cloud, his eyes all black, no white, no pupil, no life, and his mouth worked, closed and opened, speaking, pleading, and his hand reached, reached, reached for her but never could she grasp his hand and pull him to safety. Brighid woke as Calum drifted down into the inky depths, woke screaming his name, gasping in the dark silence of predawn.

There would be no more sleep, she knew; she would meet him in the waves again if she tried to sleep. Instead, she lit her lamp and mended rends in dresses and darned the holes in her stockings and bided her time until it was light enough to milk the goats and put them and the sheep out to pasture. All the while, her mind was on the dream she'd had. Calum, reaching for her, sinking into the depths. As much a confirmation of his demise as she was likely to get, although she would never have admitted to such superstition out loud.

Her nearest neighbor, taciturn old Mr. Malloy, had traded her some lobster traps for a few pails of milk, and had shown her where and how to place them, so she brought a large pail down to the shoals with her skirts tied high and her hair braided tightly to prevent tangles in the mischievous wind of the morning. Scrambling across the rocks and down into the thigh-deep pools, she hauled up the first trap, and found a trio of angry, tentacle-waving crustaceans therein; the next few traps were empty, and the last pair held four more each, which made for a tidy enough haul that Brighid made a mental note to bring Mr. Malloy some of her goat cheese, which was nearly done aging.

With her lobsters ticking and clacking and climbing claw-upon-eyestalk in the bucket, Brighid picked her way carefully back across the spit of surf-slick rocks and then slid down a sandy embankment to the beach proper, and there pulled up short, breathless in fright and shock.

A monstrous harbour seal was beached not half a dozen paces away, dark eyes wet and fixed on her, whiskers twitching. It was on its side, its tail in the surf, a flipper in the air waving listlessly. She set down her pail of lobsters and inched toward the seal; he—the mighty beast was a he, she was somehow certain—was staring at her. She could feel his gaze.

Urrrr—Ur-ur-ur-urrrrrr. He sounded…weak. Troubled. In pain.

Brighid—fearful of the size of the beast, which was

well over six feet in length and weighed several hundred pounds, easily—inched incrementally closer, keeping her eyes on his. His wet skin was mottled dark gray, speckled with a spray of white spots around the base of his tail.

A few inches closer, and Brighid was nearly close enough to touch him, should she reach out her hand. He growled again, a throaty rumbling that was somehow non-threatening. His eyes were round limpid pools of ink, shining and glimmering with emotion and intelligence. Closer and closer yet, and the seal did not move. Brighid knew she was being foolish. Seals were ungentle creatures, despite their playful reputation. Males could be territorial, and downright dangerous if threatened, and this close, Brighid was at his mercy. But his bark as she laid a trembling palm on the top of his neck was pained, a beseeching murmur. His flipper waved again, flopping listlessly back and forth.

Brighid, shaking all over, moving slowly and keeping a wary, cautious eye on the beast, shuffled toward the wavering flipper. The seal shifted abruptly, rolling away from her, causing Brighid to yelp in fright and stumble away. But he made no other move so she crouched beside him, one hand on his slick, soft wet skin, trailing across his body as she examined him. There, underneath his flipper, was a huge, wicked, curved fishhook, all of a foot long, speared directly through his flipper and skin near his body. A nasty barb at the tip prevented the horrible hook from sliding out.

"Oh my, you poor creature," Brighid crooned. "You've been hooked, haven't you?"

Urrrrr...urr-ur-urk.

"You just wait here, won't you? I have just the thing." She patted his thick neck. "I swear you can understand me, can't you? I'll be right back. Don't you move, all right? I'll help you."

Urrrrrrk-ur-ur-ur.

Once again, his bark felt eerily and even preternaturally like an intentional response. Brighid shrugged off the shiver that shuddered down her spine. She snatched a lobster from the pail and tossed it toward the seal, who barked again, excitedly, and flopped toward the snapping, clicking crustacean, and then fierce canine teeth crunched and the lobster became a meal for the seal.

Brighid shuddered at the sudden violence, but then turned away and ran as fast as she could up the shore toward her home. Up the dunes she scrambled, dune grass slicing and prickling and stabbing at her calves. At the back of her little house—a small, snug, squat structure of piled stones and hand-hewn timbers and jagged, overlapping, mortared hunks of slate for the roof, built with love and skill by Calum and his eight brothers, most of whom lived several counties over, now, and couldn't spare a month's journey to help her—sat a huge old wooden chest, the wood rotting and the metal straps rusting. Within were Calum's old tools: a hammer, an adze, a saw, a handful of nails...and a pair of thick-handled, blunt-jawed pliers, with enough of a blade to the jaw that it should probably snip through the barbed tip of the hook, if she could summon the strength.

Along with the pliers, she fetched a strip of cloth and a jar of salve, and then jogged back down to the beach where the seal had been. Upon her return, she discovered that the seal had, in her absence, knocked over her pail of lobsters and devoured them all.

"Oh, you naughty beast!" She scolded, with an amused huff. "You've eaten all my lobsters! That was meant to be my dinner, you know. Not very nice of you, was it?"

Ur-ur-ur-ur. If a seal's bark could be said to be almost apologetic, that one was.

"Well, no matter. I'll rebait them later, and catch more. I suppose you need them more than me, anyway." She knelt beside him once more, set the cloth and salve to one side, and grasped the pliers in both hands, pinching the tip of the hook just beneath the barb in the heavy, bladed jaws. "Now, hold still, yeah? I don't want to hurt you further. I may not be strong enough to cut through this."

She applied all the pressure she was capable of, but the pliers only bit in the slightest amount. Letting go, Brighid sank back into the sand with a huff. A moment's rest, and then she bore down once more, grunting with exertion, feeling the hook give just a touch, this time. Unclenching the pliers, she examined her progress: she'd managed a pair of fairly deep divots on either side, but wasn't even halfway through, yet. She rotated the pliers so the blades would sink into new spots, and bore down again. And again. Rotate back to the original location, and she squeezed the handle with all her might, sweat dripping from her nose, hands aching, the seal watching, breathing, not making a sound or moving a muscle.

"Good boy," Brighid murmured to him. "Nearly there, now. A bit more and we'll have it, won't we? Keep still a moment more, and I'll have you patched up good as new."

It was more than a moment or two, but eventually and with much groaning exertion, Brighid managed to snap the ugly barbed tip of the hook away, and then carefully slid the hook back through the seal's flipper. When the hook left him, the seal barked in pain, flinching away, rolling onto Brighid's foot, throwing her to the wet sand, her ankle twisted.

Immediately, he rolled away, flipper waving, whiskers twitching, barking in a low growl.

"Oh it's fine. I'm fine," she said, pulling herself to her feet and brushing her shins and thighs clean of the sand. "A little twinge, is all."

Urrrrr-ur...ur-ur-ur. The seal flapped his flipper, and lurched toward her.

He was bleeding profusely, she saw. She crouched and let him wiggle closer to her side. "That's it, a little closer. You need to have that patched up or you'll be a meal for someone else, with more teeth than you have, and we wouldn't want that, would we? No, indeed."

She had a moment of self-consciousness, realizing she was talking to a seal as if expecting him to understand her and respond, but…it felt as if he could. And it wasn't like she had anyone else to speak to, anyway, was it? Nor was there anyone to see or hear her folly.

She scooped a generous palmful of her homemade healing salve and gingerly spread it over the jagged hole in the seal's injured flipper, topside and bottom, and then wrapped the strip of cloth around several times, tying it tight.

"There. It's the best I can do, as I'm no nurse, nor a doctor for animals—a what would you call it? A veterinarian, isn't it?" She stroked his wet fur from the top of his head down his back, and he growled in his throat, a pleased sound, it seemed to her.

"If you want to thank me, bring me fish," Brighid said, standing up and backing away. "With my husband lost, I have no one to catch fish for me, and I'm dead tired of mutton."

Urrrrr! Ur-ur-ur. Urrrk ur. Flopping backward a foot or two, the seal then wiggled around to face the sea, tail flapping, flippers slapping at the damp sand. Brighid watched, feeling an odd kinship to the seal. A sense of…recognition, even. Familiarity, perhaps, although that was the most foolish notion she'd ever had, and well Brighid knew it. Yet the feeling persisted, and she couldn't quite banish it.

Splashing into the water, the seal dove and shot away, then leapt and splashed down, and then poked his head out of the water, eyeing her from a distance of a dozen or so feet out. She waved, a hand lifted, her copper hair fluttering in the breeze. An eyeblink only, but when Brighid saw him again, she would have sworn instead of a seal, she saw a man, treading water, just his eyes above the surface, long black hair spread out on the waves like spilled ink. Those eyes, staring at her, they were limpid and dark and intelligent, and familiar. Another eyeblink, and there was a seal's tail spraying the sky with diamond-bright droplets, and then the sea was empty again.

Taking her empty pail, Brighid returned home, built up her banked fire, and stirred the stew she'd made that morning.

That night, she dreamed again.

But not of Calum.

Of *him*, that man she'd seen the day prior. His lean, hard, powerful body. The long black hair, the taut muscles. She hadn't seen his face, but she knew he'd be as handsome as his body had been beautiful.

Not that it mattered. It was all conjecture. But where had the man come from? Where had he gone? He'd swum away and hadn't surfaced. A seal had, but…

Stories her mother had told around the fire when Brighid had been a little girl bubbled up from deep in her memory.

Selkies are real, Brighid, her mother had said, her dark eyes wide, firelight playing on her features. *Of that I'm absolutely sure. I've seen one. I came across a woman on the beach, and when she saw me, she dove into the water and swam away and only a seal appeared. I saw her again another time, too. They're real, Brighid. Don't you let anyone tell you any different. You find one, you find the skin of a selkie left behind when they change, they'll be trapped on the land and beholden to you for as long as you have it.*

She'd never really believed her mother's stories, though. Fireside tales, a mother entertaining her daughter during the long lonely evenings. Not real, not true.

But she'd seen it herself, a man vanishing into the waves, and only a seal appearing out in the surf. Could it be real?

She woke restless, irritable. Hungry, and sick of mutton stew. Missing Calum. Hating the endless days alone, knowing Calum wouldn't be returning, knowing she had a life in front of her that would be the same as the years since Calum shipped out: Alone, herding goats and sheep, fixing fences, doing everything alone, making her way as best she could, one day at a time, until she grew too old to do it all.

She had fences to mend, sheep that needed shearing, wool that needed carding, and the garden needed weeding, but Brighid found herself instead wandering down between the dunes to the edge of the sea. It was another gray day, the sky heavy and leaden, the sea churning and wild and angry, petrichor thick in the air. Gulls surfed the wind currents, and sandpipers skittered toward the retreating waves, pecking at the slick wet sand and then darting away from the onrushing waves. Way out, far in the distance, a fluke tipped up out of the water and then dipped back down beneath the surly gray water, and then a plume spouted white skyward. The cry of the gulls was mournful, it seemed to Brighid, their harsh discordant caws striking her nerves. She wandered the shoreline, carrying her shoes, letting the bitter cold water lap at her feet.

Yet, even after she'd wandered nearly half a mile away from her section of the shoreline, the water remained empty, the shore barren. Eventually she had to return home and attend to chores. Yet as she hammered nails into a fence post and carded wool and yanked weeds, she continued to feel at loose ends, vaguely unsatisfied for reasons she couldn't pinpoint. She felt her loneliness more acutely than ever.

Again that night, she dreamed of the man she'd seen. Wondered what his name was, where home was for him, what his voice sounded like. What his hands would feel like on her skin. She dreamed he was in her home, crouched before the fire, a blanket around his shoulders. She dreamed of his eyes, dark as the night sky, intelligent and still somehow animal, watching her as she fluttered around the house, cooking, cleaning.

The next day, and the next, and every day for the

following month, she wandered the shoreline just past dawn. She trapped lobsters, and thought of the seal who had knocked over her pail.

And then, when she'd begun to give up hope of seeing the man or the seal again, she wandered down to the shore in the minutes just before sundown, when the sun was just barely peeking up over the horizon, and the air was still warm but swiftly cooling and the light golden-scarlet and the wind gentle in her hair. And there he was, the seal. Breasted upon the sand, his tail flicking at the waves as they skirled around him. She knew it was him. Even if the strip of cloth hadn't still been tied around his flipper, she'd have known him. The preternatural way he stared at her with those limpid eyes. The way he remained still as she approached, just watching her, unafraid. Knowing, somehow. Welcoming, greeting.

Brighid knelt in the wet sand a few feet away from him. "Hello again. Are you well? How's your flipper doing?"

The seal flapped the flipper in question, splatting sand, barking.

She shuffled closer to him, reaching slowly and carefully. "I'm just going to slip this off you, now, okay?"

Another bark and a flap, tail slapping. He was massive, this seal. It hit her all over again as she crouched beside him. Huge, long, heavy, powerful. Those teeth, when he barked—they flashed white and sharp. Predator's teeth. He was still, however, as she unknotted the wet strip of cloth and tugged it off of him. He'd healed completely, with only a puckered scar remaining.

"There now, good as new." She shuffled back away from him, the makeshift bandage in hand.

Ur-ur-ur-ur.

"Oh, 'twas nothing. A bit of help for another of God's creatures. I still wouldn't mind if you brought me a fish or two, though."

Urk! Ur-ur.

He twisted around and carved under the waves, as graceful in the water as he was ungainly on land. She watched his dark form slice through water and vanish, and she found herself sitting in the sand, thinking of all the work that awaited her, and wishing she could dive into the ocean after him and swim with him beneath the waves and splash and catch fish and sun herself on a rock somewhere off shore.

She daydreamed, sea foam and icy water licking at her heels, the sun now past the horizon, the light hazy and red and golden.

Exhaustion snuck over her; the evening was warm now, and she wore a thick wool sweater of Calum's, and she was just so tired. She felt herself sinking down to the sand, pillowing her head on her arms, slipping into drowsy peacefulness as if in a dream, a return to girlhood when she could lay in the grass in the summer sun and let the warmth soak into her skin and bathe her closed eyes with a gentle yellow heat and drowse and feel time skip and hop and slip as she napped like a cat in a window.

There was movement. She was dreaming, though. Dreaming of Calum, returned. Scooping her up in his arms and carrying her to bed. Tucking a blanket around her shoulders. Watching her with large dark mysterious eyes.

Calum's eyes were gray, though, weren't they?

She fluttered her eyes, and saw craggy, swarthy features, a jaw like a cliffside, deep-set eyes like chips of blackest night, scars criss-crossing his cheeks, a thick black beard braided with strands of seaweed, long black hair around burly shoulders. Bare skin, a hint of a stomach, and then her eyes slid closed and when she opened them again, she was in her own bed and the house was empty.

Her door was open, though. Banging in the wind, the light of a full moon shining bright on the wood planks, staining a line of wet footprints into silver pools.

"I'm dreaming. I must be dreaming." She rose from her bed, traipsed across the room to the nearest footprint.

There were grains of sand in the print. And her arms, her shoulders, her cheek were gritty with sand. It was in her hair. In her clothes. She followed the footprints outside into the night—there were flattened patches of grass, blades twitching upright still. It was a considerable distance to the next print, and the next, and then she was following impressions in the sand, where the edges of the impressions still slid in on themselves. Running, now, Brighid tripped and slid down the dune path to the sea and there he was, standing in the waves, hip-deep.

Watching her.

"Wait!" Brighid called, splashing knee-deep into the water toward him, uncaring that her skirt was getting soaked.

He hesitated, his posture that of a man about to dive into the water. He said nothing, waiting. She approached, the water at her thighs and then her belly, her clothing wet and sticking to her skin, the water icy cold. She was close enough that she could have touched him. The water did nothing, this close, to hide his manhood, although he was utterly unashamed of his nakedness.

Now that she was mere inches away, she had no idea what to say to him. She met his eyes, and he didn't look away, but his gaze was...alien. Animal. Other than human. An animal soul in a human body.

A momentary tableau, two pairs of eyes meeting, and then he twisted in a flash of dark skin and splashed into the sea, feet kicking the surface, and then he was gone. Brighid remained belly-deep in the frigid water, waiting, watching. Long minutes passed, and then, far, far, far out, a head surfaced. Too distant to make out anything but a vague shape, but she felt his gaze. And then another splash, a flash of a tail, and then the sea was just the sea, calm and tranquil once more.

Days passed, and Brighid continued to walk the

shoreline in the mornings, and sometimes in the evenings as well.

One day she went to check her lobster traps, and her pail was gone.

The next day, it was back, sitting in front of her back door, full of fish. Cod, mackerel, tuna. Massive, fat, freshly caught.

The next morning, she left her pail on the sand near the rocks, where she'd first tended to the seal, where she'd first seen the naked man. By evening, it was gone; the next day, it was returned once more full of enormous fish.

For months, through the bitter winter and into spring, she would leave the pail on the beach in the morning and find it by her back door, full of fish, by evening. Those fish would sustain her for days, keep her fed, and prevent her from having to slaughter any more sheep.

And then, one night there was an awful storm, the kind where the wind blew so hard the windows rattled in their lead panes, and the thunder shook the foundations, and the rain clattered on the roof and walls and windows, and she could hear the sea roaring and churning. It blew angrily well past dawn, and then the sun rose and burned away the clouds, and trees had been downed across fences and sheep were missing and the goats were huddled together under a cluster of trees, bleating piteously.

It took Brighid hours to right everything, using Shem, her horse, to haul away the trees and then replace fence boards and find her sheep and herd the goats to a different pasture. It was evening before she found time to trudge exhaustedly down to the sea, which was still crashing loudly, whitecaps smashing onto the sand. Seaweed and driftwood littered the beach, enormous shells washed up from the depths, the corpse of something long dead water-bloated, bones showing through partially-eaten flesh. Farther down, near the rocks, a dark shape.

Something alive, moaning low, writhing. A seal. *Her* seal, as she thought of him. She recognized his mottled coloring and the spray of whitish dots near his tail, and the scar on one flipper. He was injured again, this time grievously, a huge jagged spar of driftwood speared through his tail, high up, oozing blood.

As Brighid approached, the seal growled, wobbled toward her.

"I know, I know. I'm not sure I can fix that here. You need proper care, I think."

Another low rowling murmur, weak, piteous. Brighid knelt beside him, examining the injury. "This is bad, I'm afraid. It's not something I can just put salve and a bandage on." She moved toward his head, petting him carefully. "You know, I have a belief that you're a selkie. If you are, you could change, and I can help you to my house and care for you there."

Silence, and a profoundly intense stare from the seal, his eyes searching hers, looking for…she didn't know what, but she met his gaze steadily, not looking away.

And then he shimmied awkwardly, with difficulty and grunts of pain, into the water. Flapping, splashing, and disappearing beneath the waves. Not very far, not very deep; she could make out his form, but only a darker shape in the gray-green waves. There was...was it a flash of light, or her imagination? And then a roiling in the waves, and the dark shape slowly became lighter, thinner, smaller, legs flashing, kicking, an arm, long hair and that beard, and those eyes as he clawed back toward land, gasping, growling in pain. The spar was now lanced through his left thigh, high up, the jagged tip protruding out of the front of his thigh, the end dragging in the sand behind him. He was on his side, trying to keep the spar from dragging in the sand, clawing with both hands.

In one of his fists was...something dark, and familiar. Fur? A hide, or a loose skin. Dripping wet, mottled and speckled. She crouched near him, propped her shoulder under his arm, and heaved him to his feet.

"It's not far," she said, "but you know the way, don't you, then?"

He didn't answer, just hobbled gingerly in the direction of her home. His injured leg dragged in the sand, and his weight pulled her down, slowed her, weakened her. She stiffened her spine and bore up under his massive weight. Calum was no small man, and she'd hauled him home drunk from the pub more than once before they'd moved to this farm on the coast, but the remembered weight of Calum seemed much, much less than this man. He just felt…dense, as if every pound of weight the seal carried, this man did as well. He was so heavily muscled as to defy belief, a massive, compact, hard, powerful man. And he was nearly limp, barely able to keep on his feet, even with her assistance.

They had to pause to breathe at the foot of the dunes, and Brighid looked back at their progress here and realized he'd left a trail of blood in the sand, a thick dark reddish-brown stain in the sand, blood sluicing down his thigh and off his foot and into the sand. After a few minutes of rest, Brighid worked herself to her feet, snugged her shoulder under his once more, and they painfully, slowly, laboriously dragged their way up the dune path. By the time they reached her back door, Brighid was sweating profusely and gasping for breath, every muscle screaming in protest.

He was barely conscious, now, deadweight crushing her into the ground. The spar—a hunk of wood cast off from some long ago shipwreck—was easily three feet in length and nearly a foot thick. It was smooth from being tossed in the briny waves for so long, but the pointed tip was jagged and razor-sharp. She got him inside, and to her bed, where he collapsed, his breath a pained whistle, groans emerging from his lips every few moments. He was bleeding everywhere, laying on his side, facing the wall, away from the doorway, the spar trailing down to the floor.

"I have to pull this out of you and stop the bleeding before you die from blood loss," Brighid said. "I need a few things first, though."

She hung a cook pot full of water on the hook in the fireplace to boil, and then cut up an old bedsheet into strips and set them in the water to sterilize. She gathered all the rags she had, and another sheet, and brought all of this, along with the freshly boiled bandages, into the bedroom.

After examining the wound, she leaned close to the man's ear. "I'm going to pull this out now. It will hurt quite a lot, I'm afraid." She shoved an old leather belt of Calum's between his teeth. "Bite down, and do not be afraid to scream. There's no one to hear but me."

Gritting her own teeth, Brighid took hold of the spar at the back of his thigh, a handful of rags close by. She braced her hand on his buttock, sucked in a steadying breath. "Ready? On three, then. One—two—*three*."

On the last count, she drew the spar out swiftly but carefully, and he screamed, an animal roar of agony as blood squirted out of the wound. He stiffened, and his hand clawed around his thigh, his fingers trembling. She gingerly moved his hand away and wadded a rag against the hole in the back of his thigh, and then another against the front side wound, and then swiftly wound a strip of bandage around the rags to bind them in place, tying it so tightly he snarled in protest.

"I'm sorry, I'm so sorry," she murmured to him,

crooning. "It's got to be tight to slow the blood flow."

He was groaning and growling and snarling, the sounds utterly inhuman, totally animal. When the bandages were tied, she settled a blanket over him, as much to hide his nakedness as to keep him warm—although he was now shivering and shaking. He moaned low, a guttural sound, weak, pained.

Brighid left the rags on the bed and tossed the bloodstained hunk of wood outside, and then sank down into the grass, cross-legged, exhausted, breathing raggedly, night having fallen to bathe everything in darkness. Allowing herself to rest only for a few moments, Brighid forced herself back to her feet and inside, to check on her patient. He was asleep on the very edge of the bed, his back to the room, the blanket draped over his mammoth form. Her heart caught; a man hadn't been in her bed in over two years, nearly two and half years now and the sight put her heart in her throat and fear in her belly.

Calum she'd known. She'd grown up with him, born and raised in the same village, courted and married in that village and then moved to Dublin together, and then here. Calum had been familiar. Marrying him, going to bed with him had been…home from the very beginning.

This man, this nameless selkie, this creature from the ocean, part beast, part human…he was utterly unfamiliar.

Brighid was beyond exhaustion, having put in a full

day's brutal work before finding him on the beach. Now she was…just done in, completely. And there was only the one bed, nowhere else to sleep save the grass outside or the hard floor.

Cursing under her breath, Brighid resigned herself to sharing the bed, because she desperately needed the rest. Her dress was sodden, however. She dug a night-gown out, checked to see if he was sleeping, and then quickly stripped out of her wet clothes, down to skin. She felt a shudder run down her spine as she tugged the nightgown on, and when she emerged from the neck hole, discovered that he was awake now, and watching her carefully, the fur clutched in both hands now, like a child with a favorite blanket.

"What am I going to do with you?" She asked, mean-ing it rhetorically. "You probably don't even think of na-kedness as anything much, though, do you? You're cer-tainly unbothered by it."

He didn't answer, only stared at her, and his eyes roamed her form, flicking from head to toe several times, scrutinizing her openly. He'd seen her before the gown was on, she was sure.

"I have to sleep," she said. "I can't very well kick you out now, but I also can't manage sleeping on the floor either. So I'm sharing. Do you understand me?"

Another long, curious, blank stare.

Brighid sat on the edge of the bed opposite him, meeting his gaze. "Do you speak English? Do you speak at all? Do you understand what I'm saying to you?"

He nodded, once.

Brighid laughed. "Well hell, man, I asked you three different questions, and I get a single nod in response?"

The intense, piercing, animal stare once more.

"Well, you nodded, so you understand English just fine, clearly. Can you speak though, or no?"

A long stare, and Brighid thought she was going to get more silence.

"I...speak." His voice was hoarse, gravelly, rough from extreme disuse. "Not well."

"Sounds fine to me." She slid a little further onto the bed. "What's your name?"

Another of those silent, intense stares that seemed to be a primary form of communication for him.

"Your name?" She touched her chest. "I'm Brighid."

He only shrugged, and shook his head.

"You don't have a name?"

He glanced at the ceiling briefly, a gesture of thought; he made a hoarse two-tone barking noise in his throat, and then shrugged again.

"Your name is...that noise?"

He shrugged, and then nodded again.

"Well, that's not going to work. I can't make that noise now can I?" She thought for a while, tapping her chin with a forefinger; all the while he stared at her, unblinking, a steady, intense gaze that no human could sustain. "How about Murtagh? Means skilled in the ways of the sea, which I feel is somewhat…erm, appropriate, given who or, um, what you are."

This got her the tiniest of smiles, a ghost of a smile at the corners of his mouth.

"Right. Well. I'm going to lay down, and you're going to stay there on that side, and you're going to keep your hands and your feet and your—" she glanced downward, an embarrassed suggestion, "—everything else, to yourself, you understand, Murtagh?"

"Yes." He murmured the word, a single syllable that felt heavy, thick, deliberate.

His voice wasn't accented in any way that she recognized, but merely as if words at all were a foreign concept to him.

She laid down then, under the blankets, whereas he was on top of them with a different blanket covering him. Layers between them. And still, she didn't fall asleep for a very long time, feeling him beside her, sensing him, smelling him. He smelled of man and of the sea, brine and musk. His breathing was steady but not sleep-slow, and she felt his stare.

"You're staring at me, Murtagh." She didn't look at him.

"Yes."

"Why?"

A silence. And then: "You…save me." Another silence. "You appear much good."

Brighid laughed. "I'm not sure what the means."

He was silent awhile, again. "To look upon you. It is good."

Brighid felt heat burn in her cheeks, and her pulse flutter. "Oh. I…thank you."

"Yes."

"Have you seen many women? Have you ever spoken to a woman? Like this?"

He grunted, a noncommittal or unsure sound. "Not as this. I see them. They swim from land, and I see them. Some with the coverings, and other times without the coverings. I like to see them better without the coverings. More of the skin. The body. It is good."

"I suppose you would." Brighid laughed. "Still a man, I see."

"Always am I man."

"Are you…a man, or a seal, or both?"

Another grunt. "This, that, all. I do not know. I am in the sea, the sea is in me. Her voice, her salt, her magic. She is everything."

"Have you ever been…" Brighid paused, realizing her question might be rude. But then, he wasn't human in the sense of understanding social mores, was he? "…with a woman?"

"To mate?" There was a hint of a smile. "Yes. She does not know I am this. A selkie, as you call me. Only that I am a man, coming from the sea, and she likes to look upon me, and touch me, and we…do this. In the sea. I show her my way. The currents, the waves, my breath. Not like upon the land. Not very good, like that."

"Isn't it cold?"

"Not with me."

"I—she couldn't hold her breath as long as you can."

"I swim deep, very deep. To swim so deep, I do not breathe for a long, long time. As man, as seal—it is the same. I breathe for her." He paused. "For you."

He'd caught her slip up, then.

"She never knew you were a selkie?"

"No. She teach me this words. To speak as you. Before, I only—" he growled and barked, exactly like a seal, as if the sounds still lived inside him. "As this."

"So it was something you did, with her, over time?"

"She live as you, near the sea. She see me, we do the mating. I come back, swim to shore as a man. Many times. Until she does not come down to the sea again."

Brighid shivered. "How old are you?"

He was silent, and she realized he didn't know what this meant.

"How many seasons have you lived?"

"I swim to the winter hunting sea…many times. Too many for the counting. More than the changeless ones. Many, many more. The sea, she lives in me, and I live in her. Long time. Long, long, long time. Before you, after you."

A vague answer that somehow left her feeling as if he was possibly ancient. His presence felt…*old*.

"Your man. He who lived here with you, before."

Brighid's heart caught. "Yes?"

"You wait for him." It was a question, but not a question. "To return to you from the far place."

"I—I don't know."

"No more waiting. He sinks down to the deepness, and he does not rise up again. No more breath."

"You know this?"

"The sea, she whispers her secrets, if you can hear her voice."

"I don't know what that means."

"Your words, this human speaking. It does not speak all the trueness of the sea, of the living of her, the feeling inside her. You do not know, for you are not of her, as I am."

Frustration boiled through her, because it felt like he was sharing something monumental, but she couldn't understand his convoluted usage of language. "I'm sorry, Murtagh, but I'm not following you."

"Follow? I am here."

"No, I mean…I don't understand what you mean."

"Oh. I mean—" he exhaled sharply, as if frustrated himself. "I ask the sea, and she tells me. I see you much with him, your man, and then he leaves on this shell upon the sea, and you are much alone. Much sad. Waiting for him to come back in his shell upon the sea. He will not. The sea knows him, now. She has swallowed him. He joins the many who breathe only the darkness of the deeps, now."

"He's dead, you mean."

"Dead is not living, not breathing?"

"Yes."

"Then he is dead."

A sob ripped out of her, the first she'd allowed herself since he'd left. Until that moment, she had refused to weep for him, to mourn him, for fear that to mourn him too soon would somehow mean she was being unfaithful to him. Giving up too soon.

But then...how did she know Murtagh was telling the truth? How could she believe him? He was a stranger from the sea, a real live selkie, if what she'd seen could be believed. Yet...if she believed he was a selkie—which the evidence of her eyes demanded—then it wasn't so great a stretch to believe that he could somehow communicate with the sea herself, that he might somehow have inside knowledge, so to speak, of Calum's death.

Tears were dripping down her cheek. She could still just barely make out Murtagh's form in the darkness, the shape of him dimly lit by the starlight from the window behind her. Murtagh reached out a hand, extending a thumb toward her cheek. She shied away, but then allowed him to smear her tear onto the pad of his thumb. Another tear slid down her cheek, and his thumb traced its path. Another tear fell, and his thumb pressed delicately against her tear duct.

And then he pressed his thumb to his lips, tasting her tears. "You make the sea from your eyes."

She sniffled. "It's called crying."

"Crying. Why do you do the crying?"

"It means I'm sad. For Calum. My man. My husband."

"Husband?"

"Mate…my mate."

Silence, and the shine and shimmer of his eyes fixed on her. "You are crying because you are sad your mate is dead."

"Yes."

"I felt sadness when this woman no longer came down to the sea to mate with me. I felt much pleased when she came down to the sea."

"We…Calum and I were mated for life."

"Always him, only him?"

Brighid nodded against the pillow. "Yes. Always him, only him."

"And now he is dead. Will you choose a new mate?"

"I…don't know."

"I could be your mate. Not for always, but for some of the seasons. I must swim to the winter hunting seas, but when I return with the warm currents, I will be your mate again."

Brighid laughed. "Such a male. No, Murtagh. That's not how human mates work." She frowned. "Well, not for me. For some, it is."

"My hurt is strong. No more of this talking."

Brighid let out a slow breath, and turned away to face the window, watching gray-white shreds of cloud skirl across the moon, obscuring and then revealing, occluding stars here and there. Behind her, she heard Murtagh's breathing even out and slow, and she knew he was asleep.

Soon, so was she.

When she awoke, he was watching her.

He watched her as she prepared breakfast, and he watched her as she changed into a clean dress, and he watched her as she changed his dressing.

He watched her, and watched her, and watched her. She went about her chores, and he rested. She helped him to the outhouse, which he found detestable. She read to him from a book, which he found fascinating. When she stirred the fire to life in the fireplace, he was fearful but fascinated, his animal instinct warring with his human nature.

Another day passed thus, and another. He healed faster than a normal man might, Brighid reckoned. He was still unable to be on his feet for more than a couple of seconds, but that was more than she'd have expected for anyone else after so short a time.

A few days became a week, and a week became a month, and then two. His command of the structure of English never really improved, but he learned new words all the time, and he became ever more articulate.

At no point did he ever let go of the fur pelt; it was always, always clutched in one hand, or tucked under his arm, cradled against his ribcage. He was fiercely protective of it.

One night, as they lay in bed, him above and she under the covers, Brighid found herself staring at the pelt curiously. She reached out a hand, tentative and cautious; Murtagh's warning snarl was pure animal.

"I'm sorry. I'm just curious." She withdrew her hand, watching him.

He tucked the fur deeper underneath him, out of sight. "It is not for you."

"I know." She kept her distance, but let the question she'd been harboring bubble out. "The legends about selkies…they say if you don't have your pelt, you can't change back, that you won't be able to return to the sea."

He snarled again. "*Not a pelt.* That is the skin your human hunters take from my changeless brothers. This—" he clutched the fur tightly, squeezing it in gesture. "It is…it is *me.*"

"I'm sorry. I won't touch it, I'm just…I'm curious, I guess."

"What you say is true. Without it, I am only a man, and I cannot speak to the sea, and she cannot speak to me. I can hear her, but I cannot speak to her. She speaks, but I hear only the waves, not her voice. If I do not speak to her, I cannot change back, and I will be like your man, but on land. What is your word for sinking under the waves?"

"Drowning."

"Drowning. I will drowning here on the land.

Already, the beast craves the sea. The drowning is soon. I must touch the water, see her, feel her. Hear her."

"You can still barely move, Murtagh. I don't know how it works when you change back, but you're not healed enough yet to swim. You'd barely make it down to the water as you are now."

He rumbled, a seal's growl of unhappiness. "I cannot change back yet. But I must touch the sea." There was a pained note of desperation in his deep, guttural voice. "I must. She calls me."

Brighid fashioned a crude crutch, the next day. Wrapped his leg tightly, and tried to convince him to don a pair of Calum's old trousers, but Murtagh refused.

"I am not a man, to wear a man's clothing."

It was growing ever more difficult for Brighid, having him around naked all the time. She found her gaze wandering to him throughout the day, whether he was covered by the blanket or not. And now, upright, her shoulder under his arm, her crude crutch under his other, assisting him slowly down toward the beach, his skin was warm against her, smooth and firm. His manhood swung between his legs, and she tried to not stare, but the battle was a losing one, for her.

If he noticed her gaze, or felt it, he gave no indication.

When they finally, after a long, exhausting trek, reached the water's edge, Murtagh tossed the crutch aside, gingerly unwrapped the dressing and handed the bundle of cloth to Brighid, and then hopped on one leg into the waves, and then when he was too deep to hop any longer, he sat down in the water and used his hands to push himself deeper, until the waves lapped at his throat and chin.

She was grateful to be away from him, because his proximity, the feel of his muscles and his flesh created a dark, dangerous fluttering in her belly, made her thighs clench and her breasts ache, in a way she hadn't felt in so, so long. It felt like a betrayal to Calum to feel such things, and she attempted to push it away. Yet the longer Murtagh remained in her home, the longer he slept in her bed—even separated by layers of blankets, and even though he had made no move to touch her in any way—the harder it became to ignore the feelings.

"Come." Murtagh's voice called out to her. "Come feel the sea with me."

It was a warm day, the sun bright, the sky clear blue, the wind a gentle breeze. She let out a breath, gathered her skirts up around her knees, and waded in to her calves.

Murtagh watched, and frowned. "No. You cannot feel her with the clothing over your skin. You cannot breathe her breath, you cannot feel her."

"I'm not taking off my clothes in front of you, Murtagh."

"Why?"

She had no answer for that. Modesty was not an idea he would understand. She'd tried, and he'd only given her the blank, uncomprehending stare.

"Just…because."

Murtagh stared. "You fear me." His lifted his head, his nostrils flaring. "I smell your fear."

"I'm not afraid of you, Murtagh."

"Your words do not agree with the scent of fear." He remained where he was, watching her. "What do you fear?"

"It's not fear, exactly."

"I do not understand, then. I smell fear."

"It's hard to explain."

He shook his head. "She said that. When she did not wish for me to understand."

"What wouldn't she want you to understand?"

"Why she couldn't come with me, out into the deeps. Down deep, away, to the winter hunting sea. I could breathe for her. I could teach her to hear the sea. But she would not, and I did not understand why. She only would tell me that it was hard to explain."

"Some things *are* hard to explain, Murtagh."

"No. You do not *want* to. This is not the same as *cannot*. Not as I am understanding your words to mean."

He was cunning. She couldn't argue with his logic. "Fine. I don't want to explain some things to you."

"Why?"

"Because it is painful and confusing. Because I don't understand them myself."

"Try."

"I'm not afraid of you, not like a…like prey fears the predator. You are a man, and I am a woman. I had a husband, a mate. Now I don't, and I'm lonely."

"I am here. You are not lonely anymore."

She laughed. "I suppose that's true."

"I am a *male*, not a *man*." He lifted the fur. "I am this." He tapped his chest. "And this. I am both."

"It's just…you say the sea told you Calum is dead."

"Yes."

"I can't just…forget him."

Murtagh sighed, and lay back in the waves so he was submerged completely and then rose up again, a peaceful, contented expression on his rugged features, water sluicing down from his beard, his hair pasted to his shoulders. "No forgetting. I do not forget her, the woman from beyond the dunes. Never, never will I forget her. She was sad, and much alone, and her body was not strong. I think she became dead, and so no longer came down the sea to mate with me. This is sad, inside me, that she is dead. But I do not forget. Also I do not cease to be alive. She has become dead, not me. Must I remember her and only her, for always? What if I choose also to remember you?" He gazed at her steadily, and his dark, sharp predator eyes were fierce and intense and wise. "Remember your man, your Calum. But also be alive. Breathe the sea. Breathe your land. Touch the wind. Touch the sea. Feel the life in all things."

"Murtagh—"

He did not look away, did not stop to hear her protest. "Feel the life in me. I am here. I am alive. I am a male, and a man, and I am here. He is not. He is in the deepness of the sea, breathing only darkness. I breathe life. Remember him, but also be alive."

"What if it's not that simple for me?"

"Life is life. It flows like the currents—always, always, always. A death does not slow the currents. We must swim, or the darkness will be our only breath."

Wisdom of the wild. Simple, practical.

She'd mourned and waited for three years. She knew in her heart and soul that Murtagh was telling the truth, that Calum was gone. So why could she not...be alive?

Slowly, hesitantly, Brighid reached up and unbuttoned her dress, baring more and more flesh with each button undone. Murtagh's gaze was steady and as mysterious as ever, unreadable. When the buttons were all undone, she lifted the garment off and set it with Murtagh's dressings, the whole weighed down by the crutch. And then she was naked, standing in the breeze and the sunlight, with Murtagh's gaze openly perusing her.

She waded deeper, and even on such a warm day the water was icy cold, making her bones ache. Deeper and deeper...closer and closer to Murtagh. Who watched, never looking away, not moving a single muscle as she waded up to her thighs. And then she was standing beside him, the water at her thighs, all of her bared. He'd watched her change more than once, despite her attempts to change when he wasn't watching, but this was different. There was no privacy in that small home, being only one room. Here, it was the open sea, the beach, the sunlight, and her own choice to strip naked so he could look at her.

"Go under. Feel her." Murtagh's voice was low, the words nearly inaudible.

Brighid waded deeper, and then, with a deep sharp breath, dove under, feeling the icy waves close around her, and she heard then only the silent roar of the undersea world, muted and muffled and so loud, somehow. He was there. Beside her. Toeing off the seafloor with one foot, the other leg trailing behind, his hands pulling at the water.

He reached out, and took her hand. His eyes were wide and round and not quite human, so dark, a seal's eyes in a man's face. "Listen."

"For what?"

He shook his head. "Not *hear*, as to hear the birds or the waves or my words." He tapped her chest, a brief but heart-palpitating contact of his finger just above her breasts. "Listen."

She held onto his hand and closed her eyes, and tried to listen, but she only heard the waves, the gulls. She felt him, though. So close. His hip touched hers, and his hand was huge and strong. She heard him, felt him. Only him.

"Do you hear her?" He asked, after a while.

She opened her eyes and met his gaze. Shook her

head. "No. All I hear is you."

"I was silent."

"No…" She tapped his chest as he had hers. "All I heard was you."

A ghost of a smile, then. He drifted closer. She could just barely touch the seafloor with her toes, enough to keep her chin above the waves, which sometimes lapped against her nose and mouth so the taste of the sea was on her lips. And then all she could taste was him, his mouth, the brine on his lips and the heat of his breath, and his hands were closing around her, carving a hot wild path from her shoulder blades to the small of her back and paused there, as if to give her time to absorb the reality of his touch. She couldn't breathe and didn't want to, because this was like coming alive all at once, after so long being…something in between alive and dead.

God, the ache. Her thighs quaked and clenched and she nuzzled closer, deepening the kiss, telling him with her body and her mouth and her hands burying in his beard that this was okay, more than okay, that she needed it. And then his hands slid down to cradle her buttocks, and she was gripping his arms and his shoulders and tracing the mighty muscles of his back and clutching his backside and she felt him nudging against her, his manhood pressing hot and hard against her womanhood.

Brighid gasped at the feel of him, whimpered.

Murtagh broke the kiss. "Breathe me. Trust in me."

"What?"

He swelled his lungs to capacity, blew the breath out and sucked in an even greater inhalation, and then locked his mouth against hers and tumbled them backward together under the waves. Fully immersed, the cold burned, and then she felt nothing but Murtagh, his hands scouring her skin and his tongue on her teeth and his legs propelling them powerfully out into the currents. Where was his hide? His hands were all over her, so he wasn't clutching it. Had he set it aside? Hidden it? She didn't know, and the ability to think about it eroded as his kiss pressed breath into her lungs, as his hands ignited fiery desire inside her. Even injured he could swim with strength and grace and power that was very truly inhuman; he was carrying them together out into the depths, twisting them together beneath the waves, farther and farther from shore.

Brighid clung to him and kissed him back and kicked her legs with his. The waves rolled above them and Murtagh's powerful strokes carried them effortlessly. And then he was pressing against her entrance, and she moaned into his mouth and took him within her, and then she could hear the sea.

Her song was deep and sorrowful and wild and joyful and exuberant and melancholy, a complex and multilayered creation of the many miles and leagues which makes up the sea, from the shores of Africa to China, from America to Ireland, and everything in between, as Murtagh moved with her, breathing for her, breathing through her, as his hands and lips and manhood fused with her skin and her mouth and private aching heat, she heard the sea in his movements, she heard the sea in his voice, she heard the sea in his movements. He was the sea, a creature of her, in her, from her. A being coalesced of pure oceanic power, distilled essence of the brine.

Brighid wept at the voice of the sea. Her words were in a language Brighid did not know but somehow still understood, but as if hearing Gaelic spoken by a Scot, or through a translator. Unclear, but recognizable. The sea was inside Brighid, in her soul, in her blood, in her brain. In her bones and muscles and sliding through her most tender flesh. The sea was loving her.

As their bodies merged and collided and slid and moved, Murtagh took them deeper and deeper until pressure weighed upon her ears and eyes and bones, and he twisted and rose up once more, gliding through the water with Brighid clutched in his arms, swimming with her in a graceful ballet, a mating dance at once animal and human.

Breathe me feel me touch me hear me

That was the song of the sea.

Swim play eat drink live love laugh cry dive drown breathe breathe breathe me know me

The sea whispered to her. Sang to her. The crash of surf on a distant shore was the melody, the rolling waves in the far wild depths was the rhythm, the tides a counterpoint, the song of the whales and dolphins and the chatter of seals and otters and the cry of gulls and albatross and the shimmering flash of schools of fish, these were the chorus. And Brighid heard it all. She could sing this song; her voice longed to join in, her body knew the dance, her soul knew the ageless tune.

And then they broke the surface and the sand was under her feet and the surf was crashing around them and their joining was lost, and the song was lost.

Murtagh was gasping for breath and his man/seal inky black eyes were fierce and intense. "Did you hear her?"

She couldn't speak. Only nod, whimpering. "Yes," she managed to choke out the word. "I heard, Murtagh. I heard her."

His smile was predatory and playful and happy. "You heard. The sea, she speaks to you. This is good."

And so it began.

As he grew in strength, he helped her with chores, and they made their way down to the sea and swam and joined together and Brighid listened eagerly to the song of the sea, which she could only hear when tumbling in the waves with Murtagh inside her.

Days, weeks, months...and then Murtagh was as healed as he was going to be, a limp forever in his step, but his strokes under the sea were as effortless and powerful as ever.

And then, one day, Murtagh was out checking lobster

traps, and Brighid was cleaning her little home. And she found, tucked inside an old pot that had been shoved behind the stove, Murtagh's sealskin.

It was silky, still damp, somehow. Thick, soft, and velvety. She didn't remove it from the pot, only stroked it gently.

A thought occurred to her. She could hide it again, and Murtagh would stay with her.

She felt him needing the sea. Needing his freedom. He was restless. He would wake in the middle of the night and stand on the dune, staring out at the moon on the sea.

Her hand in the pot, fingers buried in the fur, Brighid heard a step behind her.

Murtagh's eyes were wild and angry and fearful. He was utterly still, tensed. "Brighid." His voice was a deep, dark rumble. "That is mine."

"I know, Murtagh. I found it by accident." She didn't want him to leave. She didn't want to lose the song of the sea, or the way he felt, the beauty of their song together beneath the waves.

"Would you hide it from me?" He took a step toward her. "Trap me here on this shore, with you?"

She shook her head, feeling a tear trickle down her cheek. "No, Murtagh." She forced herself to stand up, to turn away, showing him her empty hands. "No. I wouldn't ever do that."

Brighid left the house, and walked down the path

with the dune grass tickling her calves and the sand skritching underfoot and the breeze in her hair and the sea in her nostrils and the gulls overhead.

He was going to leave.

She felt it.

His step was silent on the sand, but she sensed him behind her. "She calls me. Cries out to me."

"I know."

"Swim with me."

She held back a sob. "No, Murtagh. I can't handle that kind of goodbye."

"I meant…swim away." He pointed, away out to sea, south. "Far. Down deep, to the winter shores."

"I can't."

"I can breathe for you, Brighid."

She shook her head. "No, Murtagh, it's not that. I know you can. But…you belong out there. I belong here."

"Our song together is beautiful music."

"It is."

"I would sing that song with you for always."

"I cannot live in the sea, and you cannot live on the shore."

He breathed into her hair. "Never before have I cursed my nature. Now I do."

"No, Murtagh. Your nature is…beautiful. You are of the sea, and she is of you."

"You are of me, and I am of you."

She shook her head again. "It can't work."

He growled, an animal sound of displeasure. "I will return, then. When the summer currents call us back, I will return here. This will be my summer shore. You will come down to the sea, and we will swim together and sing the song of the sea."

She nodded, her breath catching. "Okay."

He strode past her, his sealskin clutched in one hand. Waded into the waves, naked, as the first time she saw him. As he always was. Nude and beautiful, masculine perfection. Deeper, until he was waist deep, and then he paused and turned around. Stared at her, and now she saw a world of emotion and intelligence and personality in that animal stare. No goodbye, no one last kiss, no sentiment. Just that silent stare, and then he dove into the waves and there was a gentle flash of greenish light under the waves and the surface roiled, and then the pale form of his naked body darkened and then there was only a seal, twisting in the waves, head poking up over the surface, dark eyes staring at her. And then another a splash and a flip of his tail and he was gone, streaking away out into the sea.

Brighid let herself sob, then.

But only for a little while.

The surf lapped at her feet, as if to comfort her, and perhaps it was her imagination, but the icy water didn't make her bones ache like it used to. She waded a little deeper, hiking her skirts up around her waist, and she felt the tug of the currents. A split second decision had her stripping the dress off and diving naked into the water and she felt the sea around her, heard, perhaps, a distant note of a song, as of the strains of a violin from a window across the city.

She swam, and the sea welcomed her.

Her tears mingled with salt of the brine.

She could almost hear his voice, the bark and growl of a seal joining his brothers and sisters on a long southward journey.

Eventually the shore called out to her, the bleat of goats and sheep, the waving grasses and the warmth of the sun and the crimson glow of sunset on the horizon and the crackle of a fire on a cold winter night.

He would return. The tides would bring him to her, and she would swim with him. And until then, she could dive down beneath the waves and hear his voice in the song of the sea.

25

Cape Town, South Africa

February 14, 2016

I start out drinking alone. It's Valentine's Day, but neither Marta nor Jonny consider it a holiday, since neither of them is American, and Valentine's Day is a distinctly American holiday. Jonny is out on the town and has been for a solid week, coming back to the boat only occasionally to repack his overnight bag with fresh clothes. We decided to stay in Cape Town for a while, mainly, I think, because every once in a while Jonny just needs to…sow his wild oats, you might say. Jonny is Jonny. I'm not sure what he does when he's gone like this, but it's how he's been since I've known him. He's not the type to go on crazy benders, so it's not just about drinking, I don't think. Women? Maybe. He's reticent to talk about himself, and I don't push it.

Marta is I don't know where. Doing Marta things, I guess.

So I'm alone on the boat for a change, which is nice. It means I can wallow. I crack open a bottle of scotch and pour myself a tall drink, and I take it to the trampoline between the hulls and think about Ava. About everything that went wrong. About how much I miss her.

How lonely I am.

I want to call her.

I don't, because I agreed not to. I'm planning on getting drunk, just like we used to, just like I promised.

One drink becomes two, and it's harder and harder to think about Ava. About the pain in her voice when we spoke at Christmas. How much that conversation hurt. How awkward it was. We used to be able to talk about anything, endlessly. And now we can't get through a merry Christmas conversation? What went wrong?

I don't know what to do.

I can't go back. I'm not cut out for life on land. This, out on the ocean, this is the life I was meant to live. But I still love Ava…that hasn't changed. I realized that when we spoke. I love her. I'll always love her. But…what if she's right? What if Henry's death was life or fate or God stamping **THE END** on our relationship? I just don't know how to fix things, how to reconcile with her. She won't come to sea with me, and I can't go back to that life.

I miss her.

Fuck, I miss her so bad.

I need her. I need her kiss. I need her touch. I need her presence.

I'm drunk.

The stars are spinning, wheeling, and the boat is rocking beneath me—although since it's a boat, that's normal, but it seems more unstable than usual. Is this my third drink or my fourth? Can't remember.

Nothing matters.

I should just move on. Take the wedding ring off, get a lawyer back in the States to draw up divorce papers. What's the point? Does she even miss me? Didn't seem like it. Seemed like she was in pain, sure, but did she miss me? Does she want me back? Does she want to fix things? Does she want to find a way for us to be together?

I think of the short story I wrote the other day, which I wrote only for me, for Ava—it's saved in with the other letters I've written her, all of which I've also printed out and sealed into a waterproof, crushproof, fireproof file box. That story, "The Selkie and the Sea"…it's us. Me, Ava, our relationship. It just poured out of me, emerging whole cloth. Ava, if she ever reads it, will understand the symbolism I used in it. I mean, it's not hard, it's not like I disguised them. Do I even want her to read any of this stuff I'm writing her? I don't know if I do. It's more for me, to help me sort things out in my own head and heart. I'm not sure I'm capable of sharing them with her. If I'll even see her again.

God, that thought hurts more than I thought it would.

I hear feet on the deck, shuffling slowly and carefully down the companionway to the berths below. Dismiss it as Jonny, coming back for more clothes. Sip at my scotch and enjoy the drunkenness; it's easier to give in to my feelings, like this. Easier to admit I'm going crazy with horniness, crazy with loneliness, crazy with grief and mourning and confusion. It's all too much and I can't handle it all. I'm trying to take it one day at a time and let myself heal and let myself feel things, but then that conversation with Ava at Christmas just fucked everything all up again.

I shouldn't have called her.

But I had to, didn't I?

I feel someone beside me. Twist my head, peer dizzily; it's Marta.

"Hey." She smiles at me; she's drunk too. "Fucking Valentine's Day, no?"

"You too, huh?"

She nods. "I was in love with an American, once. A captain. It was his favorite holiday. He was always very elaborate about the dates he took me on for that day. Roses by the dozen, or more. *Chocolat*—" she says it the French way, "flowers. Extravagant gifts, since he was very

rich. I was a deckhand on his yacht, and it becomes...
something more. At first just sex, and then more, and
then I was in love with him, and he spoiled me."

"Sounds nice."

She sighs. "*Oui*. It was." Her accent is much, much
thicker than usual, and she doesn't usually sprinkle her
conversation with French words. "Until he found a new,
prettier, younger deckhand, and I could accept that he'd
moved on and stay aboard his yacht with the excellent
berth and excellent pay, or I could jump ship in Jakarta
and figure out what to do next on my own."

"Hello, Jakarta."

"Yes, exactly. There was no real choice to make. He
was not shy about his relationships, with me or with her.
So I ended up in Jakarta for a month, until I found a new
berth. And ever since, I have hated your stupid American
romance holiday."

"It is pretty stupid."

"So why are you drunk and alone on this day, hmm?"
she asks, taking my glass from me and sipping.

As she takes the glass from me, our fingers brush.
I jerk my hand away a little too fast, and even drunk, I
know she notices.

I shrug, and take it back from her, making sure our
fingers don't touch. "It was my...Ava's and my thing. We
both hate Valentine's Day, Ava especially. Had it ruined
for her by a nasty ex, like you, and she just refused to
have anything to do with it. So we'd...on Valentine's Day

we'd both take the day off and spend it drinking, eating, watching movies. She wouldn't let me buy her anything, not a damn thing. Not even a fucking candy bar. We'd spend it together, getting wasted. And then, at midnight, when it wasn't the holiday anymore, we'd have sex. But not until after midnight. It was like a weird reverse celebration, I guess."

"I like that plan." She takes my glass again, and this time intentionally brushes my fingers with hers, letting her index finger trail along mine, her eyes on me. "So that's what you're doing, then?"

I nod. "Sort of. Getting drunk alone, being pathetic."

"Well, you're not drunk alone anymore. I am drunk too. And if getting drunk alone is pathetic, then I am that as well, since I sat alone in a bar, drinking far too much merlot." She hands the glass back and rolls to face me. "So now we are drunk and pathetic together."

Goddammit. She's wearing…not much. A tiny pair of what might be loosely termed workout shorts, which cover even less of her ass than usual, and a bikini top. Which she's spilling out of, especially lying on her side as she is. My eyes betray me, latching on to the spillage for longer than is probably acceptable.

When I finally turn my eyes back to hers, she is smiling a strange, secret smile.

She tilts her wrist, checking her watch. "It is nearly midnight. Only two minutes until the change of the hour."

"Marta, I—"

"Christian, I think you think too much. Expect too much of yourself. Of others. Of her. Of life."

"What do you mean?"

"Things do not have to be so complicated. You sailed away from a mess that was your life. From someone who seemed able to let you simply sail away. Does that not make you free to do what you want?"

"Maybe."

She takes the now-empty glass from me, shimmies up the trampoline to set it aside, and then slides back down. Closer than before, her knees brushing mine, her breasts all but totally spilled out of the tiny little triangles of her bikini top, her face inches from mine. "I think it does. What reason do you have to remain faithful to a relationship that is over? It is over, is it not?"

"I don't know."

"There is no reason for you to be lonely."

"What do you want, Marta?"

She shifts closer. Tugs at the laces of my swim trunks, the only thing I'm wearing. "This. You. For tonight only, perhaps."

"I don't know if I can, Marta."

She has my trunks open, and reaches in, grasps me. "Why not? Because of the whisky you have drunk? It has not affected you adversely, it seems."

I groan at the feel of her touch, a warm firm delicious sensation. "No, not that."

She slides her touch up, and then down. "Then what?"

"I just…" My mind isn't working. My heart is saying something, loudly, but my body is in control. The whisky has numbed me to the cry of my heart.

Give in to this, some part of me whispers.

You know you want it.

What's the harm? No one needs to know.

It's over anyway. You might as well seek comfort where you can find it.

There's something wrong with that logic, but I'm too drunk to figure out what and Marta's hand on me feels too good.

Her lips fumble clumsily at mine. Her kiss is…god, I don't know. It's a hot, erotic kiss. Drunken, sloppy, eager. Her hands are busy, pushing my trunks down, and then she guides my hand to her breast, a warm silken weight that leaves me groaning in delight. Instinct takes over. Need. I'm touching her. She's naked, somehow, and so am I. I'm touching her, making her moan.

But…something is off. I don't know what. I need this. I need more. But I can't shake a vague but potent sense of wrongness. Her mouth, kissing me—her kiss is skilled and eager, even drunk, but it's not…*right*. I don't know. And even though her touching, reaching, stroking, squeezing, caressing hands feel wonderful on my hungry flesh, I just…god, I want this, but it feels…she's not…

Words fail me, even in my own head. I'm too drunk to make sense of what I'm feeling.

"Christian…" Marta murmurs.

Slides against me, rolls so I'm above her, nudged against her entrance. She pulls at me, urging me. I gaze down at her. Blonde hair spilled on the trampoline in a golden spray, wide brown eyes stare back at me, eager, expectant, ready. Her body is toned and lush and soft and lovely. She feels good beneath me. She's ready. She wants this. I want this.

I blink, and for a moment, I see Ava. Short thick black hair always in her eyes. Blueblueblueblue eyes, Ægean blue, stark stunning azure. Svelte, athletic figure. Small, high, firm breasts, dark areolae, prominent nipples. Nipped-in waist, a taut round ass. Strong legs. God, the way Ava wrapped those long legs around me, it drove me wild. She wasn't all that tall, but most of her height was leg. She'd gaze up at me as I moved in her, blue eyes fierce and wild, hips pivoting madly, fingers scratching down my back—I'd have scratch marks for days after sex, and given how frequently we had sex, I always had scratch marks. Her eyes, god her eyes. So blue, so expressive. So much love in those eyes.

I blink again, and it's not Ava, it's Marta. Blonde hair, not black. Brown eyes, not blue. Large, heavy breasts with pale, small areolae and flat nipples, more curve to her waist, to her buttocks. Lying beneath me, heels hooked behind mine, staring up at me in confusion.

"Christian?"

I growl. Roll away. "I can't." I climb to the nearest hull and haul myself up, crawl to the railing and stand up naked and stare down at the sea. We're anchored offshore a ways rather than in a berth at the marina. The waves lap restlessly against the hull, slapping, slapping.

My cock aches.

I feel Marta behind me. "What is the matter, Christian?"

I shake my head. "I can't do it. I'm sorry."

"Why not?"

"I just can't."

"Did I do something wrong?"

I sigh. "No, no. God, no. I mean, I wanted it. I *do* want it." I twist in place, stand facing her. She's still watching me. "But I just can't do that."

"I do not understand."

"I know, and I'm sorry."

"Please, explain."

I clench my teeth; she's naked, and my balls ache, and I still want her, I need release now more than I ever have in my life. My body is at war, with itself, with my mind, with my heart. "I looked down at you just now. I was about to…I was nearly inside you, and I…I looked down at you—" I break off, tear my gaze from hers because it's too hard to say this with her intense brown eyes on mine. "I saw her. I saw Ava. Then it was you again, but…if we did this, Marta…"

She sighs and rolls onto her back and slides down the trampoline, almost out of view. "You would feel guilt. You still love her."

"Yes."

"Damn it." She slaps the trampoline angrily. "Dammit! Why are the men I am attracted to always unable to give to me what I want? You are a good man. A strong one, very handsome, smart, a wonderful sailor. And in love with someone else! Still, even after everything. I do not know all that has happened, but it is much, and very painful."

"Marta, I'm sorry, I—"

"*Non.* It is what I have come to expect." She rolls over again and climbs up the netting to eye me. "I would not wish to cause you guilt, or more emotional pain. I do not want to make this thing worse for you. I thought you wanted this. I was mistaken, and I am sorry."

"I did, I *do*. But…it wouldn't be fair to you."

Her gaze flits down between my legs, where I am still painfully aroused. "I wish I could at least make you feel a little better."

Temptation rifles through me, a strong burn. "Marta, I…" A groan of frustration rippled out of my chest. "No. No. I can't make sense of anything right now, and I'm drunk and confused and I don't want to risk doing anything I'll regret later. I don't want to pull you into my mess."

"I don't mind a mess." Her voice is sultry, suggestive.

I laugh, bitterly. "You're not making this easy for me, Martinique."

"Why should I? I want you. I want this. Very, very much I want this. If you were happily married, or in a relationship which was going well, I would never have gotten on this boat. I am not that woman. You are alone. You are hurting. You are lonely. You are needy. I can help with all of that. I do not ask for commitment. Although, you and I, Christian, we both love the sea. We are content to live out there—" she waves a hand at the sea behind us, "to never have a permanent home except a boat. The sea beneath and the stars above, it's all people like you and me need, Christian. We could be happy together, I think."

Somehow, she's gotten close all over again, and the sound of her voice and the lure of her words is mesmerizing, and then she's touching me again and it's been so long and I am so aroused that it takes but a few moments only before I feel myself nearing release.

But the feel of her hand...it isn't Ava's hand.

I knock her hand away at the last second. "No, Marta. Please, no. Not like this."

She stands up, naked, and walks away. "You are stronger than any man I have ever met, Christian St. Pierre." Then she's gone, and I hear her door close.

"Not strong enough," I say to the lingering scent of her presence, the fading warmth of her touch.

I ache.

God, I ache.

I close my eyes, take myself in my hand. The image that arises in my mind's eyes is Ava.

A memory.

I've just woken up. Dawn breaks golden on the horizon—we've spent the night out on the beach, wrapped up in our favorite fleece blanket. Ava is cradled in my arms, her head on my chest, snoring gently. I just hold her and watch the sun rise. And then, gradually, Ava stirs. Murmurs sleepily under her breath. Nuzzles against my chest. Her eyelids flutter, and those iridescent blue eyes of hers meet mine through a haze of black hair. She smiles up at me. Wiggles, and now she's pressed against me, her warm skin flush against mine, her thigh over mine, her hand on my stomach. The morning air is cool beyond the blanket, but nestled here together underneath the fleece, we're warm. She just smiles happily at me for a moment, breathing and staring, loving me with her gaze.

And then her grin shifts.

Becomes…eager. Predatory.

She takes me in her hand and fondles me to life—which takes barely an instant, the moment of touch igniting a fire in me. I let her touch me, do what she wants, assuming she'll touch me a little and then when I'm ready, climb on top of me and ride me in the dawn's light.

Instead, she keeps touching me.

I'm grinding into her hand, and she's watching me, gauging my reactions, my breathing, my eyes. She knows when I'm close, and she ducks beneath the blanket, and I feel her mouth on me, hot and wet and sliding around me, taking me deep, and I have absolutely no chance of holding out. She doesn't want me to. She brings me to gasping, ragged, bursting release. Swallows, and swallows, and then her hands are on me again, caressing me to shivering shuddering wracking paroxysms.

Ava emerges from beneath the blanket, a smile on her face and come dripping from the corner of her mouth, which she wipes away with a thumb, and then licks the pad of her thumb, her eyes on mine. "Good morning, love," she murmurs to me.

Then, in the memory, she'd then pushed me down under the blanket and I'd made her scream so loud the gulls had cawed in response.

Now, I return to reality only grudgingly and I've made a mess of myself.

I don't even think twice before stumbling naked to the swim platform at the stern of the boat and dive into the sea. I let the waves close over my head and I scrub myself clean in the salt, burst gasping to the surface, and swim away from the boat a ways. Wondering how I'll feel about all this in the morning.

If I'll tell Ava what happened—what almost happened.

I wonder what she would say—what she *will* say.

Because I know I'll tell her…at some point.

I swim until I'm weak, and then I climb back aboard and stumble wet and naked to my room and the shower.

I fall asleep thinking of Ava, and I dream I'm a selkie, and Ava has stolen my sealskin so I'm trapped in a be-tween-land, trapped on an island surrounded by the sea but never able to become my true self. She taunts me, seduces me, teases me, teaches me love, and keeps the sealskin hidden, and when I wake, I miss her more than ever while somehow feeling angry and resentful toward her because of a dream.

Or resentful because of reality.

I don't know.

God, I don't know.

26

EPISTLE #4

(Or is it #3? Does the short story count as an epistle? I'm not sure.)

February 16, 2016

Ava,

It's taken me two days to put these thoughts in order in my own head well enough to be able to even write them down here.

I nearly had sex with Martinique. I was getting drunk alone on V-Day, late. I drank and I lay on the boat thinking of you. Of us. Of all that's gone wrong and how to fix it and just...everything. Missing you. Regretting all the pain and mistakes. Wondering about you. What you're thinking. What you're feeling. If you miss me.

And then suddenly Marta was beside me, not wearing much, as drunk and melancholy as I. It began innocently, discussing why we were both so drunk on Valentine's Day—me, because of you and us, and she because of an asshole ex. And then she was kissing me and I was kissing her back because it's been so damn long since I've had sex, since I've felt the touch of a woman, since I've felt release brought on by something other than my own hand. I said *nearly*, however.

I didn't.

I stopped.

It doesn't make it right that things went as far as they did, because you and I are still married. I don't know what this is, what we are, but I'm still your husband, legally and emotionally. You are still my wife, legally and emotionally. We're in a fucked up place, to be sure, but... damn it, I still love you and I'm not ready to move on and I don't want you to move on. I don't know how to fix us, but I'm not ready for someone new.

I was drunk, and it felt good.

But I stopped because even though it felt good, it didn't feel *right*—both in the sense of morally and ethically, and in the sense of *wrongness,* meaning...god, it's hard to put into words. Like lying in a stranger's bed and trying to sleep, or wearing a shoe on the wrong foot...just wrong. Not correct. Unfamiliar and thus uncomfortable.

She wasn't you.

That's what it came down to. She wasn't you, Ava.

I couldn't keep going, couldn't go through with it because she wasn't you. And you know, for the sake of total honesty...I *wanted* to keep going. I *wanted* to be able to just move on, get over you, get over us. It'd be easier, in so many ways. Trying to fix all that's wrong between us is going to take enormous amounts of work on both our parts. We both have to want it more than anything. It's going to be so hard, Ava. We've both done things, wrong, painful, stupid things. Regretful things. Decisions that will make reconciliation so much harder.

But it's the only real choice for me.

Except...I don't know if it's even possible.

I can't live on land any longer. My life is out here, on the sea. It's where I belong, Ava. I can't just give that up, get over it, or forget it. And I know you won't sail with me. So what's the answer? Maybe there isn't one. I don't know, Ava. Answers are not coming to me.

I just know that I can't move on so easily.

What if you have, though? What if you decided to see someone else? Would you tell me? You promised to tell me.

I made a mistake, a drunken mistake, and in so doing, sort of made a lie of what I told you on the phone, that I wasn't thinking about doing anything with Marta. But the thing is, and the reason I say *sort of*, is that it wasn't a conscious decision, a sober, clear-headed, *I know the consequences and I'm going through with it anyway* decision. I was drunk and she was drunk and it just started happening before I knew what was going on—and yes, I know that's a classic bullshit excuse, one I've never used in my life, but in this case it's just true. I could have stopped it, I think. Gotten up. Recognized the temptation and left the situation. I should have, I know this. I feel guilty, and I hate it. Knowing it will hurt you and make you angry with me when you find out.

I have no intention of keeping secrets.

I'm probably going to go too far with this, but since I'm not sure you'll ever read any of these anyway, I'm going to put it all down.

Marta was beneath me, all but begging me to push inside her. I was about to, I wanted to, it would have been so, so easy. But then…I blinked. And I saw you. It was you beneath me, Ava.

The way I remember you, from so many times I cannot count them all, could not even begin to. We had a lot of favorite positions, didn't we? You enjoyed most having your legs over my shoulders. I hit you inside in just the right way, and you always came within minutes like that. Doggy style. Standing up, you bent forward over the bed. Cowgirl, reverse cowgirl—those were my favorites, you know. You above me, riding me. Taking me deep, taking control, your hips sliding and rocking, your breasts bouncing, your hair wild and in your eyes. My fingers dimpling your hips as I gripped you and pulled you down onto me, harder and harder. But when it came down to it, missionary was what we went to as our default. It just… it was the most intimate. The other positions were erotic and allowed for different angles and different sensations, but for raw romantic love-deepening intimacy, missionary is just the best. It's not boring. It's not routine. It's not vanilla. It's the most meaningful. It puts our bodies together so we are wrapped up in each other, pressed as close as two bodies can be, from toes to hips to chest to lips. You always wrapped your legs around me, hooked your heels behind my back or my thighs and clutched my shoulders, clawed your fingernails down my back. You would kiss my throat as I moved above you. Dig your fingers into my hair. Bite my earlobe. Whisper encouragement in my ear—*yes, yes, yes, yes, Chris, don't stop baby, don't stop, oh god Christian you feel so fucking good.* I wrapped my hand around the back of your neck and kissed your face and your throat and your breasts as I moved, and when the release billowed through me, you always knew. You felt it, in the way I moved, in the way I breathed, in the frantic roughness of my thrusts. I didn't have to say anything, although I often did. You just knew. And you would beg me to keep going, to give it to you, to come so hard. You would touch yourself, then. You would wait until I was close, because you have a hair-trigger orgasm, and when I was close, you would reach between us and I could feel your knuckles against me and your fingers moving on your clit and you would gasp desperately and your hips would flex and slam and your hot wet sheath would tighten around me and you would scream and scream and scream as we came together.

I need that, Ava.

The intimacy, the familiarity of *us*. Of you, beneath me, wrapped around me.

In that moment, in that blink of an eye, I knew. She wasn't you, and that's all it took for it to just feel completely alien and foreign and unfamiliar and wrong, and I couldn't do it. I could never go through with it, not with her, not with anyone. I'll spend my life celibate before I betray us like that again, Ava. It was a betrayal, too. I know this. I hate it. I want to take that moment back, unkiss her, untouch her, eradicate the feeling of her hands on me, erase the memory, erase the reality.

Ava, forgive me.

I may never forgive myself.

If we cannot reconcile, what then? What will I do? I don't know if I'll ever be able to move on from you. I'll always belong to you, Ava. I cannot fathom ever being able to touch a woman without thinking of you. I shudder now, at the hazy drunken memory of what I did. I've washed and washed, but I cannot wash away the guilt or shame.

I was achingly hard, when I stopped things. Marta walked away, and I was painfully hard, and all I could think of was you.

One of the mornings we spent waking up together on the beach. How you touched me, and then instead of climbing onto me, you took me in your mouth and gave me a morning I'll never forget. Cannot, will not. I thought of that morning, and I came all over myself. Alone. The stars were my only witness.

I don't send these letters to you, I print them and I save them, but sometimes I have moments where I forget I haven't sent them and wish for a response from you, and get angry that you haven't, and when I remember that I haven't spoken to you or sent these to you, I wonder if I should.

Perhaps if you read these, you would understand.

But I can't.

I'm not done yet. There's more to say, I feel. What, I don't know.

I love you, and I hate you. I miss you, and I want this to just be over. I have to see you again, but dare not return.

The contradictions are a messy tangled war inside me, and I know not how to mediate the conflict.

Part 3

27

Email from Ava to Christian

April 9, 2016

Chris,

I've sent a package of letters to Port Elizabeth, South Africa, c/o of the postmaster there. They should have arrived a week or two ago, but I knew you wouldn't be there yet, so I'm just now writing to tell you.

I'm still not ready to email, which is why I sent you the letters. Respond in kind, if you're so inclined. Or don't.

A series of letters written on a computer and printed out, from Ava to Christian; undated

Christian,

I'm losing my mind, and I don't know how to stop it. I shouldn't be writing to you, but I am. I'm friendless, loveless, and lifeless. You're out there somewhere, and still you're all I really have. I hate my reliance and dependence on you, emotionally and otherwise, and that reliance is something I'm coming to recognize. Since you've been gone, I've had to learn how to do so many things. You've always taken care of me. It's the little things, honestly. The way you'd always wake up first, make coffee, and bring me a cup in bed before going on a run or heading into your office to write. Now, I have to make my own coffee. Some mornings, I still wake up and expect to smell coffee brewing. Expect to see you with my favorite mug in hand, a smile on your handsome face, set the mug on my bedside table and kiss me stupid.

You left me breathless, most mornings. And then you'd leave, just like that, and I'd be all breathless and turned on and crazy, and you were just oblivious. Did you know that sometimes, if I was horny enough, after you kissed me and left like you always did, I would touch myself? It's a dirty little secret of mine. I'd masturbate thinking of you, usually of the last time we fucked.

Another dirty little secret: I still masturbate and think

of you. I shouldn't, I sometimes think. You're probably fucking that French deckhand, but I'm not ready for a man, yet. I'm still hung up on you. The thought of going to a bar and picking someone up seems...well, for one, like a lot of damn work. Also, just stupid. I mean, I'd have to get all done up, wearing something sexy—and I don't feel sexy—and then I'd have to find a spot and let a guy come chat me up and let him take me back to his place and I'd have to decide whether to go through with it. I most likely wouldn't be able to. I'd freeze up, I'd panic. I'd...dammit, I'd think of you. I'd think of us.

You, above me. My feet on your shoulders, your thick cock driving into me, filling me, making me crazy. I can't come like that, and you know it. I need clit stimulation, but it doesn't take a lot of that to make me come. So you'd fuck me until you were close, and then I'd touch myself and I'd come. I'm a screamer. You said, once, that I sometimes leave your ears ringing, because I'd bite your earlobe and scream into your ear as I came.

Do you remember the time you made me squirt? God, that was so fucking hot. We were both pretty tipsy. We'd been bingeing *The Walking Dead*, and you just looked at me, and that was it. One look was all it took. You set down the popcorn and took my wineglass from me. I know you remember this. I pretended to be more drunk than I was, and acted like I wasn't sure what was going on, what you wanted. Surprised when you ripped off my yoga pants, shocked when you tore my shirt off. I giggled—not faked at all, by the way—when you dragged off my underwear and tugged my tits out of my bra. Too impatient to unclasp it, I guess. You ate me out. Right there on the couch. You were fully clothed, and you just…you fucking devoured me. You used your fingers inside me, scraping and rubbing my G-spot and your tongue circled around my clit wildly. I screamed and screamed and screamed. You made me come four times in a row and wouldn't let up, and I just kept coming like a string of firecrackers, except each one was a stick of dynamite. Your fingers went crazy, and I was clenching like a vise and just coming and screaming, and you didn't stop. And then your mouth got tired, I suppose, so you used your hands, your fingers inside me and the heel of your palm on my clit, and the next orgasm was a little longer in arriving, but when it did, it was a nuclear detonation compared to the dynamite explosions before.

I came, screaming, hoarse, and a stream squirted out of me and splattered your chest. I couldn't help it, couldn't stop it. Everything inside me was squeezing, under insane pressure, so much heat, so much tension ratcheting through me. I broke apart. That's what that felt like. An orgasm so powerful it was painful, a true shattering.

When I could breathe again, when I could move again, I yanked your dick out of your pants and climbed on you and clung to you as I rode you to your own orgasm. There was no finesse, no changing positions or slow rolling or leaning back to ride you so my tits could bounce for you. I clung to you for dear life and fucked your orgasm out of you as hard and fast as I could, so I could feel your cum inside me.

I fucking miss that, Chris. You, inside me.

Your cum dripping out of my pussy, sliding down my thighs as I walk to the bathroom to clean up. Do you think of that? Or have you moved on? Are you filling that French girl's pussy with your cum? Am I just a wayside memory? Something from the past?

Now I'm horny from writing that. I'm going to go masturbate. And yes, Christian, I'm going to think of you. I'm going to picture your cock inside me. I'm going to imagine sucking your dick, and taking your cum on my chest. Tasting you, half-drunk, before fucking you into oblivion.

Oh, the things I'm going to do to you…

In my dreams. In my imagination.

And yes, Christian, I do wish it could be reality.

But then I'd have to face my other emotions toward you, and those are ferociously complex.

Chaotically yours, but still yours (for now…)

Ava

Chris,

I cannot make sense of my hatred for you. It conflicts with my continuing love. Even now as I write, I can feel myself channeling you, writing like you. My sentences sound like yours. I don't like it. The longer we're apart, the more messed up about everything I get.

I really do hate you. HATE. But it's a complicated hatred. It's not a hatred like I'd have for a cheating ex, or one of those nasty, vicious, gossiping popular girls I went to high school with, or someone who abuses children or animals. It's not like that. It's…god, I don't know. I'm trying to figure it out. That's what this letter is going to be. It may be a rambling mess, but it's all I know how to do to make sense of this.

YOU FUCKING LEFT ME. That's an enormous part of it. You sold off property, arranged for bills to be auto-paid, bought a sailboat, and left me. Yes, I get it. You were dying. You were contemplating suicide. I was all but catatonic and then unresponsive to you and then just downright cold. OUR SON DIED. How was I supposed to deal? Couldn't you have just gotten a condo on the other side of town? Or gotten a houseboat? Or a sailboat, but stayed, like, within 3 miles of me? I needed you. I know, I know, I fucking know—my actions demonstrated the opposite, but I was crumbling. Shattered. Dead inside. My son—*our* son—had died. I held him in my arms as he died, Chris. He was just a baby. His death ruined me. I didn't know how to continue. How to keep living. I wanted to die. That's why I stopped eating, you know—hoping I'd die. Instead, I slimmed down to a weight I haven't been since high school. But I didn't die. I never thought about suicide in the sense of shooting myself or cutting my wrists or something. It just never even entered my head—I just…I wanted to not be alive anymore, without having to kill myself. I don't know how else to put it. Life without Henry was—and is—utterly barren. I still some days wish I could just not wake up. Keeping sleeping. Join Henry in the darkness of never.

You'll love that turn of phrase.

I hate you for leaving.

I hate you for being able to leave in the first place. It's a separate thing. It's…you being able to sail away from me at all. I know I pushed you away, blamed you for things that weren't your fault, acted like I hated you, because I did. I needed someone to blame, and you were it. But I thought…FUCK, I thought you could take it. That you'd forgive me and we would find a way to heal together, Chris. I needed time. I needed you to keep loving me. To keep supporting me. I needed you. I just needed you. I needed you to know that I still loved you, still needed you, still craved your presence, even when I acted as if the opposite was true.

It's not fair. I know that. It's not fair of me to have expected that of you, to expect you to understand all that without even a single hint of any of it. I KNOW, okay? I do. But it's still my truth. I needed you.

And you sailed away from me.

You planned it all out. It wasn't a spur of the moment thing. You went through a lot of preparation to do it right. To take care of me even as you left me. How could you do that? I just don't get it.

I hate you for calling me on Christmas, because it was exactly what I wanted, what I needed, and nowhere near enough. I need to scream in your face and slap you and rage and rage and rage. I need to anger-fuck you. I need to shove you down on the floor and claw you bloody and ride you until neither of us can move or breathe, and then I need to slap you and curse you and be angry some more. And then I need you to kiss me and hold me and comfort me and tell me—

Tell me—

Tell me I'm not alone anymore, Chris.

TELL ME I'M NOT ALONE ANYMORE.

I'm alone.

I don't want to be alone.

I hate you because I'm alone. I'm so goddamn lonely, and it's your fault.

I know it's mine too. But I hate you for it.

I hate you calling me on Christmas, because for a moment, I heard your voice and it was all okay. I heard your voice, and I was home. You were calling me from the store, to ask me which kind of spaghetti sauce you should get. Which wine to get. How many packages of ground beef we need. If I wanted you to get rocky road ice cream, chocolate peanut butter, or both. But instead, you were calling from some isolated godforsaken island in the middle of nowhere, with no intent of ever returning, and you were wishing me a merry fucking Christmas.

Related: I hate that I still love and find comfort in the sound of your voice. When you called, when I first said hello, and you said hello back…that moment of forgetting before reality set in, the sound of your voice was all I needed to be okay. I hate that the sound of your voice can turn me on, can comfort me, can bring me back in time, can soothe me and wash over me like waves of sonic love.

I hate you for that too.

I hate you for taking that French girl on the boat with you. I have this feeling something happened with her. I can only guess, but that guess is a knife in my gut. I know I shouldn't let emotions fly over a conjecture, or a feeling in my stomach, but there's no one to talk me out of it.

Most of all, I hate that I can't hate you as much as I want to. I hate that I still fucking love you so much.

I hate that there's no clear solution to our conundrum. Even if we could forgive each other, what then?

I hate you, Christian. I really do.

But most of all, I don't.

It's complicated.

Complicatedly (still) yours,

Ava

I went on a date—I went on several dates.

With my therapist. Who is now no longer my therapist—he referred me to a colleague, a female. A better choice for me, overall. She's a divorcee, a survivor of sexual abuse, a marathon runner, and a crossfit athlete, as well a licensed physiologist and therapist. I admire her, and I respect her. She listens, and she forces me to confront my bullshit head-on.

My former therapist, Craig, he's good-looking. Funny. Quiet and reserved, but when he finally loosens up a bit, he's a lot of fun. We went for Italian and then drinks afterward, and I had a lot of fun. More fun than I ever thought I'd be able to have.

I lied to Craig, though. I told him you and I had gotten a divorce, because I knew he wouldn't go out with me otherwise.

He didn't kiss me, or try to.

Truth? If he'd have kissed me, I'd have let him. I'd have kissed him back. I'm desperate for physical attention, affection, for touch. He was a gentleman, though.

And then we went out again, and he still didn't try to kiss me.

A third time, no kiss.

And then, on the fourth date, he kissed me. It went from zero to sixty instantly, from a hesitant first kiss to clothes coming off in my foyer. I told you I'd tell you if anything happened, so that's what this is: Something happened, Christian.

He kissed me, and I enjoyed the hell out of it. He touched me. Groped my boobs and my ass, got my shirt and skirt off, had my bra off, and his hands were warm and strong and his kisses were eager.

I touched him, Christian.

I had his cock in my hand, and I was stroking him. Kissing his mouth, and enjoying his touch, and thinking *yeah, I can do this.*

And then…it all went wrong.

Nothing he did, though. It was all me. I was touching him, stroking him, and his cock just…didn't feel right. Didn't fit in my hand the way yours does. He didn't move the way you move. Didn't groan the way you groan. He didn't touch me the way you touch me. My skin didn't light on fire the way it does when you touch me. My heart didn't palpitate. My brain didn't short out. I couldn't lose myself in it the way I lose myself in our touch. I couldn't do it.

I told him to stop, and he did.

I told him I was sorry, that it wasn't going to work, that I wasn't ready; he said he totally understood, no big deal.

It was a big deal though.

I told him I'd lied, that you and I hadn't divorced, and that we hadn't even discussed it or anything. He said he knew, or rather, that he strongly suspected.

I told him I didn't think I could go out with him again, because I just…I'm not ready.

And once again, he was understanding. Polite. Sweet.

Once upon a time, you would have fought for me.

If you wanted me and I was dating someone else or separated from someone, you wouldn't have stopped until you'd gotten me to leave them for you.

Now, you're just gone.

Damn you.

And fuck you.

You possess me, Christian. You possess me in the sense that you own me, you have me, in that I am yours; you also possess me in the sense that you are like a fuck-ing poltergeist inside me. I cannot exorcise you from within me. I'm trying, goddammit, but I can't.

I hate you for this as well.

Damn you,

Ava

Chris

I nearly called you just now. It's 4am and I'm ham-mmered. Drunk too much wine. Malbec. You're favorite wine. I want to talk to you. Your stupid voice makes me feel all bettre. I'm so drunk damm it. Typing is hard the letters on the keyboard keep swimming. Just keep swim-ming, just keep swimming, what do we do we swim swim swim. That's all I'm doing is swimming. Just keep swimming, just like Dory. I'm not strong enough, Chris.

I had your number dialed, all 134094h9948uu4 dig-its of it. It took like five minutes just to dial that stupid phone number. I had my thumb on the little green phone symbol and then I didn't push it. I refuse to drunk dial you. I'd break down. I'd ask you to come home. I'd tell you how fukcing much I fukcing love you. I'd cry. I'd tell you how bad I need your dick. It's like drug withdrawal, only for your penis. That's a metaphor. I don't mean just your penis. I mean all of you. You fucking me. That's the thing I'm in withdrawal from. Just you. Stupid, amazing, beautiful, talented, kind, loving, thoughtful, big dick and talented tongue and incredible hands—YOU.

YOU>

Instead of calling you I opened my laptop and I'm writing this. I'm going to hate reading it in the morning, or whenever I figure out how to get out of bed and op-erate my body again. I drunk three bottles of wine. All by muself. Thinking about stupid you, stupid Christina.

Have I told you lately that I hate you? Because I hate you.

I'm so goddammed lonely.

AVA. This is to you, Ava. When you read this, do what you're telling yourself to do. SEND THIS LETTER TO CHRIS. He needs to read it. For because of reasons. I can't make anysense any no more. Words ar4e hard.. But it's important. Chris has to read this.

So he knows what he's doing to m.e

I'm not strong enoug.gh

Good night nobody.

Christian,

I'm including that drunk letter. I was right: you do need to read it. You need to read all of these. I wonder if you'll write back. If you're writing to me.

Knowing you, you're probably doing something melodramatic and stupid and romantic, like writing journal entries but calling them letters to me you'll never send. You probably have a fancy name for them too. What's that bible term for letters? Epistles. I would bet all the bottles of wine in the rack—23 bottles: 10 cab sav, 6 malbec, 6 pinot noir, and 1 merlot—that you're writing a bunch of "epistles" to me, but not really to me. You'll vent your bullshit into those letters and never send them. And then, in a fit of rash impulse, you will. And you'll regret it, because you're violently private about your journals. If you've written it for a novel, you'll let others read it, but a journal entry? You'd die first.

I'm doing the same thing, writing down my most tumultuous, complicated, messy, emotional private inner thoughts and addressing them to you. The difference is, I'm sending them to you. I have the manila envelope addressed already, to the postmaster in Port Elizabeth where you said you'd be. When I decide I've got enough letters to send, I'm folding them like real letters, and stuffing them into the envelope, and I'm taking the package to the post office and stamping it and sending it.

I can't take much more of this, Christian. I'm in hell. Life is hell. Living is pain. Loneliness is agony. I don't know what to do. I don't know much longer I can take things as they are. No, suicide will never be an option for me. What will I do? Shave my head, get a bunch of tattoos, and join a band? I've thought about that. I love singing. I could do it. Sell everything and take the cash and drive away? Where would I go? Vegas? LA? New York? Probably Boulder, Colorado or Portland, Oregon, where pot is legal. I think I might try pot again. It went badly for me the last time I tried it, but becoming a stoner sounds like fun. A nice escape. Something to drown myself in. Become a shut-in stoner. Watch daytime TV all day—which I already do—eat shitty food—which I don't do, yet, I'm still too health conscious for that—and smoke marijuana all damn day. Write rambling and elaborate blog posts and maybe another novel. My prose would probably be improved.

In all likelihood, I'll probably just sell everything and start over somewhere. I'd pick a small town, somewhere obscure. Sedgwick, Maine; Port Arthur, Texas; Eureka, California.

All of those are by the sea. I never even Google Earth-ed anywhere not on the ocean.

That's your fault, too, probably.

I spend a lot of time on the beach, staring out at the sea, like an old sea-wife, hoping for a glimpse of your ship returning home.

God, I'm losing it. I'm losing it.

Desperation is a discordant song within me: the warm-up of a symphony.

I am undone.

Wilderness is my soul.

Flight, feral and of muted voice.

Let me off this mad calliope,

give me stable breath and solid world and brazen un-varnished truth.

Laughter.

Hot wild mad sex in the deeps of endless night.

Screams in the dark, heat in my belly spearing through my veins and boiling effervescent into my skin and muscles and

building like a tsunami approaching shore, becoming a violent release.

This

Give me this.

I need it.

You do not. Cannot. You are not here to give me this. You are nowhere and thus I am nowhere

Thus I am nothing

Thus I may only perish, one day at a time

Reality is a shitstained shadow I cannot evade.

Hatred is exhausting.

You

You

You you

You you you

FUCK YOU

I LOVE YOU

I FUCKING LOVE YOU

But god I hate you

God, I hate you

This is as close to breathing as I can get:

gasps in the dark,

waking in the moonless starless silent succumbing drowning depths of an endless night from which I cannot wake,

from which there is no escape—i sigh, and I gasp, and I die, and I wake still alive, hating it every single moment of life because life is pain and life is loneliness and love is a sham and a lie and

These words pour out, a waterfall, a deluge, a soul-scouring acid-bath.

It is four in the morning and I cannot sleep, as I have not slept since—

Since

Him—

Since the harsh knifing scything flatline beep in the tear-humid

purgatory

of the

Pediatric Oncology Ward

Where I died

Where you died

Where we died

Where the once vibrant dancing brilliant hopeful animated being that was US

Died

Everything died that day

And then I died again when you stepped from the sundrenched dock wood onto the fleeing deck of your escape

I am a wraith.

I am a shadow lost amid a wilderness of ghosts.

Mothwings beat in the silvergraced gleam of the gloaming;

THEY are alive.

A frog belches throaty somewhere under my bedroom window,

 calling for his mate;

 She intones her reply in a hopeful chirrup;

 THEY are alive.

A bat flits silently, tipping and tumbling and devouring and agile;

 Something enormous and dark breasts the waves,

 far out, spraying plume skyward;

 The shadows, the stars, the moon, insects in the grass,

 people sleeping next door

 and across the street

 and around the city;

 THEY are alive.

I am a lichyard creature

 shuffling and dragging myself between mossy headstones,

 suffering a pretense of half-life.

 I wish, I wish, I wish, Christian,

 I wish it was harder to blame you.

 I wish it was easier to forgive you.

 I wish it was easier to forgive myself,

 The universe,

 God,

 Fate,

 Life.

 There is no forgiveness.

Only suffering:

my capacity for suffering is maxed out,

the architecture of my soul is nothing but a pile of rubble and ruin.

I have nothing left, Christian.

nothing

left

Email from Christian to Ava

April 11, 2016

Ava,

Your last letter in that packet has me worried. I know you didn't want me to email back, but I had to, after reading those letters. I miss you. I'm in Port Elizabeth and everything is a mess. The weather is not cooperating and Jonny is AWOL, and Marta and I, well...you'll understand when you read the letters I've written you. But now, after that poem you wrote, or proem, or whatever you want to call it...I hate this.

 I really hate this.

Please email back.

Always yours, even now,

Chris.

Email in Christian's inbox

April 11, 2016

Delivery to the following recipient failed permanently:

Amstpierre@hmail.com

Technical details of permanent failure:
The server tried to deliver your message, but it was rejected by the server for the recipient domain. The error that the other server returned was: 550 550-5.1.1 The email account that you tried to reach does not exist.

"The phone number you are trying to reach is no longer in service. Please try your call again later."

Port Elizabeth, South Africa

April 14, 2016

It's four in the morning, and I'm unable to sleep. She's deleted her email address. Shut down her cell phone. I'm not sure what to do. I'm horribly worried for her. She's never had the best relationship with her parents and rarely sees them even though they only live a few hours away in St. Pete. She has an older sister whom she was close to growing up and still corresponds with her regularly, but Delta lives in Chicago and is a single mom, so it's unlikely she'd be able to visit Ava in Ft. Lauderdale.

If anyone could be there for Ava, though, it'd be Delta.

I call Delta, but she doesn't answer. I leave a voicemail, but I expect nothing back from her; I've never been Delta's favorite person, for reasons I've never totally understood.

I'm terrified for Ava. The poem, I mean…damn. That was intense. She used to write poetry a lot back in the day, but not as much as of late.

What do I do? Ava has always been unpredictable…at least, she used to be. Now I'm not sure I know who she is anymore. The Ava I knew loved to eat, and always took her nutrition pretty seriously. Not eating at all? That's not like her. But then, neither was getting day drunk, but that became a constant reality.

Henry's death shattered us both. Altered us totally. I'm not the same man I was. I haven't reverted to the person I was before Ava and success found me, but neither am I the man I was before Henry's illness and death.

What do I do? What do I do? Abandon the journey and return? Find Ava and fix things, if they can be fixed?

I hear noise, footsteps, muttering in Spanish. I'm in the saloon, sipping tea when he stumbles in. His shirt is ripped, his eye is turning black and blue, his lip is split, and his knuckles are a mess, and he's three sheets to the wind.

"The hell happened to you, Jonny?"

"Bar brawl, *amigo*. You should see those *pendejos*, though. Thought they could take Jonny Núñez. No *gringo pendejos* can take me. Not even four of 'em."

"You all right?"

"I'm good, man. I'm good." He grabs a pair of beers from the fridge, twists the caps off, and hands me one. "What you doin' up at four in the morning?"

"Can't sleep."

"Well, no shit. You're awake, therefore you can't sleep. Why, though?"

"Ava. She closed out her cell account and deleted her email address. Even her blog is down. Just a pinned post saying she was taking an indefinite leave of absence for personal reasons. Sent me a bunch of letters all together. Lots of intense stuff."

"So you're worried about her?"

I nod. "Yeah."

"So?"

I frown at him. "What do you mean, so?"

"So what's the problem? You love her, you're worried about her, you go back. Jump on a flight back to the States and check on her. I can watch the *Hemingway* for a few days."

"If I go to her, I'm not sure I'd be coming back, Jonny."

He rests his elbows on his knees and hangs his head, nodding. "Ah. I see." He glances at me. "Do what you gotta do, man. I'll be all right no matter what."

"Will you, though? I feel like I'm a bad friend. Seems like you got shit going on of your own, but I've been too occupied with my drama to ask you about it."

Jonny waves a hand dismissively. "Nah. I get like this every once in a while. Got no home, no family, no roots. I live my life on the sea, always have and always will. But sometimes I just get…homesick for a home I won't ever have. Not a big deal. Get drunk, fight some bitches, fuck some bitches, and get back out to my one true love: *el mar…el mar hermoso.*"

I have the fireproof, waterproof safety box full of my letters to Ava. "You're gonna call me crazy, but…will you make me a promise?"

He eyes me silently for a moment. "Anything it's within my power to do, it's yours, *mi hermano.*"

I hand him the box. "If anything happens, give these

to Ava."

"Chris, *amigo*—what do you think is gonna happen?"

"You know what the sea is like even more than I do, Jonny."

Jonny hangs his head again, nodding sloppily. "*Sí*, this is true. She is a capricious mistress, as they say." He takes the box from me, and the key that opens it. "What's it, then?"

"Letters." He glances quizzically at me, and I tap a thick envelope on the table near my hand. "Those are the originals. I've got backups with me. I'm planning to bring them to her myself. I know I've got to go back, but I'm just...part of me doesn't want to. I just got back out here, and I'm worried if I go back to Ava, I'll never get back out onto the sea again. But..." I sigh. "I know I have to go see her. I have to try to fix things. I can't just run away from it all. I needed time to heal, and I think I'm as healed as I'm ever going to get. At least...until I've either repaired my marriage with Ava or gotten closure from it."

"So we sail back to Florida."

I nod. "Yeah, sorry."

Jonny waves me off again. "Eh, no sorry needed. I've been east before, nothing out there I haven't seen. I'm with you to the end, Chris, no matter what. You know that."

I drain my beer, reach out a hand, and he claps palms with me, which turns into a standing hug. "I don't know what I'd do without you, Jonny."

"Get lost and be lonely."

I laugh, slapping him on the back. "There might be some truth to that."

He guffaws, pulling out three more beers. "Where's Marta? Get her ass up, we need to do a toast to rounding the Horn twice in a month."

I let out a breath. "Um, Marta's gone, actually."

"Gone? Gone where?" he asks, popping open two of them.

I shrug. "Not sure. Another berth."

"Wait, like off the ship and *gone*, gone?"

I nod. "Yeah."

"What happened?" He eyes me, putting away the third bottle. "You didn't. Tell me you didn't."

"I didn't."

He wipes his brow with a dramatic flair. "Whew. Thank god. I was gonna have to kick your ass."

"I almost did, though."

"Fuck, *amigo*. You told me that wasn't a problem."

"It wasn't. Until it was. Valentine's Day, I was drunk and lonely and melancholy, and so was she, and then she kissed me and things got out of hand. I couldn't go through with it, though. I was sober enough to know what I was doing, drunk enough to not care in the moment. Figured things were over with Ava, might as well feel good for a minute, right? Wrong. I was *this* close to having sex with her, and I realized I just...*couldn't.*"

"Why not?"

"She wasn't Ava." I shrug.

Jonny just eyes me. "She wasn't Ava? That's it? I don't get that, man."

"She didn't...feel the same. Didn't kiss the same, didn't touch me the same, didn't...she wasn't Ava. I *wanted* to be able to have sex with her, because it'd have made it easier to stay out here. I think I knew even then, deep down, that I was going to end up going back, and I didn't want to. I really don't. It's going to be hard. It's going to suck. I'm going to have to face myself, and my emotions, and hers, and everything. Going back means giving up sailing, for the most part, unless she's changed enough to want to try again, which I doubt. But Marta, man. She was gorgeous, and cool, and a great sailor. We could have been good together. But I couldn't go through with it."

"So she left?"

"It was...I think it was necessary. For both of us." I shrug yet again. "I think she had feelings for me, and that would've made things impossible. Things were getting awkward and difficult between us, and I also think she realized I was going to go back to Florida and Ava, and she wanted to go her own way, in that case."

"Glad you controlled your dick, even if it was at the last second."

"I think it was more a case of my dick controlling me, but in a good way for once."

Jonny laughs. "I think that may be the first time in history a man's dick has led him *out* of trouble 'steada into it."

"Truth, brother, truth."

"So." Jonny holds his bottle up toward me and I clink mine against his. "To rounding the horn twice in a month."

"We're crazy, you know that, right?" I ask, laughing.

"Always have been, always will be." A pause. "When we leave?"

I shrug. "Day after tomorrow, today, whatever you want to call it. Get some sleep, check things over, and leave next dawn."

"Sounds good. I'm crashin', then."

"I'm gonna try to do that myself, again."

It takes a long time for me to finally fall asleep. Well past dawn. And when I do, I dream of Ava.

Except, in this dream, she's on the shore, reaching for me. Pleading. I can't hear her, though. All I hear in the dream is a roaring, rushing wind, and snatches of her voice. In the way of dreams, I'm seeing her clearly, up close and in perfect detail, but she's somehow far away. As if I'm seeing her through an impossibly powerful telescoping lens. She reaches out, pleading with me. Weeping, begging. But I can't make out her words. She's so thin she looks sick, frail. Her black hair is whipped by the wind into her eyes, and sticks to the tears running down her face. She falls to her knees in the sand,

and a storm surges around her, hurling sand in stinging curtains, flattening dune grasses, pressing her clothes against her nearly skeletal frame.

Please, Chris, please. Please. Please. Please.

Please what, Ava? What?

I'm coming. Wait for me. I'm coming.

She shakes her head, reaches out across the ocean. I could grasp her hands, but I'm incorporeal, without a body, only a soul in the wind. Her agony, her terror is palpable. She's desperately trying to tell me something, but I don't know what.

29

From Christian's journal

April 18, 2016

> I see you
> From across the horizon
> From a thousand thousand thousand miles away
> From half a league away
> From countless leagues away
> I see you
> I feel you, too
> Your soul throbs like a drum and I feel it pulsing
> Crashing behind your breasts
> Aching as I ache
> The sea is my home

But you are my soul
This ship is my place in the world
But you are my breath
And I have not filled my lungs since…
Since our world was shrouded in darkness
Since I tossed a handful of soil onto a too-small coffin
I cannot breathe
Because you are my breath
And you are nowhere
You are nothing
You are no one
I know this, love
Because I too am
Nowhere
Nothing
No one
I fly to you, love
But the sea is wide
And the winds cannot carry me fast enough back to your arms
But with each league crossed I ask a tumbling million questions
Do you love me still?
Will your arms curl around me as they used to,
With soft warm strong gentle ceaseless affection?
Will your words wound me or warm me?
Can the shattered mirror of our love be pieced back together?

Slivers are missing

Shards have scattered across the floor

Glass dust drifts in piles across the marble

And even with all the pieces, all the slivers, all the shards,

I fear the whole, once repaired, will not show a true reflection

Or perhaps, more fearfully, it will show a more than true image

Of me

Of us

Of you

As we are now,

Postmortem

Undead

Lichyard creatures shuffling and dragging ourselves between mossy headstones, suffering a pretense of half-life

As you so accurately put it

You used those words for yourself

But in so doing described me, descried the truth of me

From 2600 leagues away, you see the shape of me

The truth of me

12,500 kilometers

8000 miles

The distance between you and me

It feels too massive a distance

And at once not enough
So many questions
with only the cry of gulls for answer

30

Somewhere in the Atlantic Ocean

May 15, 2016

It's been smooth sailing, up until today. We rounded the Horn without any issue whatsoever, and we're making incredible time back across the Atlantic. Favorable winds, no trouble. Jonny and I sail in perfect synch, needing very little by way of communication.

Until today. We're nearly back to Florida when things go sideways on us.

It started out innocently enough. A stiffer wind than usual, the kind of wind that has something cold in it, something sharp. A wind that just...smells of trouble. I know we both noticed it, but neither of us wanted to say anything. He caught my eye, and I sniffed the wind, and he furrowed his brow. He pulled the sheet a little tighter, and we tipped a little as our speed picked up.

Just a wind.

But then, after a few hours, the stiffer-than-usual wind picked up even more, and Jonny had to let the sheet out again or risk tilting too much. With only two of us and little enough ballast, it's game over if we tip. So we let out the sheet and it snaps and bellies taut, bulging pregnant. Even with the sheet let out, we're fairly flying across the waves, which are growing larger with every passing moment. A bit of a lift and smack at first, that's all, white spray crushed skyward by the hulls. And then the lift is accompanied by a momentary pause as we drift over the crest, and then we're rocketing down the side of the wave like the first drop on a rollercoaster. Then the lift is preceded by an upward coursing, and the wave crest curls and we're thrown downward once more. The sky, once blue and clear, is now obscured by a seething mass of scudding thunderheads. Flashes of lightning crackle and spear and lance and dance all around, and the waves grow larger and the winds blow harder.

"This is no good, *hermano*." Jonny says.

I study the wall of clouds approaching us from every direction. "Yeah, no shit."

We exchange long glances, and then Jonny eyes the storm. "You got a storm sail, yeah?"

I nod. "Of course."

"Think we may need it."

"I've never used one," I point out.

Jonny just laughs. "Me neither." He gestures at the thunderheads, low and dark and laced with lightning. "But with the speed she's blowing up, I think this may be the time to try it out."

"Fine by me. I'll follow your lead on this."

I haul out the storm sail, silently thanking all the sailing forums I read which advised that, if I did pack a storm sail, to resist the temptation to stow it somewhere out of the way, on the logic that if you *do* end up needing it, you'll likely need it in a hurry. Jonny and I have the fluorescent orange sheet raised in minutes, and the mainsail reefed. By this time, though, the storm is in full rage. Rain pelts sideways, blowing cold and hard, like needles of ice. Wind howls, and the waves rise ever higher, curling crests swelling to breathtaking heights.

Jonny and I have sailed through any number of storms, including a typhoon off the coast of Okinawa. Of course, that was a much larger ship with a full crew and a captain with thirty-six years of open ocean experience. This is just Jonny and me and *The Hemingway*, and what is shaping up to be one hell of a preseason hurricane.

Jonny opens a storage compartment and comes up with two life vests, hands me one and dons the other himself. I take it from him, fasten it on. In all the years I've been sailing, that typhoon is the only time I've put on a vest, and the fact that Jonny thinks they're necessary now scares me.

I can read a storm almost as well as he can, and I know he's not overreacting. Especially not when a monster wave roars toward us, lifting our bow to the angry sky until we're nearly vertical. It crests and we abruptly tip over the wave crest as if it were a fulcrum, and our tack down the back of the wave into the valley is so fast we begin to heel. Our starboard hull lifts completely clear of the water, and then we're smashing into the bottom of the trough between waves, halting our momentum momentarily, and the hull smacks down hard enough to jolt us both.

And then we're slicing up the front of another wave, higher than the last, its peak towering twenty feet high easily, and this time, the downward rush is even faster and we heel even harder despite the tightly reefed mainsail. I'm holding on as hard as I can to the wheel, braced, ready for the smash at the bottom.

Lightning sears across the sky, a deafening roar of thunder blasting so loud my ears ring. Wind and rain are one, a single violent entity, turning all the world into a single wet wall of stinging, blinding, crushing ferocity.

The crash at the bottom never comes.

The next wave is so hard on the heels of the previous, it lifts up beneath us and tosses us like a piece of driftwood, sending us spinning, airborne, and then the crash comes.

I'm ready for it. Braced. Clinging to the wheel for dear life, desperately trying to keep us under some kind of control, even as the wind tries to blow us over and the waves crash and sling and roar and the currents rip at the rudder. I'm ready for the crash, when it comes.

But sometimes, the crash is so violent there is no readiness.

I hear the crunch of the hulls hitting water, and the jolt is an earthquake tremor felt at the fault line, the hand of a mighty god shaking the world like a snow globe. Or, just shaking me.

Throwing me.

I'm airborne, spinning, tumbling, pinwheeling in the wild rain-soaked sky, seeing lightning beneath me and waves above me and then thunderheads to my left and waves to my right, and then a flash of orange storm sail in front of me and then the crest of a fifty-foot wave obscures *The Hemingway* and a peal of thunder drowns out my scream, drowns out Jonny's shout. I hit the water hard enough to knock the breath from me, and then a wave slams down over me, burying me under a mountain of briny lightning-lit jade. My lungs scream but I dare not allow myself to breathe. I haul at the water with shaking arms, kick with trembling feet. Swim toward the lightning—the only hint of up I can see. Another flash, and another, and I'm swimming in place as the waves toss and churn, and then I'm spat out, arms flailing as I breach out the side of the wave, gasping, sputtering, hacking, sucking in a breath as hard and fast as I can and clamping down on it before I'm plunged into the water again.

I roll with the churn, and I pray to deities I'm not sure I believe in. Thrown skyward, fight to breathe, plunge under again. Stop trying to swim, conserve energy. Focus on not aspirating seawater. The churn claims me again, and again, and again.

I know the odds.

Lotteries are won more frequently than sailors survive being thrown overboard during a storm at sea.

Hypothermia.

Exhaustion.

Thirst.

Those will all kill me, assuming I don't just drown in the sky-spearing waves.

I fight.

Ava.

Ava.

Ava.

I see her face, almost as if her features are carved into the wall of the waves, or painted on the boiling black sky. She was warning me, in that dream. Pleading with me to put off the trip, to wait, to stay, to fly home, pleading with me. But it was a dream, and I couldn't hear her, couldn't make out her words.

Another moment of free-fall, breathing salt spray and rainwater and blessed oxygen, coughing and gasping and splashing down and feeling the lifejacket pull me up so I can gasp another breath and then a wave smashes me under and I spin and tumble in the churn like a leaf caught in whitewater rapids.

How long has it been? Five minutes? An hour? I can't tell, there is no way to mark the passage of time when existence is nothing but fighting for the surface and sucking at the air and rolling with the churn and gasping as rain batters me and lightning sizzles and strikes and thunder pounds and waves rage.

Already I'm exhausted. I cling to awareness by a thread, knowing if I give in to exhaustion, if I succumb to weakness, I will die. I'll drown in the waves and breathe the sea spray and if I'm ever found, I'll be a waterlogged corpse washing ashore somewhere in Africa.

Or, knowing the caprice of my mistress the sea, Brazil.

No.

Not like this.

I have things to say to you, Ava.

I'm not ready to bathe in darkness, just yet. I fight, and I fight, and I fight.

The storm rages on, endlessly. Day, night, which is it? Have I spent hours tossed by the wind and waves, or minutes? I'm dizzy and thirsty, surrounded by water and yet parched. Still storm-thrown. Abused by the waves, assaulted by battering walls of rain and slicing skeins of wind. Thrown and buried, churned and spat free.

Gasping, sputtering, praying.

Not to God, or the gods,

But to Ava.

It's a simple prayer.

Just her name, whispered in the clanging, dizzy, aching confines of my skull, over and over and over again.

Ava,

Ava,

Ava,

Ava,

31

Ft. Lauderdale, FL

May 16, 2016

"Authorities are saying that this is in fact a tropical cyclone, despite the fact that hurricane season doesn't officially begin until June first. According to the NOAA, this is one of the worst storms on record, and it's still picking up steam as it heads our way. Already, this extremely rare preseason storm, officially named Hurricane Dorothy, has claimed several lives, and as it closes in on Florida authorities are saying to prepare for the worst." The weather anchor, a trim, neat man in his late forties, works up a grim expression. *"Folks, it's time to batten down the hatches. With more information on how to be safe during a hurricane, here's Melanie—"*

I shut off the TV, toss the remote aside. Try not to think about Christian, but fail. Is he out there, in that? Or is he safe in the Indian Ocean, making his way toward Indonesia? I wish, just for a moment, that I hadn't been so rash, that I hadn't shut off all my communications. But I had to. I had to. I couldn't breathe. I couldn't function. The thought of seeing him, hearing his voice, reading his words, it sent me into a downward spiral, and the only way out was to cut myself out his life completely. Don't let him contact me. I sent him my goodbye. He abandoned me and didn't look back, and now I have to start over.

I listed the condo.

I bought a prepaid cell phone and called my sister, Delta, and asked if I could come visit her for a while.

I haven't seen Delta since Henry's funeral. She took two days off, all she could afford, and by that time I was already drowning in my grief, too lost in my sorrow to even see her, much less interact.

We used to be close. We've exchanged emails on a weekly basis for years, and would talk on the phone a few times a month. But I never made the time to go see her, and she couldn't come to me because she's a single mom trying to support her five-year-old son on her own. Now I need her, and I regret not making time for her.

She told me she only had a couch to offer, but it was mine if I wanted it.

I have a suitcase packed. Snacks in the car, bills paid,

mail held.

But, this morning, as I'm about to leave for Chicago, I turned on the news while I ate breakfast, and learned of the hurricane heading this way, which started far out in the Atlantic, and a heavy feeling hit my gut.

A feeling of fear, of foreboding. Dark, heavy as a ball of lead, thick, acidic. Burning.

I remember the dream I had a month ago, of Christian. He was in the cockpit of his boat, feet kicked up, a hand on the wheel. Sails bellied full of wind, the sun setting golden-red in front of him. But he didn't see the monster. It was right behind him, trailing behind his boat, ink-black cloud-claws traipsing and slithering across the surface of the sea, reaching for his boat. A lightning-sharp talon went tap-tap-tapping on the stern, but Christian didn't see it. Didn't hear it. Didn't turn around to glance behind him. The monster was a thing of storm clouds and lightning, towering a thousand feet in the air, eyes flashing evil, mouth a gaping black maw with gnashing teeth like scything waves a hundred feet high. It followed just behind Christian, prowling, stalking, hunting. And he didn't see it.

I cried out, begging him to look behind. *Watch for the storm, Christian.*

Then I woke up, and dismissed it as a stupid dream.

And now, Hurricane Dorothy is raging her way across the Atlantic.

There's no reason to worry, I tell myself. He's safe.

He's not out there. He already crossed the Atlantic, already rounded the Horn. He's not out there; he's not in this.

I don't even try to tell myself not to worry about him, that I shouldn't care. I do.

I have my prepaid cell, and the minutes card. For emergencies. I have his sat phone number written down on a slip of paper, which is on the island counter in front of me.

I can't help myself. I have to know he's okay.

It takes several minutes to enter all the correct numbers, but eventually the line rings.

And rings.

And rings.

And rings.

No voicemail, just an end to the ringing, an abrupt silence.

With the hurricane on the way, I should leave now. Stick to the original plan. Get away from this condo, from the memories. From myself. Spend some time with my sister and nephew.

But I can't.

The feeling of foreboding overwhelms me. Takes me over. Settles inside me, sinks in claws like roots.

My cell vibrates in my hand, and I answer it without looking at the number. "Hello? Christian?"

"Um, hi, Ava. It's actually Delta."

"Shit." I breathe out a sigh of worry. "Sorry, Delta.

I'm just trying to get hold of Chris, and he's not answering. I thought you were him."

"Sorry to disappoint, sis."

I try to laugh it off. "No, not at all."

"Hope you don't mind me saying so, but you sound… off."

"I'm just worried, is all."

There's a silence. "I know things have been rough for you since…"

"You can say it, Delta: since Henry died."

"Right. I want to help any way I can. I mean, obviously, you've been struggling. I haven't wanted to bug you about things, and I figured you'd reach out when you needed me."

"Delta, I'm sorry, I just…you can't imagine."

"No, I really can't." Her voice is thick with sympathy. "If Alex ever…god, no. I can't even imagine." Another silence. "How are you coping?"

"I'm…not."

"What about Chris?"

I choke. "I know you read my blog, Delta."

"So it's true? He just…left?"

I try to breathe, and don't quite succeed. "Yeah. Yeah, he did."

"What a bastard. I thought better of him than that."

"It's…it's more complicated than that, Dee. It's not all on him."

"I don't give a shit what you may have done or said

or whatever, Ava, there ain't a single reason that would excuse his ass just up and leaving you alone like that."

"You don't know, Dee," I whisper. "You don't know."

"Sounds like you're defending him, almost."

"I…I don't know. There's too much for me to cope with…and I was so…and he—" I fight a sob. "I need you, Delta. It's so hard, and I can't breathe and I can't do this anymore."

"I'm here, honey, I'm always here. You know that. Get your skinny ass to Chicago, okay? My house is yours for as long as you need. Me and Alex, we'll take care of you."

"I…I can't leave. Delta."

"What?"

"There's a hurricane out there, and I just…I know it sounds stupid, but I have this feeling, a bad, bad feeling, and I can't shake it. I'm scared for him."

"He's out there? Where the hurricane is?"

"I don't know. Last I knew, he was going around the Horn."

"I don't know what that means," Delta says.

"Sailing around the southern tip of Africa, into the Indian Ocean."

"So he shouldn't be in the hurricane, 'cause that's in the Atlantic, right?"

"Right. But I still just…if something happens, and I'm not here? I shut off my phone and my email. I wanted to—I needed space from him, from us, from everything.

I was going to go see you, take a road trip. Get away. But I can't. He doesn't have any way of contacting me and he's not answering his satellite phone and…I just have to stay, Delta. I've never felt anything like this."

"Mom always did say a woman's intuition was never wrong." I hear a small voice in the background, and Delta's muffled answer. "Look, I've gotta get Alex to school in a minute."

"I'm sorry, Delta. I shouldn't be bothering you with all this. You have to take care of Alex."

"Nonsense, girl. I'm your big sister, of course you're gonna bother me with it. It's what we do." She says something else to Alex, and then returns to me. "Listen, honey, if you feel that strongly about staying, then you have to stay. And if you need me, then I'm gonna be there."

"You can't take any more time off work."

"That's my business, not yours. You're getting a visit, okay?"

"I can't ask you to come all this way, Delta. And what about Alex's school?"

"He's five, Ava. What's he gonna miss? Snack time, recess, and gluing construction paper to more construction paper." She emphasizes her point with a snort. "We're coming, and that's that. God knows I need a damn vacation anyway."

"If you're sure."

"Of course I'm sure. I've got your back, Ava. No

matter what."

"God, I love you, Dee."

"I know you do. Now, get a bed made up and stock up on wine. You'll see us in a couple days." I heard her in the background, talking to Alex. "Hey buddy, guess what? We're gonna go see Aunty Ava down in Florida. How's that sound?"

"YAY! Ava Ava Ava! And Uncle Chris?"

"He's gonna be gone. He's on a long business trip, okay, buddy? It's just gonna be you and me and Aunt Ava."

"Can we go now? I don't even like show-and-share anyway. It's dumb."

"Sure thing, kiddo." Back to me, then. "I'm gonna let you go. Gotta get packed and all that. Love you, honey."

"Love you. Drive safe. See you soon."

I sink onto a stool at the island, setting the phone aside.

I realize I forgot to tell her the hurricane was about to hit here. Maybe it will have blown over by then. Or maybe it will blow itself out before it gets here. I should tell her to wait until I know what's going on.

There's a tick-tick-ticking on the window, and then a flurry of rattling. I glance up, and the sky is dark. Black. Angry.

Too late to flee, now. Not that I would have, anyway.

I need to be here; I'm suffocating here, but I can't leave.

Can't breathe, can't leave.

Delta is coming.

I hope the storm blows out before she gets here.

Outside, palm trees are waving their shaggy heads, nodding, dipping, bending sideways in an ever-strengthening wind. I've lived my entire life in Florida, so this isn't the first hurricane I'll have sat through. I know the drill.

Yet as the storm begins to rage, all I can think of is Christian.

32

Somewhere in the South Atlantic

date unknown

Sky and sea. Waves and lightning.

It continues, a torment unending. Breath is a gift, each time I draw a lungful.

Ava.

If I live through this, I'll…

What? I don't know. So much. Love her. Forgive her. Beg her for forgiveness. Hold her. Tell her…everything. Spend a month whispering all the truths within me to her.

A light, then. The sun? No; rain still stings my face as I tumble down the side of a mountainous wave. But there is light bathing me, too steady and constant for lightning. I hear a noise, like thunder, but not. Thunder cracks as lightning spears, sound and strike concurrent. The other noise…it's a grumbling. A deep, bass murmur.

Shouts?

I can't speak, have no strength to speak. All I can do is gasp for breath when I feel air on my face. Can't even wave my hand. It might be a dream, a taunting of my subconscious, creating fictional rescue where there will be none. I am doomed to float and tumble thus in the storm-tossed sea until I drown, as punishment for abandoning Ava when she needed me most.

The bass murmur is louder, feeling almost real, now. And I'm imagining voices. Shouts snatched by the wind. Something smacks the water near me, and I hear frantic shouting, but I can't make out what they're saying, or it's not in a language I know. I'm so dizzy, so thirsty. I stopped being cold long ago, which something deep in the recesses of my brain tells me is a sign of acute hypothermia. I manage to roll toward the thing that hit the water.

It's orange. Round. A life preserver? White lettering. A white cross. I hook an arm through it, still certain I'm hallucinating. But as I cling to the imaginary orange disc, I feel myself being pulled through the waves. I sink as a wave slides past, drop fifteen or twenty feet into the trough and then water closes over my head. Not for long, though. I'm pulled up. It's all I can do to cling to the orange circle. Is this real?

The bass grumbling is powerful now. I twist in the water as I'm drawn forward. There's a massive dark shape shrouded in the darkness, a shadow obscured by wind-blasted sheets of rain. A bow. A long, long, long body. A superstructure, lights dim yellow. How close am I? I hear the propeller chopping at the water. Feel the pull of the mighty ship's enormous draft as I near her side. I wrap my other arm around the preserver, clinging with every last shred of strength I possess, which isn't much.

I'm airborne.

Dangling.

Twisting.

Drawn upward, my grip fading.

And then, from behind, the rushing of something even more massive and mighty than the boat. A rogue wave, towering so high overhead that I can tip my head backward and see it. How high? Too high to measure. A colossus of the sea. Rushing, reaching. The tanker or cargo ship or fishing scow or whatever it is that I've dreamed up or am being rescued by—I'm still not sure whether this is real or not—tips sideways as the wave soars at her, bobbing, heeling, sliding down into a canyon between waves, and I'm thrown skyward. I've wrapped the rough fibers of the line around my hand and my arm, tangled it around me so I cannot release it even if I tried. A good way to lose an arm, but better than that be thrown aside this close to rescue, only to drown. I tumble and wheel, spin and twist, and the wave smashes against the enormous ship, and god, how did they even see me in this? I'll owe the sharp-eyed observer my life, and a lifetime of drinks, should I make it out alive.

I hear a crash, the ship righting itself as the wave smashes past, not even cresting yet. And I'm swinging, still, shoulder wrenching almost out of the socket, hand searing in pain, burning, arm constricted. But I've got the line, and I'm swinging on it, arcing back toward the ship.

I get a glimpse of the ship as I hurtle at her.

I slam full-force into the side of the ship, and I feel something break. Agony lances through me, washes over me. I feel myself being dragged upward, and I feel rivets and sheet metal, ice-cold from the waves and wet and slimy.

Darkness surges up from within me, shadows armed with claws of excruciating anguish.

PAINPAINPAIN. All is pain.

I can't even groan past the pain.

Movement stops.

I settle against something solid and unmoving, and yet I still feel as if I'm being wave-thrown, tumbling and rising and dipping, and I can't breathe for the agony in my lungs. Broken ribs, and my left arm and leg have been shattered and set afire. My right arm is still tangled in the lifeline, and I peer blearily down my torso, and see blood and things bent in directions arms shouldn't bend.

Thoughts come slowly.

"Est-il en vie?"

A second voice. *"Oui, mais pas longtemps."*

A face, garbed in yellow rain gear. *"Assurez-vous qu'il ne meurt pas."*

I shake my head. I try to speak, but it comes out in a moan. Hands grab me, and the agony as they lift me is just too much.

Darkness spins around me, in me, through me, and I tumble into it.

"Ava…"

Was that my voice? Cracked and rough and grating and so weak?

I should be shivering, but I'm too cold to shiver. Not cold at all, maybe.

There's nothing.

I hear Ava's voice, but I know it's in my head. *Christian. Come back to me, Christian.*

I'm trying, my love. But I'm tired, now. So tired.

The darkness is warm.

I can't fight anymore.

Ava?

33

Ft. Lauderdale, FL

May 19, 2016

Christian?

I hear him, I feel him. He's out there.

I need him.

Do you hear me, Chris? I need you. Come back. Come back.

I fade into the drowsing silence. The storm has quieted, here. I'm huddled in my bathtub. A slab of the ceiling or the wall fell in, covering the tub. Protecting me, trapping me. My breath is hot and close. I have a bottle of water, which I had clutched in my hand when I realized the storm was destruction incarnate, flattening buildings, hurling roofs and car hoods and street signs, and that this truly wasn't a ride-it-out storm, and that I needed shelter. So I huddled in the tub, sport cap pink Hydro Flask in one hand. And then the ceiling or wall fell over on top of me, sealing off the tub from the world outside. I heard the storm continue to rage, felt the walls shudder and shake, heard the wrenching squeal of tearing metal and crashes and juddering joists.

I cannot move. If I lie on my back, my nose touches the soggy drywall imprisoning and shielding me. To drink, I have to lie on my side and tilt the bottle just so. It's nearly empty, now.

I've been trapped for…I don't know how long.

Hunger is a distant memory; I know how long I can go without food, although I have less excess fat to live off, now.

Chris…I think of Chris.

Remember his face. The feel of his hands. The rough murmur of his voice in the small, quiet hours, as we laze in the afterglow.

The silence that pervades, now, is total. I can hear my heart beating in my chest. Hear my breathing echoed back to me. A tick and a rumble and a faint hum, then silence again.

Time skips and hops, stretches like taffy, contracts like a Slinky. I count my breaths, and lose track at one million eight hundred and ninety-four thousand five hundred and sixty-something.

Start over.

I'm tired.

How could you leave me, Christian? I love you, god I love you. Come back. Please come back.

34

Somewhere in the South Atlantic

date unknown

Ava?

I should never have left.

I am pain. There is no me, no body, no self, no consciousness, no past present future, only raw, blazing, endless agony.

It gives me something to focus on, other than sorrow and fear.

I can't open my eyes.

I can't move.

My breathing is assisted, somehow. For which I am thankful, since I'm too weak to manage even that.

There is only silence. And warmth, like a heat too great to fully understand, or too cold and too deep to fathom. Nothing makes sense.

Only that I need Ava.

I have to find her.

I have to go back.

Ava.

Ava? God it hurts.

Ava…

Epilogue

Somewhere in the Atlantic Ocean

date unknown

It takes me a few minutes to completely wake up, and when I finally do, it's a hazy, groggy, troubled awareness. I moan, and the rough, scratchy sound of my voice tells me I've been asleep for quite awhile.

"He's waking up." A male voice, American accent. "Hey, can you hear me?"

I moan again. "Nnnngh." It's not a word so much as an attempt at a word. *"Agua…por favor…"*

"Sorry, man, I don't speak Spanish."

"Dude. Even if you don't speak Spanish, that much at least has to be obvious." This is a second voice, also male, much younger, and it's not until now that I realize they're speaking English and I used Spanish. "He's thirsty. Agua? Aqua? Water? Duh."

"I may be your brother, Dane, but I'm still the captain. Show a little respect."

"Sorry, Dom."

A silence, and then the first, older voice. "Well? Get him some water, dipshit."

"Oh, right."

I realize, at this point, that I haven't opened my eyes yet. I'm in no hurry to do so, though, since everything hurts. My head is throbbing, my throat is on fire, my bones ache, my muscles are sore from head to toe, and I think there's something broken in my left leg. I feel a hand slip under my head, and something plastic touches my lips.

"It's a sport cap. You just gotta suck on it, okay, bro?"

"How do you know he understands English, Dane?"

"Oh, good point." The second voice clears his throat. "Um. *Agua*, dude. I got some *agua*. El drinko, *ese*."

"Dane, you idiot. None of that was Spanish except *agua*. I may not speak Spanish, but even I know 'el drinko' ain't fuckin' Spanish, moron."

I would laugh, if it didn't hurt. I try to lift my hand, but it's too hard. I manage to wrap my lips around the cap and pull until ice-cold, pure, filtered water fills my mouth. As badly as I want to gulp it down greedily, I've been through enough shit to know better. Instead, I let the water sit in my mouth, let the dried-out tissue soak it up. Swish it around, let some trickle down my throat, and I could cry in relief.

"This guy knows what he's doing, at least." The first voice, in a lecturing tone. "Notice how he didn't gulp it down? He let it sit in his mouth, and he's swallowing it slowly. If you've gone without water for a long time, like you're close to death by dehydration like he was, you gotta go slow or you could make yourself sick. Same thing with food."

"Not...not my first rodeo," I manage, my voice raspy and hoarse. "And I speak English. Better than the two of you, I think."

A laugh from the first voice. "Probably true."

I open my eyes. I'm in the cabin of a boat. Wood paneled walls, bare ceiling, pipes visible. Narrow, hard cot under me, thin pillow, scratchy green military issue wool blanket over my torso. Not much else in the cabin aside from a battered bureau attached to the wall on one side and a metal desk attached to the opposite wall. There are two men in the cabin with me, although "man" is a bit of a stretch for the one. The older man, Dom, is tall, well built, rugged looking, with a messy, curly, wild mass of jet-black hair bound back in a low knot at the back of his neck, and a long, well-groomed beard; he is midthirties, probably, with hard, intelligent gray eyes. The younger, Dane, is probably not even eighteen, and clearly the older man's younger brother. Similar build but twenty years younger, less filled out. Same wild, curly black hair, and the beginnings of a beard, more of a straggly attempt than a real beard, same gray eyes but young and eager and excited.

I wiggle my toes and fingers, roll my head on my neck, shrug my shoulders, taking stock. My left leg throbs like a motherfucker, a deep, burning pain centered around my thigh, but I can move it and wiggle my toes, which tells me it probably isn't a break but some other injury. Everything else seems to be fine.

"I wouldn't move around too much," Dom says. "You got pretty fucked up."

"For real. Miracle you're even alive," Dane adds.

"My leg?" I ask.

Dom shifts closer, twitches the blanket aside to reveal thick white bandages wrapped around my thigh, low, near the knee. "Nasty gash to the quad. Took a good thirty stitches. You'll be limping for a while."

I eye him. "You do the stitches?"

He nods. "Did eight years in the Navy as a corpsman on a hospital ship. I can set bones and stitch shit up, basic triage stuff."

I try to lift my hand again, and this time succeed. "Well, thanks." He takes my hand and we shake. "Jonny Núñez."

"Dominic Bathory, and this my brother, Dane."

"How'd you find me?" I am trying like hell to remember, but things are foggy.

I remember the hurricane hitting, like the fist of God smashing in from nowhere. I remember the monster rogue wave knocking us flying, and Christian going overboard. He was just gone before I could even blink, before I could do a damn thing, just snatched by the sea. He had a life vest on, and the motherfucker can swim like a fish, and he's one of the toughest bastards I've ever known, so if anyone can survive going overboard during a hurricane in the spring in the Atlantic, it's him. But... the chances aren't good.

After that, it's all a blur. The storm raged for so long. It was all I could do to stay on the ship, to keep her from being flipped. I remember thinking I was going to drown while still on the damn boat. I remember... not much else. The ocean around me. Seawater in my mouth. Dark sky above, lightning. Struggling to breathe. Swimming.

Did I go overboard too?

"That was a bitch of a storm," Dominic says. "Came out of fuckin' nowhere. We were running ahead of it, but it overtook us. I thought for sure we were gonna flip, but we didn't. That bitch blew for three damn days, man, and when she finally blew past us, we were so far off course it's not even funny. Well, when I finally figured out where the hell we were, we'd been blown way the hell west, luckily for you. We took some damage, lost some nets, had a boom snap off, lost our radio antenna, so we gotta put in for repairs. Then yesterday, right around dawn, we came across a catamaran. Flipped, swamped. Surprising it was still afloat, but those cats are tough as hell to sink, right? And you were laying on the hull, passed the fuck out. You had a rope wrapped around your waist, and a metal box in your arms, in a damn death grip." He shrugs. "So we took you aboard, I stitched up your leg, and hoped for the best. I don't have an IV or fluids or I'd have pushed some fluids."

A thought hits me. "The boat. She sank?"

He nods. "Sadly, yeah. No way to save her. Too bad, too. She looked like a gorgeous boat. I got you off, and we had to keep going. Saw her going under, though. Got you off in the nick of time, I'd say."

"I owe you my life, then," I say.

Dominic shrugs again. "Hey, something tells me you'd've done the same thing."

"Sure, of course I would've. But you still did it. So thanks."

"Buy me a beer or ten when we put in to port and we'll call it even."

I laugh. "I hope my life is worth more than ten beers, but you can count on that much, at least." I peer around the room. "The box. You mentioned I had a box with me. Where is it?"

Dane crouches near the cot and reaches under it, coming up with Christian's box. I take it from him and rest it on my lap, breathing a sigh of relief. I've got the key on my gold chain necklace, next to my crucifix. I have a vague memory of slipping that key onto my neck-lace when I realized I may not sail out of the storm; I also put Christian's tiny little laptop into the box, so that much of him at least would survive, the letters and everything saved to his computer.

Dominic lifts his chin in the direction of the box. "Mind if I ask the importance of that?"

"The boat was my friend's. He went overboard during the storm. The box has some letters for his wife, which I'm supposed to deliver in the event of my friend…" I shrug, not wanting to even say out loud the possibility.

I want to believe he's still alive out there somewhere.

Dominic nods, his expression serious and grim. "Anything's possible, but…"

I sigh. "I know." I rub the back of my neck. "I wonder where Christian ended up, then?"

"Assuming he made it, there's no way to tell. A body can get pushed a long-ass way."

I feel a tightness in my chest. "He fuckin' made it, okay? He had to."

Dominic holds up his hands. "Hey, I hope he did. I'm just saying. You gotta know the odds."

"Never tell me the odds!" Dane says, glancing as if to gauge our reactions.

I stare at him blankly, and Dominic huffs and shakes his head, giving his brother a playful shove. "He's a *Star Wars* geek. Don't mind him."

I shrug. "Never seen it. Heard of it, though. Is that

the one with the bald guy? Picard?"

Dane groans and slaps his forehead with his palm. "Oh my god. No. Picard is *Star Trek*. Totally different."

"Oh. So *Star Wars* is the one with the big hairy monkey dude that makes the weird noises?"

"Chewy. Chewbacca. And he's a wookie."

I snort. "Okay, *ese*."

Dane blushes scarlet. "I didn't know you spoke English, okay?"

"Pro tip, buddy? Never call a Spanish speaker *ese*, okay? Just makes you sound stupid. Ninety-nine percent of us don't even use that word, never have, and never will. I think only gangbangers in LA actually use it in what you might call a non-ironic sense."

"Oh."

I laugh. "You even know what non-ironic means?"

Dane shrugs. "Not exactly."

Dominic chortles and smacks his brother on the back. "What'd I tell you, Dane? This cat speaks better English than either of us."

"Yeah, well, I learned from you, so what's that tell you?"

"It tells me I got saddled with the job of raising a ten-year-old brat by myself and at least you can read and write and count to twenty without taking off your shoes."

"I wasn't a brat."

"No, you were a holy terror. You heard the phrase

sleep with the fishes on TV and thought it sounded like fun. I had to jump in and rescue you from shark-infested waters of the South Atlantic in the middle of the night."

"I fell in, you dumbfuck."

"You were mumbling about wanting to sleep with the fishes."

I'm watching their fast-paced, nonstop exchange like a tennis match, finding myself entertained, despite everything, and slowly sip water.

"I was sleepwalking! I didn't know what I was doing."

"Yeah, and I had to lock your door from the outside every night for six months so you didn't sleepwalk off the fuckin' boat again."

"And how is that my fault?"

"Too much TV?"

"Just because you're a goddamn Luddite who wouldn't use GPS or radar if you didn't have to doesn't mean I can't appreciate quality cinema."

"You watch Star Wars a dozen times a week."

"Because it's one of a dozen DVDs on this godforsaken bucket of bolts."

"Well I'm sorry I can't afford to supply you with a wider variety of *quality cinema*, Dane. I *am* trying to keep you fed and clothed and halfway educated, none of which is exactly easy when my job keeps me out in the middle of the ocean."

"That wouldn't be a problem if you'd just take us back to New England. You could lobster and I could live with Bobby and Bo."

"I hate lobstering, and Bobby and Bo are lazy pot-heads. You'd never leave the couch except to go on munchie runs."

"They both work full-time jobs!"

"At Pizza Hut and McDonald's."

"Work is work."

"Wrong. A job is a job, but you're smart and you're a talented mechanic. You could go to college, or trade school. You can have a meaningful career. Those jack-asses will work dead-end hourly wage jobs for the rest of their lives, and then they'll be fat and unemployed al-coholics just like their piece of shit old man is now. No, Dane. Even if we did go back to Gloucester, you would NOT be living with goddamn Bobby and Bo."

"At least I'd have a home that didn't fuckin' float! There's something to be said for dry fuckin' land, Dom."

"Yeah, there's something to be said for dry land: it sucks. You know why? Because PEOPLE live on dry land, and people fuckin' suck."

Dane snorts. "Like I said, you're a Luddite and an antisocial recluse."

"I'm not a Luddite."

"You have GPS navigation, but you still chart courses by hand."

"Yeah, and if the GPS goes down, I won't be lost, because I have charts and I know how to use them."

"You don't have a cell phone, a laptop, an iPad, or

even a CD player. Who the hell doesn't have a CD player? I mean most people, nowadays, actually, since they have a cell phone and listen to internet radio and buy music on iTunes like civilized human beings."

"I like things simple."

"Yeah, simple like you."

I can't help a laugh. "You guys fight like this all the time?"

Dominic kicks open the door to the cabin, picks Dane up bodily, and tosses him out of the cabin, then closes the door behind him. "Yes, we do. He's difficult and stubborn and hates everything."

"So...a teenage male?"

"Yeah, exactly."

"Thanks again for..." I shrug. "Everything, I guess."

"It's what anyone would do." He eyes me. "So. Where are you headed?"

I touch the cold metal of Christian's box. "Ft. Lauderdale, I guess."

"That's home?"

I shake my head. "Nah. That's where my friend's wife lives. I was supposed to give her this—" I tap the box, "if Chris didn't...if he doesn't...you know."

"Should I contact the Coast Guard? Get search-and-rescue going?"

"He went overboard in the first few hours of the storm, and it's been days." I blow out a conflicted breath. "I mean, for the sake of my conscience, I have to at least have them look, right? But…like you said, we both know the odds of him having survived."

"You gotta file a report at least. You know? Have them search a grid around the coordinates where he went missing."

"I only know the general area. It hit so fast, I didn't really have time to check our coordinates."

"Better than nothing. People beat the odds all the time, man."

"True, true."

Dominic helps me to my feet, gives me his shoulder to grab onto as I hobble out of the cabin and up to the cockpit; by the time I struggle up the ladder, I'm gasping and sweating, shaking and weak. My leg is more messed-up than I thought, and I think I'm still incredibly dehydrated. Not in good shape at all, that's what I am. I get on the radio and give my report to the Coast Guard, with as good a last-known location as I can manage and a description of Christian.

I'm on a deep-sea fishing trawler, on the smaller end of medium size. I can see crew scrambling around the deck, repairing, tending to nets, coiling lines, and a dozen other busy-work activities. It's a sunny day, calm waters. I can feel the rumble of the engine, which is strange to me after spending so much of my life on sailboats.

I'm content to sit in an old, cracked leather chair in the corner of the cabin, watching Dominic converse in low tones with the older guy at the wheel. The door leading from the cockpit to the deck is open, letting in the smell of the brine-laced breeze and the sounds of the ocean, the low murmur of the voices of the crew, the trilling call of an albatross.

I still have the box.

I should stay out here, make the Coast Guard criss-cross the whole damn Atlantic looking for Chris.

But I sit here in the cabin, tapping on the lid of the box, and I hear his voice in my head. *Give her the box, Jonny.*

It's damn near impossible to find someone lost at sea within the first twelve hours, but after three days? He's either dead, or he got rescued by someone. Those are the only two possibilities. I mean, a distant, *distant* possibility is that he washed ashore somewhere on the African coast, or that he's still floating out there somewhere and the SAR crew will find him.

But after three days without food or water? Not good. Not good.

They'll look, and they won't find him. I'll bring the box to Ava in Ft. Lauderdale and we'll have a memorial service, and I'll go back out to sea. What else is there to do?

I hate it, though.

I should look for him.

But where do I even start? And how? I'm barely alive myself, *The Hemingway* is probably at the bottom of the Atlantic by now, or is being hauled for scrap by scavengers, and the tiny bit I did own is gone with it. I don't think my wallet even made it with me. I don't know what I'm going to do about myself, as a matter of fact. I wasn't exactly flush with cash to begin with. I have some bank saved up in a Bahamian account, but it ain't much, and I gotta go there in person to get it... only I need ID for that, which means I'd have to go back to Columbia to get a new one, or at least a Columbian embassy somewhere. Passport, wallet, my clothes, everything I owned was on that damn boat, man.

Jesus Cristo. What a mess.

"You look like you're deep in thought," Dominic says to me.

I sigh. "I'm just starting to realize that my friend's boat sank, and that all my shit is gone."

"Sorry I couldn't tow the cat or something, Jonny. We're barely limping along as it is. The storm fucked up the engine and we don't have the parts to fix it."

"Nah, not blaming you. But my passport, my wallet, my clothes, everything I own was on that, man. I didn't have much, but what I did have was there. Now it's gone."

"Sucks, man. I've been there."

"Yeah?"

He nods. "After getting out of the Navy, I realized I'd spent eight years on a boat and never actually saw anything but a few harbors. So I joined a deep-sea dragging crew. Similar circumstances. Out-of-season storm, boat capsized, most of the crew was lost. I survived, along with a couple others. Lost everything. Another reason I don't own much. Shit is expensive to replace, so if you don't have shit to replace, won't be a problem."

I nod. "Yeah. Always been my philosophy, too. But losing my passport is a pain in the ass, because I don't go back to the country of my birth if I can help it."

"I might be able to swing as far north as Ft. Lauderdale."

"Get me close, and I can make it the rest of the way on my own. I can't ask you to go that far out of your way."

A crewmember appears in the cabin, a kid even younger than Dane, blond-haired and blue-eyed and eager looking. He hands Dominic two mugs of coffee, and Dominic extends one to me.

"I gotta get Dane to Charleston anyway. He's eighteen in a month, and he doesn't know this yet, but I've got an old Navy buddy who's gonna take him on as an apprentice. My buddy is a shipwright, builds fancy yachts and shit."

"That's what Dane wants to do?"

Dominic nods. "He's talked about college, but I think he's mostly ruled it out. He's a hands-on guy, not a school guy. Bully, my mechanic, says Dane has a hell of a knack for anything mechanical, and I think with the right opportunity, he could really get somewhere in the world. He ain't gonna get that stuck with me, dragging the

Atlantic. This is what I wanna do, not him. So I called up my buddy last time I was ashore and set things up. I need to have him in Charleston sometime soon."

A stocky, swarthy man in greasy coveralls appears in the doorway. He's as wide as he is tall in a muscular way, and his hands are black with grease, as is his face, except two clean patches where a pair of goggles had been. "Cap. I think I got 'er patched. Might be able to get a few more knots out of 'er now."

"Ah, Bully. I was just talking about you." Dominic gently nudges the throttle forward, and the engine grumbles and rattles but we surge forward noticeably faster. "Sounds rough but serviceable. Good work."

"My ears was burnin', but I thought it was just sparks." Bully eyes me. "This the feller we fished off that cat?"

"I was just saying that you think Dane has a natural gift for mechanical work. And yeah, this is Jonny."

"Name's Bully. Glad you made it." Bully nods. "Dane? Boy can weld and solder, and any little thing I put in front of him, he can figure out. He fixed a hydraulic jack on his own without so much as a howdyadoo from me."

"Think we can make it to Ft. Lauderdale on your patch?" Dominic asks.

Bully stares out the windscreen, head cocked to listen to the engine. "Got a bit of a hitch in her step still. I wouldn't care to give you any guarantees, but I think we could make it, prob'ly. Of course, if she goes out again and I don't have the spare parts I need, we could be in a world of hurt."

"Will she hold, Bully?"

"She'll hold."

"Get me your list. We need a new antenna anyway, so I'll pick up the parts you need while we're in port to drop Jonny off."

"If I can shut her down completely for a few hours, I can check her over more thoroughly. Poor old girl's been through hell last few days."

"Sounds good. Thanks for the update, Bully." When he's gone, Dominic glances my way. "Ever work a trawler before, Jonny?"

I tilt my head side to side. "Not specifically. But there ain't much I can't do. Been at sea my whole life." I tap the bandage around my leg. "Might be a bit limited for a minute, but I'll pull my weight."

Dominic nods, eyeing me thoughtfully. "Something tells me you will."

Ft. Lauderdale, FL

May 20, 2016

When I get to Ft. Lauderdale, it becomes quickly apparent that the hurricane blew past us and hit the Atlantic seaboard, starting here, probably, and smashing her way north. The city is a mess. Flooded, houses missing roofs and walls, or knocked down entirely, high-rises battered, signs missing, cars abandoned everywhere.

It's chaos, still. No cabs, no public transit. Work crews are everywhere, working furiously to clear the mess.

Dominic is out in the bay, making himself useful doing transport work for the dock authority; he's agreed to wait for me to finish my business with Ava, and then I'll join his crew for the trip north to Charleston. It's a good crew, and I don't mind the work. Not as peaceful or challenging as sailing, but it's a change of pace and I like it.

In the meantime, with the city in tatters, finding Ava could prove difficult.

I have the address, and I'd planned on simply catching a cab from the docks, but now it seems I'll have to go about this the hard way. A huge portion of the roads are completely flooded, so nobody will be driving anyone anywhere anytime soon. I have no cell phone, which means no easy access to GPS or anything helpful; not sure cell service is working at the moment anyway. I walk a few blocks inland from the docks, which is tough with my leg still a bit sore; I'm doing my best to skirt flooded spots, but a lot of my journey is made trudging through icy calf- or knee-deep water. I'm standing at an intersection, trying to figure out the best course of action when I hear a motor of some kind; I turn to locate the noise and see a flat-bottomed, fan-powered, airboat approaching from the south, one man in the pilot's chair at the wheel, a few others clustered around him. The airboat's fan slows and the craft glides to a stop in the murky water beside me.

"Where ya headed?" the pilot asks. He's an older man, white-haired with a neat white goatee, decked out in hip-waders.

I shrug. "Not sure exactly. All I got is an address, but I don't know the city." I hand him the slip of paper with Ava's address scrawled on it in Christian's handwriting.

The man takes it, stares at it, and then pivots this way and that in his seat, as if orienting himself. "Well shit, you ain't but half a mile off, though you're headed in the dead wrong direction." He hesitates a moment. "That area was the hardest hit. Can't say I know that exact building, but most of 'em around there are...not in good shape. Climb aboard, stranger. I'll run you there."

I trudge through the water, my legs bumping into debris and detritus, chunks of wood, bits of insulation, a child's plastic toy phone, a strip of siding. I climb as gently and carefully as I can aboard the prow of the airboat, clutching the box I'm meant to deliver under one arm.

"Checkin' in on family?" the pilot asks me, shouting over the fan.

"Not exactly, but sort of."

"Well that's about clear as mud," he answers with a laugh.

"It's complicated."

He makes a face and nods. "Meanin' quit askin' s'many damn questions?"

My turn to laugh. "Pretty much."

Only half a mile or so, he said, but we take a long, winding, slow, circuitous route. He drifts slowly down the flooded roadways, peering into open doorways and windows, slowing to a stop here and there, hopping out and peeking in for a closer look.

"What are you looking for?" I ask him, finally.

"Anyone who might need help. Times like this, you gotta do your part. Folks need help, and I'm in a position to help."

"I see."

We take on another two people, a young black woman and a wildly overweight older white guy, both picked up from the first-floor window of an apartment building. Finally, the pilot takes a right turn and the sea is shining and twinkling in the bright sun, and the beach stretches away in both directions out of sight. The beach is ruined, flooded, littered with trash and washed-up wreckage, and seaweed and driftwood and who knows what else from the deep sea, along with other garbage and rubble from the city. The rivers are surging, the docks are gone, boats are lodged into the sides of buildings, and on end and upside down and bobbing free, drifting by mooring ropes. It's a dangerous route we take, now, dodging between wrecked boats, crossing surging river currents trying mightily to dump excess water into the sea. The condo buildings here are ruined, completely. Wrecked totally, most of them. It's hard to believe there could even be survivors in them at all, but each building is a humming hive of activity, volunteers and firefighters and police and construction and rescue workers, placing sandbags and hauling at the rubble with bare hands and any available tools.

The pilot halts at an intersection, catching at a pole that had once held stoplights over the road. "This here's as near as I can figure. One'a them buildings," he says, pointing at the condo buildings facing the beach. "Not sure which, but if you ask around, I'm sure you'll find the right one." A heavy pause. "May have to help dig to figure out if your friend or relative or whoever is…you know, all right."

I nod, and hop into the waist-deep water, feeling the current pulling hard against me, trying to haul me out to the sea. I cling to the pole with one arm and the box with the other, and the pilot lets the current tug him away before hitting the throttle.

I aim for the nearest condo, wading across the road and climbing up the sand dunes. A policeman, wearing his uniform pants, gear belt, and a white tank top, is directing a group of civilian volunteers as they form a human conveyor belt to haul rubble away from the building.

"Excuse me, officer," I say. "I'm looking for—" and I read him the address.

The officer points down the beach. "Two down, that way."

"Thanks."

It's a long, laborious journey to the correct building, and when I get there, my heart sinks. I've been doing my best to keep my emotions at bay, but seeing the ruined condo building and knowing Ava was probably in there when the hurricane hit...it's hard to have hope. The entire front half of the building, facing the ocean, has collapsed. It looks as if the hurricane winds picked up something enormous and slammed against the condo, and the resulting impact caused several floors to collapse, compacting downward, smashing out windows and columns. The back half is more or less intact, but most of the windows are shattered and the lower stories are flooded and littered with debris and are wind-damaged.

There's a massive rubble pile already, just inside a four-foot high wall of sandbags keeping out the floodwaters. At the edge of the pile is a kind of staging area, a makeshift pavilion set up with a pair of folding tables underneath. A local deli has set up shop, providing free sandwiches, coffee, and water to volunteers and rescue workers, and there's another pair of tables nearby, both piled high with cell phones, wallets, purses, and backpacks all watched over by a fit-looking middle-aged man in a wheelchair, missing his legs from midthigh.

"Here to help out?" he asks me, seeing me eye the tables.

I nod, and point at the building. "I've got a friend who lives in that building, so yeah, I guess so."

"Leave your shit here, and I'll watch it." He hands me a clipboard with a sheet of paper and a pen. "Write down what you're leaving, and your name. Anybody wants to retrieve something, they check it out through me."

I set my box down on the table, and write my name a brief description of the box—*Jonny Núñez, safety box, initials engraved on it: CSP.*

I join a crew of men picking at the rubble. Someone hands me a pair of grease-stained, well-worn work gloves, and I take them and offer my thanks, and I haul at the rubble. Cinderblocks, siding, rebar, I-beams, bits of plastic and twisted metal and chunks of wood and marble and laminate and tile and drop-tile ceiling pieces and machinery and electronics. Occasionally there's a shout, and we all rush to the spot and haul like mad, and there will be a body underneath. Alive, dead, or in between.

I remember growing up on the island of Providencia, a little tiny island off the coast of Nicaragua, owned by Columbia. Storms hit us pretty frequently, and homes would be knocked down and we'd all pitch in like this, hauling at the wreckage and pulling people out and rebuilding together. This isn't new. I've been ground zero for a lot of hurricanes, more than I care to count, and I know how it goes.

So I dig with a heavy heart.

Chris is gone. I want him to be alive. I want to believe.

But the pragmatic part of me, the part that knows the odds…? It's hard.

And Ava, now, too? That's even harder to believe. A big, complicated building like this? So much weight, so much wreckage to move. I know the odds here, too.

I dig.

I move to a line of people hauling the rubble away from the building.

I help move bodies and carry wounded survivors on stretchers to where teams of medics work in a makeshift facility.

The sun goes down and diesel-powered generators rumble, providing light on the scene.

I rest, eat a sandwich, drink some coffee, and go back to helping.

Dawn comes, and then afternoon, and I rest, and go back to helping, and we've made progress and I've examined every body and every survivor, and none of them are Ava. I have her picture in the breast pocket of my shirt, a snapshot given to me by Chris.

Two days. Three. With each hour, the odds of even finding her corpse plummet.

Midmorning on the third day, a tin fishing boat propelled by a trolling motor drops off a woman, who climbs over the sandbags from the boat. She looks familiar, even though I know I've never met her before. She stands just inside the wall of sandbags, breathing heavily as if holding back tears. Shaking her head. I'm only a few feet away, working on a sandwich and a cup of coffee. I'm filthy, covered in dirt from head to toe.

She's just staring at the wreckage of the building. Then she sees me, and seems to need to say something to someone, anyone. "I don't—I don't understand how this happened."

"Hurricane."

She sniffles. "I know, but…how can a building just be…gone?"

"You never been through one?" I ask. She shakes her head. "It ain't just wind and rain. It's like…God got angry. Scary shit."

"You were here?"

I shake my head. "Not here, for this one. Others, lotsa times." I nod at the building. "Looking for someone?"

She shudders, crying, and then her head tips up and down shakily. "My—my sister. Ava. She lives—that was—is her building. My son and I were supposed to visit her, but then I heard about the storm and I left Alex with my parents, and Ava—god, Ava."

"Ava?" My suspicion meter rises. "Ava who?"

She doesn't answer right away. "Um. Martin. Ava Martin." She frowns, rubs her face. "St. Pierre, I mean. Martin is her maiden name. My name. God, I'm sorry. I'm not making any sense."

"You're looking for Ava St. Pierre?" I pull the snapshot from my pocket; it's a candid shot, printed out from Chris's cell phone, blurry, pixelated from being blown up. But it's enough to recognize her. "This her?"

The woman takes the photo from me, stares at it. "Y-yes. Why…how…I mean, I don't understand."

I take it back and stuff it back into my pocket. "I'm a friend of Christian's."

Her expression sours. "The bastard couldn't make it here himself so he sent you?"

"He was lost at sea. Same storm, I think. I came to find Ava and bring her some letters from him."

"He's…dead?"

I shrug. "I don't know for sure."

"I'm sorry about your friend, but he didn't treat my sister very well. I'm angry with him. I never liked him for her."

"It was a complicated situation, from what I know." I try to be diplomatic.

She sighs. "I suppose that's true."

I finish the sandwich and the last of the coffee. "I should get back." I gesture at the wreckage.

She just stares. "How…um—is she…will she be okay?" She chokes back another sob. "Is she alive in there, do you think?"

I shrug. "No way to know. I hope so. It is certainly possible, in my experience."

"How long has she—has she been in there?"

"More than three days, now."

"Oh my god. Ava. God please, Ava."

"If she is in a place where she can breathe and she

isn't losing too much blood, and if she has water to drink, she might survive." At my words, Ava's sister can't hold back the sob. "I'm sorry. I've been here for three days myself, working to find her. We all are. Not just her, but…" I gesture as a pair of men carry a man on a stretcher. "Many others."

"I'll help."

I point out one of the police officers, who seems to have taken charge of organizing the rescue and dig-out process here. "Talk to him. I think he can help you find somewhere to pitch in."

"I have to find Ava." She's beginning to panic. "I can't just make sandwiches and hand out coffee." Anger tinges her voice.

"That's not what I meant," I say, trying to placate her, calm her. "I just meant, helping everyone helps you find her. If she's in there, we'll find her."

"She's in there. There's nowhere else she'd be. I just talked to her before I drove here. She knew I was coming. Ava—god, she has to be okay. She has to be okay. We're going to find her. Right?"

Full-on panic, the sudden flow of babble stopping as abruptly as it started, tears streaming down her face. She's having trouble breathing. Gasping. Waving her hands in front of her face, wheezing, sobbing.

I don't know what to do. Panicking women are outside my range of expertise, but she's staring at me like I can do something, and I have to try. So I grab her arms and pull her close. It's like an instinct, you know? A woman is crying, you hold her. Maybe that's just me. My mom would cry, when I was a kid, and I'd hug her through it. Or my older sister, after her piece of shit husband ran off on her, leaving her with four kids under five—she'd cry, in the middle of the night, and I'd go to her and hold her through it. I was just a kid, but it was the only thing I knew how to do. And as a man, sometimes afterward, a girl and I would be talking and she'd start in on something or other and I'd listen and suddenly she'd be crying, and the only thing I knew how to do was grab her and pull her close and hold her.

So this woman, a complete stranger, but someone to whom I'm connected via Christian, she's sobbing hysterically, panicked, scared, worried, upset and confused, and she's grabbing at me like I'm a lifeline and she's drowning. So I hold her against my chest.

And I mutter to her in Spanish. *Hey, hey. It is going to be okay. Do not cry, little girl, do not cry.* The *little girl*, part, in Spanish it's a term of endearment. Translated into English, it just sounds condescending, but I promise it doesn't sound that way in Spanish.

After a few minutes, she backs out of my hold, wiping at her face. "I'm sorry. God, I'm—that's embarrassing. I'm sorry."

She has mascara running down her cheeks. I can't help but wipe it away with my thumb, which only smears it worse. "No worries. Don't apologize, please."

"What were you saying?" she asks.

I shrug. "The same kind of automatic nonsense any-one says to comfort a crying person. Just...*en Español*."

"Oh." She's eying me oddly. Intently. Scrutinizing.

Almost as if she felt the same thing I did, while I was holding her, comforting her.

Almost like I'd done it before. Held her. Comforted her. Whispered to her in Spanish. It was familiar, too familiar, that way the top of her head fit just under my chin, just so. It's creeping me out, throwing me for a loop. All those English slang phrases, they all fit.

She looks like Ava, in the face. Medium height, on the slimmer side of average build. North of thirty, south of forty, by my estimate. Her hair is a messy mass of ra-ven-black locks, a handful of strands pulled back around the top and front to keep it out of her eyes, the rest left loose. Blue eyes, crazy-intense blue eyes. Lots of mas-cara, too much. Lots of makeup overall. More than she needs. It's all coming off, and I want to smear it away to see what she looks like without it.

She's wearing too-short shorts, tight khaki shorts that hug her hips and cup a tight ass, which is barely held in and covered. A thin, tight purple tank top, tiny barely there straps. *McCall's* is written in glittery, sparkly, cursive on the front, right across her breasts, which are propped up by what seems to be a hell of a push-up bra, which she really doesn't need. The tank top is tied in a knot just under her breasts, baring her belly and navel, revealing faint and faded childbirth stretch marks; it's the kind of outfit a waitress would wear at a Hooter's style bar. A name tag affixed just above her left breast confirms my estimation of her employment, and announces her name as Delta. Or at least, that's what the tag says.

She notices my quick once-over. "I left to drive here straight from work." She notices her name tag, and unpins it. "It's a…well, McCall's is a shithole. Cross between Denny's and Deja Vú. Only, we don't have to actually take our clothes off—we just don't wear much to begin with." She stuffs the name tag in her pocket, and shifts uncomfortably. "I fucking hate it, but it pays the bills. It's actually a step *up* from my last job, though. We worked in bikinis. At least at McCall's I get to wear shorts and a shirt."

I hold out my hand, amused despite the way she tends to blurt out more information than I'd expect to hear from a stranger. "I'm Jonny Núñez."

She shakes, and our hands remain in contact longer than is necessary. "Delta Martin."

"Nice to meet you." I gesture. "Not under the circumstances, maybe, but it's good to meet you."

"You too."

Someone calls my name, and I wave at her, and then trot over to where a group of rescue workers is clustered. Deep under the wreckage, in what used to be the ground floor, facing the sea. Can't tell what the room used to be, since everything is smashed. They're pulling at pieces of ceiling and wall, frantic. Aggressive. You only work that hard for a survivor.

I join the effort. I hear faint thumps, regular, consistent. Someone desperately but exhaustedly trying to alert rescuers as to their presence. Whoever is down there must hear us.

"Hold on! We're coming!" someone shouts.

Delta is beside me. Pulling at a piece of drywall. "It's hard to be sure, but this seems about where Ava and Chris's condo is."

She's got long fingernails, fake nails painted bright cherry red. I take off the gloves and give them to her, and she puts them on, but not before I notice she's broken several already. One was torn off, it looks like. She works furiously, as do we all; the thumps are fading in consistency and frequency.

"Ava?" Delta calls out. "We're coming, baby. Hold on, okay? Hold on!"

A giant metal beam lies across a chunk of drywall. It takes six of us to heave the beam aside, and then we have to clear rubble off and away from around the sides. A bathtub, and whoever is here, is trapped in the tub. The drywall is still pinned down by something, the wall itself, I think, having caved in sideways.

A guy wearing a hardhat and the orange vest of a construction worker shows up with a battery-powered circular saw. He thumps on the drywall near one end of the tub. "Scoot up this way!" he shouts. "We're cutting through!"

There's a thump on the underside, right near where he'd thumped.

The saw buzzes and whines, and then zips and snarls angrily as he cuts through the drywall. He frees a section covering one end of the tub, and rips it away. Inside is a pair of feet, bare. A few inches of dirty water. Bare female legs curled up into a tight ball on the other end of the tub. The toes are painted baby blue; it's an odd detail to notice.

"Ava?" Delta chokes. "Is that you?"

A low, ragged moan. I reach in, along with the guy who'd been running the saw, and we haul her toward us. Reach down, lift her free, and I cup dirty white-dust speckled damp black hair to protect her head from bumping into anything, and she's limp. Alive, but barely. She's clutching a pink reusable water bottle in one hand, hand curled tight around it, clutching it for dear life. It's how she survived, probably, that bottle of water. Otherwise, she'd have died of thirst by now, most likely.

We have her out of the tub and the two of us are carrying her gingerly but quickly out from the wreckage and Delta is following, sobbing.

It's Ava.

Her eyes open, just a sliver, and fix on Delta. She glances at me, and then moans.

"Chris?" A wordless moan of pain, exhaustion. "Chris?"

"He's coming," I murmur. "I'm Jonny. He's coming, okay?"

It's a lie.

But it's what she needs to hear. And it just slipped out.

Delta is holding on to me as we settle Ava onto a makeshift stretcher and carry her to the medical tent.

Her hands don't let go of me.

I don't think I'll be joining Dominic and Dane anytime soon.

CONTINUE READING FOR A SNEAK PREVIEW

Of the second book in THE ONE series

By

Jasinda Wilder

I tingled.

There's never been a tingle before.

Even that day almost six years ago when I conceived Alex—which to date still stands as the hottest day of my life and one which I do not regret even slightly despite the fact that the man in question turned out to be a rat bastard and a coward and a piece of shit. Since then my life has been all messed up and screwed over and irredeemably fucked except for two factors: that I got Alex of out of it, and his conception entailed some seriously hot sex. Even then, I didn't tingle.

But I have tingles right now.

For real. Tom—Alex's sperm donor—he knew what he was doing. There was screaming, there was a lot of me calling on god, and there were at least four orgasms—for *him*. Eight for me. In a little under four hours, which included three smoke breaks and four bottles of wine, and one large pizza.

I never saw Tom again after that—although that's kind of a lie. I saw him once more, for five seconds. I was six months pregnant, and had spent the preceding six months hunting his ass down to inform him of our little "oops."

Or, his oops. He'd assured me he was "fixed." I was thirty-two at the time, and managing a restaurant… okay, well, fine, managing a titty bar. Managing, mind you, not dancing at, or waitressing at. I'd done my time carrying trays in New York, then LA, and then Nashville, and then Chicago, in my pursuit of a career as a musician. Which had gone belly up. Or, rather, never really got off the ground. I was told over and over and over and over again that I had talent, that I had the looks, but the timing just wasn't right, or some similar excuse. It just meant the years whiled away little by little, and suddenly I was thirty-two with a couple songs I'd written playing on the radio, performed by another artist, for which I got paid dick in a basket, and the only real work experience I had was waitressing, and I was going nowhere, and when I got offered a job managing a strip bar, I took it because it meant a steady paycheck rather than relying on tips.

And then I'd met Tom at the gym, and we slept

together a few times, and then a few more, and then we met at his hotel room downtown and had a magical afternoon...and I ended up pregnant.

Guess what the strip bar didn't offer? Health insurance.

Guess who hadn't ever bothered to get Medicaid because I was never sick, and thus never needed it? Me.

Also, did you know you can't get covered for pregnancy coverage after you're already pregnant? Yeah, you can't.

So guess who ended up stuck with a massive hospital bill?

And guess which strip bar didn't take kindly to me needing a few weeks off after having a baby?

There went that job.

And wouldn't you know...by the time I was able to go back to work, they'd filled the position, and only had slots open for dancers and waitresses, and the waitresses were more or less just extra strippers who would also bring food and booze out from the kitchen. So no. I had a little pride, after all.

Anyway, about six months into the pregnancy, when I was really starting to show, I finally tracked down an address—and let me tell you, that fucker did *not* want to be found—and showed up at his door. Pounded on it till he answered, at two in the morning. Naked. Just as hung and ripped as ever...and not pleased to see me.

He stared at me, as if absorbing my presence as

reality, and then his gaze slid down to my rounded belly.

"Oh, hell no," he'd snarled.

"Oh, hell yes," I'd snarled back. "And yes, I *know* it's yours."

He'd stared at me again, and then held up a finger in a *wait a minute* gesture. Disappeared. Reappeared with a check in his hand. It was a check for ten grand. Which was when I'd finally absorbed where I was—the nice, upper-crust end of suburban Chicago. A brick house, huge and beautiful. Manicured lawn. Four-car garage. Porsche in the driveway. And, I noticed now, a ring on his ring finger, which had never been there. Nor a tan line, which meant he took it off a lot.

I stood there staring at his check, and his cock, and his house, and the marble floor and the chandelier over his head, and then a young woman several years my junior descended the stairs, wrapped in a thin robe which highlighted her perfectly fake tits, and her perfectly fake tan, and her perfectly fake blonde hair.

She'd sidled up behind him, leaned against his back, stroking his chest and stomach, as if trying to tease me. "Really, Tom? Another one? Pay her and come back to bed. I want you again."

I shook the check. "He did pay me. But I'm not sure it's enough."

The woman—Tom's trophy wife, I assumed—snatched the check out of my hand, glanced at it, sniffed, and tore it up. Reappeared after a moment with another check, this one for twenty-five thousand. "There. Now leave. And don't come back. He's a lawyer, and our lawyers have lawyers, so don't think about trying anything."

"He does this a lot, then?" I'd asked. "Knock up girls and then pay them off to vanish?"

She'd eyed me up and down. "I'm not sure you count as a *girl*, honey. A little past your prime for that."

Damn. That had hurt more than I'd been willing to let them see.

"You know, if I'd known all along that it was like this, I'd have tried to get some goodies out of you."

"You were a side-fuck, Delta, not a sugar-baby." Tom had a watch on, something gold and glittering with diamond insets. He stripped it off and tossed it to me, careless of whether I caught it or not. "Here. Now seriously, get the fuck out of here."

I got the fuck out.

Took the money and the Rolex. I still own and wear the Rolex, actually. More because I want a reminder of my bad decisions and how I got to where I am than anything. It's too big, but in a fashionable way. And if I wear it with a sexy little black dress, I can pass for someone I'm not. Which is useful when you're a single mother trying to get laid.

Anyway, back to the tingles.

Jonny Núñez gives me the tingles.

I'm on the beach, sitting next to him. We both have Styrofoam cups of coffee and sandwiches, and my head is resting on his shoulder. I'm not trying to be cute or coy, I'm just completely flattened by exhaustion. He doesn't seem to mind. He hasn't said anything, and he hasn't tried to get away from my heavy head, so I'm assuming he's okay with it. He doesn't seem like a man of many words.

He's salt of the earth, is what he is. Strong. Solid. Fit. Handsome, but not flashily so. Exotic. Ruggedly sexy. Deep-set dark eyes narrowed in a permanent squint. Weathered and darkly tanned Latino skin, scarred in places. Black hair, thick and wavy and messy, dirty and unwashed at the moment, flecked with debris and mud and who knows what else, finger-combed straight back, curling around his collar. A little too long, a lot messy. Scruff on his jaw, almost but not quite a beard. A scar on his jawline going from right cheekbone through his beard to his chin. His voice is smooth, has that musical Hispanic lilting, rolling accent.

He's worked tirelessly since I first showed up two days ago, and he says he's been here since three days before that. I have yet to see him sleep for more than a couple hours at a time, and when he does sleep he lies down wherever he is, pillows his head on his arm, and dozes off immediately. Wakes up alert and energetic. Works tirelessly, powerfully. Inexhaustible. Methodically. He does the work of three men and makes it look easy, as if he could do more but he's pacing himself.

Ava is at the hospital, crowded into a room with

three others. She's dehydrated, exhausted, suffering from shock, and she has a concussion, despite not remembering hitting her head at any point. There's no way for us to be with her, given how crowded the rooms and hallways are, and there's work to be done. So we work.

I'm not aware of having made a decision to stick with Jonny and help clean up and look for survivors and bodies, but it's what I'm doing. I should be with Ava. I should go back to St. Pete and be with Alex.

I call to check in every day, and Alex sounds like he's having the time of his life with Gramma and Grampa, as he calls them. Eating sweets and junk food and watching movies all day, probably, being spoiled rotten. But god knows he deserves a little spoiling, since I can barely keep a roof over our head and food in the fridge most days, now.

I used the hush money Tom gave me as a nest egg, a cushion. I try not to rely on it, or use it unless I have to. It'll go quick, if I'm not careful. So I work all the hours I can, and provide for Alex myself. My neighbor, Mrs. Allen, is a retired widow, and she picks him from the bus and watches him till I get home. Even working doubles most days, it's all I can do to pay rent, utilities, and buy food. I've got an apartment in a decent neighborhood, for Alex's sake. It wouldn't be as tight if I lived in a shitty area, but I want him to grow up safe. I want him to go to a nice school. Get a decent education, and grow up to be a successful adult. Which means I work my ass off to afford a nicer apartment in a nicer area than I really should and can afford, but he doesn't know that, and I don't let him.

Tingles, though.

Ava always said I was easily distracted, and prone to oversharing. Which, I suppose is true. It's why I sucked at school, and never even tried to go to college. I focused on music, writing songs and honing my acoustic guitar skills, booking gigs at coffee shops and dive bars. I actually made a decent living for myself on music alone, for a while. But it just wasn't going anywhere, and I had to get a day job. Which meant I gigged less and less, and then not at all.

And now it's been, oh hey, wouldn't you know? Six years since I gigged.

I still play though. When I get home from work at three or four in the morning, Alex is asleep and I'm too wired from work to sleep yet, I get out my battered and beloved Yamaha and I tune her up and I play quietly and sing my old numbers. I even write new ones. Usually bitter Ani DiFranco-esque pieces about how men are assholes, and quasi-artistic pieces about how life is hard, told via metaphor.

Tingles, tingles.

My ear and cheek where my head rests on Jonny's shoulder tingle.

My hip, where it touches his, tingles.

He lifts a hand to munch on his sandwich, and then

lowers it, and his forearm touches mine, and my skin tingles.

Why am I tingling?

It's stupid. I shouldn't tingle. I never tingle.

I mean, after a really nice orgasm, I'll tingle for a few seconds, but it goes away. Just innocently making contact with someone has never made me tingle before.

I know nothing about him. Nothing. NOT A DAMN THING. He doesn't talk much. He just works tirelessly, like a machine. Eats, drinks coffee, dozes for an hour or two, sometimes on the rubble, or the beach, or wherever.

He listens to me, when we take breaks together.

Meaning, he watches me with those intense, inscrutable dark eyes of his and nods and asks probing questions and never seems surprised by my tendency to blab what other people might consider personal info, or TMI. I'm a constant fountain of TMI.

He seems utterly without judgment. Like, he just accepts, and listens. And I don't get the sense that he's just tolerating me, or keeping his judgment to himself.

I LIKE HIM.

Dammit.

It means he'll probably turn out to be an asshole.

I'm preoccupying myself with Jonny and the cleanup efforts in an attempt to not freak out about—well, everything.

Reasons to freak out: Ava, the hurricane, Chris, and the fact that Ava doesn't know he's dead or most likely dead, or how many days of work I'm missing and that I'll probably have to find a new job if I ever get back to Chicago, or how much I miss my Alex, and how I'm worried that he'll like living with Gramma and Grampa more than me and I'll be alone, or that I'm misreading the conversations I have with Alex and he's actually miserable and hates it there and thinks I've abandoned him. And, oh yeah, Jonny.

And liking him.

And the mantra I've had looping through my head since I met him:

Don't sleep with Jonny
Don't sleep with Jonny
Don't sleep with Jonny

I'm putting the reminder on repeat in my head, because I have to at least try to be a good girl.

But I'm not. I'm a bad girl.

I like sex and I'm reckless and impulsive and I'm a terrible judge of people—the exact opposite of Ava, in other words. She's perfect, and always has been. Excelled in school. Never got in trouble. A good writer. Sweet. Funny. Classy. Effortlessly elegant. Effortlessly skinny. Snagged Christian without even trying, and he turned out to be a mega-popular novelist with books being turned into movies and made a shitload of money and now Ava drives a fucking MERCEDES-BENZ and I'm...

just me, still.

Bad at school. Always in trouble, because I was always hanging out with the wrong crowd. Dyslexic, or dysmorphic or something, or just not book smart and can't write or read very well. Not very sweet—I'm sarcastic and sassy and rude and talk too much and spout too much highly personal information without thinking about it. I'm not classy at all—see also my previous jobs, and my current job, and my current state of dress, e.g. booty shorts and a shelf bra and a tank; not elegant, and I have to workout like a fiend to stay in shape and keep my ass from ballooning into something with its own zip code. I hate running. I drive a fourteen-year-old Accord. I have no boyfriend, much less a wealthy and successful and admittedly gorgeous husband like Christian St. Pierre.

What I have going for me: naturally big and still-perky-at-38-despite-having-breastfed tits, a beautiful voice, talent with a guitar, a knack for songwriting, and a cool name. I mean, come on, Delta Martin says music star, doesn't it? I've always thought so, but the music industry doesn't seem to agree.

That's pretty much it.

I'm good at sex, so I've got that going for me, too. I give a hell of a BJ, and I'm good with my hands, and I'm athletic and flexible enough to get into some really neat positions. Plus I've got the libido of a girl twenty years my junior.

Which is a problem, currently.

Because, as I said, I'm trying to remind myself that I should NOT under any circumstances allow myself to sleep with Jonny Núñez, because it's bad timing and can't go anywhere and he's probably an asshole or transient or both, and I've got enough on my plate to deal with, and I'm a thirty-eight-year-old single mom and nobody wants to be saddled with that baggage and I'm at the stage of my life where I'm prone to getting clingy, and now I've got to be there for Ava, because god knows she's gonna need a hell of a lot of help after the storm and with Christian going missing.

Sleeping with Jonny is a bad idea.

God, I'm so gonna sleep with Jonny, and I'm going to regret it.

Don't sleep with Jonny

Don't sleep with Jonny

Don't sleep with Jonny

"I'll make sure to keep my hands to myself, since you feel so strong about it." His voice is a low rumble, amused.

Oh no.

Oh no.

"Did…Was I saying that out loud?" I ask, straightening up off his shoulder.

He rumbles again, and it's a laugh, I think. "Yeah, you were chanting it. Been whispering *don't sleep with*

Jonny for like five minute now."

"Shit. My mouth sometimes runs away from my brain."

"Funny. I got the exact opposite problem."

"I've noticed."

"Jonny, listen, I just—"

He gazes at me, and his eyes are totally opaque and unreadable. "Why shouldn't you sleep with Jonny? Asking for a friend."

For once my mouth is shut, instead of blabbing all the reasons I've been obsessively going over in my head.

Oh, wait, nope, here we go.

"I, um. Because I want to."

"That's not a reason not to sleep with Jonny. Sleeping with Jonny is a good thing, from what I hear. And if you want to, then…presto, not a problem."

I laugh. "But it's a bad plan. For me. And for you."

"See, I'm not hearing too much by way of reasons."

"There are a lot of them, but they would just bore you."

"I don't bore easily. Try me."

"Um. All this?" I wave around us.

He shrugs. "Good enough reason for now. Later, though, it may not stick for long."

"Ava," I say. "And…Christian."

He frowns. "Gotta give you that one. Good reason."

I sigh. "And because I have a son." I sigh again, more heavily, because this is when dudes tend to check out on me.

"What's his name?"

I'm silent for a moment, because I've been stunned speechless. "Um. His name is Alex."

People don't usually ask his name. Well, okay, that's not true. Little old ladies, grandmas, grandpas, cashiers, servers, cops, security guards, etc., they all ask his name. I mean, he's a ridiculously precocious and adorable little human being. He's magnetic. But guys who want to get me naked? They don't ask his name.

So either Jonny isn't like other guys, or he doesn't want to get me naked.

Not sure which; he's a hard man to read.

I also don't want to read into this, and create things that aren't there.

Like feelings.

And potential.

And Jonny's status as possibly not an asshole like every other male on the planet.

I have an absurd desire to light a bonfire on this beach, and play my guitar and sing.

If there was a bonfire, and a guitar, I would.

I really want Jonny to know I'm, like, a person with something to contribute to the world, besides a skill with a pen and order pad, and my banging-for-any-age-let-alone-a-38-year-old body.

I want him to…

I want him *like* me.

I haven't wanted anyone to like me since my senior year of high school when I had a crush on the starting quarterback of the FSU varsity football team.

I want Jonny to like me.

Which creates a question, and thus a conundrum.

If I want *him* to like me, then I'm pretty sure I have to like myself first. That's how that works, I'm pretty sure.

And I'm not positive I do.

Which is a problem.

Or, not, if I keep to my determination that I'M NOT GOING TO SLEEP WITH JONNY NÚÑEZ.

If I don't sleep with him, it won't matter if I like him, or if he likes me, or if I like myself.

I mean, I could JUST sleep with him, in which case it wouldn't matter either.

That last one isn't really a possibility, though. I'm gonna be clingy, and I'm going to like him, and I'm going to be a problem for both of us.

Dammit.

This was supposed to be a visit to my sister, to help her through a difficult, emotional time in her life.

It wasn't supposed to create a crisis for me.

God, I'm so gonna sleep with Jonny.

Book Two in THE ONE series, coming soon

Visit me at my website: **www.jasindawilder.com**
Email me: **jasindawilder@gmail.com**

If you enjoyed this book, you can help others enjoy it as well by recommending it to friends and family, or by mentioning it in reading and discussion groups and online forums. You can also review it on the site from which you purchased it. But, whether you recommend it to anyone else or not, thank you *so much* for taking the time to read my book! Your support means the world to me!

My other titles:

The Preacher's Son:
Unbound
Unleashed
Unbroken

Biker Billionaire:
Wild Ride

Big Girls Do It:
Better (#1), Wetter (#2), Wilder (#3), On Top (#4)
Married (#5)
On Christmas (#5.5)
Pregnant (#6)
Boxed Set

Rock Stars Do It:

Harder

Dirty

Forever

Boxed Set

From the world of *Big Girls* and *Rock Stars*:

Big Love Abroad

Delilah's Diary:

A Sexy Journey

La Vita Sexy

A Sexy Surrender

The Falling Series:

Falling Into You

Falling Into Us

Falling Under

Falling Away

Falling for Colton

The Ever Trilogy:

Forever & Always

After Forever

Saving Forever

The world of *Alpha:*
Alpha
Beta
Omega
Harris: Alpha One Security Book 1
Thresh: Alpha One Security Book 2
Duke: Alpha One Security Book 3
Puck: Alpha One Security Book 4

The world of Stripped:
Stripped
Trashed

The world of *Wounded:*
Wounded
Captured

The Houri Legends:
Jack and Djinn
Djinn and Tonic

The Madame X Series:
Madame X
Exposed
Exiled

Badd Brothers:
Badd Motherf*cker
Badd Ass
Bass to the Bone

The Black Room
(With Jade London):
Door One
Door Two
Door Three
Door Four
Door Five
Door Six
Door Seven
Door Eight
Deleted Door

Standalone titles:
Yours

Non-Fiction titles:
Big Girls Do It Running
Big Girls Do It Stronger

Jack Wilder Titles:
The Missionary

To be informed of new releases and special offers,
sign up for
Jasinda's email newsletter.

Made in the USA
Lexington, KY
12 July 2017